BREATH OF DEATH
THRILLER FROM

GW00832408

Original and intriguing, it had me gripped throughout.
—Mohammed Hanif
author of A Case of Exploding Mangoes
BREATH OF DEATH
A THRILLER FROM PAKISTAN
For Peter
with fond regards
Saad
March 2013
CHLOROPHYLL

First published 2012

ISBN 978-81-8328-185-0

Published by

Wisdom Tree,
4779/23, Ansari Road,
Darya Ganj, New Delhi-2
Ph.: +91-11-23247966/67/68
wisdomtreebooks@gmail.com

Printed in India

To

WMD,

for being

who she is.

One

The headache came first. It crept up from nowhere to pierce through his forehead and pound on his temples, making his head feel like it would crack open. The headache was followed by body aches—raw and throbbing waves of excruciating soreness that washed over his body again and again.

Breakfast induced nausea. He willed himself to eat, and promptly threw up. Soon he was enveloped by fever and an overwhelming sense of fatigue. He was drowsy and lethargic, and rapidly became disoriented, finding it impossible to concentrate or think straight. The fever intensified.

These were the first symptoms. Zafar's immediate thought was panic and anxiety about missing work. A clever young lad who had worked hard to learn the tailoring trade, he had just leased a small shop and started his own business. There was even a staff of two assistants and an errand boy. A fetching shalwar kameez cut in European style—all the rage with women these days—had been hung on an eye-catching mannequin in the storefront window. Competition was intense and he needed a niche. Zafar was marketing himself as a specialist in Western fashions.

Clients were attracted; work had been secured. This was not the time to default on business promises.

At first, Zafar's mother thought he had the flu. She was looking forward to arranging his marriage soon, now that he had his own business. For weeks, she had obsessed over the shortlist, and narrowed it down to four girls after the most peripatetic hemming and hawing. She was now leaning heavily towards one of them—a distant niece whose hazel-green eyes Zafar was forever working into conversation. The girl even had some education, which along with the charismatic eyes, had been enough to land her a job as a receptionist at a travel agency. It promised to be a great match, Zafar's mother was certain. Just thinking about it made her agitated with joy. She wanted to act on it right away, wanted to draw up the guest list, scour the markets for bargains in dress and jewellery, decorate Zafar's room with jasmine and rose petals... As soon as Zafar recovered, she would get his consent and plan a formal proposal.

When her son's drowsiness gave way to a restless delirium, it alarmed her. She worried about malaria. Zafar's body burned and he was drenched in sweat. He was talking nonsense. When she held him, she felt his body tremble with rigors. With a mother's instinct, she reached out to wipe the sweat off his brow and feel his temperature. Zafar let out a wail and pushed her hand away.

The gesture was utterly uncharacteristic, and it frightened her. This was not her son, the dutiful and deferential boy she knew and doted on. She tried again, this time also offering him a glass of water, but Zafar became frantic. Wildly flinging his arms, he caught her full on the cheek, the force of the blow knocking her down flat. The glass of water flew from her hands, smashing into the wall.

The commotion brought Zafar's father and younger brother rushing into the room. They found the mother on the floor, frozen in shock. The top of her sari had come undone and her left cheek looked as if it had been set on fire. There was broken glass everywhere. Zafar was sitting on the edge of his bed, knuckles digging into the sheets, hair matted with sweat, face vacant, eyes distant and unreachable.

The deeply affectionate relationship between mother and son was legion. For him to strike her like that was as unthinkable as the sun failing to rise. To Zafar's father, it was as if the devil had taken possession of his son.

Against the rational pleadings of his family, the father—a retired pensioner with all the hang-ups that came from a lifetime of unrewarded struggle, insisted on taking Zafar to see a mufti, a religious elder. They bundled him into a rickshaw and hurriedly took off.

The mother was adamant about malaria, but the mufti looked unconvinced. He diagnosed demonic possession and ordered a beating to drive out evil spirits. A lathi draped in green velvet was brought out and ceremoniously unveiled. The mufti mouthed Quranic verses while gently blowing on the stick. An aide held down Zafar's arms while pulling up his shirt to expose the back. It was a superfluous act because by now Zafar was in a stupor and in no shape to resist.

The lathi was swung a few times before Zafar's mother exploded. Hysterical and screaming, she wrapped herself around Zafar and would not budge. The mufti complained this was interfering with the exorcism, but Zafar's father had had enough too, and told the mufti to stop. They were going to take him to a hospital. As they left, the mufti asked for two hundred rupees for his efforts. Zafar's father brought out a fifty, and the mufti pocketed it without fuss.

It was a few hours later, sometime after midnight, that the

telephone in Dr Asad Mirza's residence started to ring. It took several seconds for the disturbance to finally pierce his slumber.

'Sorry to wake you up, sir. This is Dr Farida from the ER. I'm calling you about a case that's just come in.'

'Yeah, okay...'

'It's a twenty-eight-year-old man, sir. He's been brought in with a day-long history of agitation and disorientation, and he's been completely unresponsive for the last few hours. Blood pressure is 110/68, pulse 86, respiratory rate...'

In a hurry as usual, thought Asad, even in the middle of the night. This girl always sounded like she had something more important to do that her duties as a neurology resident were interfering with. What was all the hurry for? She was a competent, responsible doctor but she was always so rushed. It could be quite annoying.

Half-asleep, Asad struggled to catch up with his assistant. He tried stalling briefly. 'Wait, hold on. Tell me again. How old did you say...'

'Okay, right,' said Farida, more deliberate this time. It was a familiar routine that always played out whenever she had to call Asad after hours. He never seemed to listen the first time. She paused for a couple of seconds, hoping that would make him more awake. A tough case had shown up. She needed Asad's full attention.

'It's a twenty-eight-year-old man, Dr Mirza, brought in by his family. No co-morbids, has apparently been in good health. They say he was fine until yesterday morning, when he complained of a headache and soon became dull and lethargic. He was probably also running a fever. Later he was confused and restless. Started acting weird around the house, fighting with the family.'

'What was he doing?'

'Bizarre aggressive behaviour. Apparently he got into a fight with his mother and hit her. That's when they took him to some maulvi or mufti or something.'

'Mufti?'

'Yes,' said Farida. 'I can't be sure because they're not telling. He's got linear bruises over his back and arms, like he was beaten or something. The family may have taken him to a faith healer. They look the sort.'

'Okay. When did he become unresponsive?'

'Well, they've tried giving him food at various times throughout the day yesterday, but he wouldn't take anything. His mother tried giving him a glass of water but it made him upset—that was when he hit her. It sounds like starting in the afternoon he became drowsy. Just became lethargic and stuporous. His brother says they've been trying to wake him up for a while now but nothing, not even a flinch from him.'

Asad's trained mind had already formed a list of diagnostic possibilities. It was second nature and something that inevitably came together towards the final months of medical school, after which it started happening subconsciously, without any real mental effort or at least none that one was aware of. Once the major points in a patient's medical history were known, a list of likely diagnoses quickly emerged in the thinking doctor's mind. It was an axiom professors had been passing on to medical students for generations.

Young guy, thought Asad, in previously good health develops headache, agitation and confusion, perhaps with a fever as well, and now seems to be in a coma—got to rule out encephalitis or maybe some kind of drug overdose.

'So what's the exam like?' he asked, feeling quite alert now.

Farida collected her thoughts to prepare a measured answer.

She was standing in the middle of the emergency room, facing a row of six beds that were reserved for the most acute emergencies. At this hour, only two of the beds were occupied.

On the bed in the far corner, a teenage girl was being treated for an asthma attack. Her mother was seated by the side of the bed but had fallen asleep, and her head and arms now lay sprawled across her daughter's legs. The girl had come in blue and gasping, exhausted from desperately sucking air into constricted and inflamed airways, but the ER's night duty doctor had been quick to recognise her condition and had started a nebulizer. It made a hissing sound as oxygen bubbled into the medicated liquid and flowed into the girl's lungs through a clear plastic mask. She looked tranquil now, all the indicators on her bedside monitor confirming that her breathing had normalised.

Three beds next to the asthmatic girl were empty. The fourth bed was occupied by Majeed, Zafar—medical record no. 109-61-79.

'He's in coma, Dr Mirza. I'm getting no response to pain, not even posturing. Brainstem reflexes are present and he's breathing on his own, but nothing else.'

'Vitals?'

'Fine, though he's febrile, 38 degrees in the axilla.'

'Have you thought of meningitis? What's the neck like?' asked Asad, hoping for a clue that would quickly put everything together.

'The neck is supple,' said Farida. 'No other signs of meningitis either. I even checked his fundi. The discs are flat.'

Asad's suspicion of encephalitis, an acute inflammation of the brain that is usually caused by a virus, was strengthened. Had the neck been stiff or the optic discs in the patient's eyes swollen, that would certainly suggest meningitis—an inflammation of the membranes wrapped around the brain. It was important to distinguish between the two conditions because the therapy was different. But such a degree of confusion and somnolence was unusual with meningitis. Ever the teacher, Asad wanted Farida to reason through it herself.

'So what's your assessment, Farida?'

'I'm worried about CNS infection, sir. I think he needs a spinal tap but I'd like to get an MRI first. I guess it could be a drug overdose too, maybe amphetamine or cocaine or something. There's no history to suggest drug abuse and he's got no needle tracks, but I'm checking a toxicology screen anyway.'

'That sounds fine,' said Asad, allowing himself to relax. He felt safe in the conclusion that they were probably dealing with a case of encephalitis, less likely one of drug overdose, and Farida was prepared for both contingencies. She seemed to be in control.

'Make sure you put him in the ICU,' said Asad. 'He could deteriorate. Start acyclovir, and just to be safe, let's give him ceftriaxone as well.'

'Yes, that was my plan. We've started D5-saline and the acyclovir is being delivered as we speak. I'll order the ceftriaxone too. Basic labwork's been sent. ECG's normal. I'll get a chest X-ray too before he goes up.'

'Good. Any other admissions?'

'Two others, both tucked in. There's a young boy with breakthrough seizures who had missed a few doses of his medication. He's fine really, but his mother was totally freaked out, so I kept him in for observation. The other one's a known case of multiple sclerosis that's flared up with right-sided weakness and a corresponding spot on her MRI scan. I'm pulsing her with steroids.'

Asad thanked Farida and hung up. His nightstand clock

said 2:21 am. His workday routine would be starting in a few hours. He got up from his bed and walked to the bathroom. When he came back to bed, his mind was still on the conversation with Farida.

A young man in previously good health, develops a headache, becomes agitated, confused, febrile, comatose. What could it be, other than encephalitis? But clinical experience cautioned against rushing to medical judgment. Could Farida be missing something? If it was a drug problem, the toxicology screen would pick it up. But the guy had fever; his family suspected it and Farida had documented it. That strongly suggested infection. The spinal tap would clinch it. Asad wished Farida had called him after the results of the tap were known, but he really couldn't fault her for calling early. She was always in a great hurry but Asad knew her to be conscientious and thorough as well.

The degree of agitation in the patient's history bothered Asad. Encephalitis could make you crazy but this sounded a bit more bizarre than the usual case. As he tried to mull the thought, it made him drowsy and he yawned. His wife was sleeping with her back towards him. Reaching across, he traced a finger lightly along the curve of her spine, but she did not stir. Asad turned over and drifted off.

Two

SUMMER IN KARACHI is brutal. The heat alone is ugly and unforgiving. Add unrelenting humidity, and the elements become merciless. The city sits on the sea but is surrounded by desert land that has been known to reach some of the hottest temperatures anywhere. When the heat reaches its peak, you feel baked in an oven and the thick, humid air gives everything an extra, hot skin. It's an effort even to lift your finger. You could get by with air-conditioning, but in this teeming, overpopulated Third World megapolis, it is a luxury few can afford.

Asad had grown up in Karachi, but a decade of living in the northeastern United States while he completed advanced medical specialisation, had destroyed his tolerance for hot temperatures. As a well-to-do doctor, he was one of the lucky few in Pakistan who could surround themselves with air-conditioned bliss. In a strange way, it reminded him of his years in Boston and the long, bitter winters endured while training as a neurologist at Massachusetts General Hospital. It was odd that Karachi's searing, unbearable heat would remind someone of impossibly cold winters in the Northern Hemisphere, but it made sense to Asad. Back in Karachi now, he craved the coolness of car, hospital, home, restaurants, shopping malls. In Boston he would seek the same sanctuaries, but for their warmth.

It had been an agonising decision, but Asad had no regrets about returning to Pakistan. He was part of a sizeable cohort of young physicians who had left the country seeking better training opportunities in America. Most of his friends had opted to stay on and settle down in the United States, where there was a perpetual shortage of physicians and overseas doctors were accommodated without much fuss.

But Asad took pride and comfort in Pakistan. In the first couple of years after moving back, he was constantly asked his reasons. Asad had quickly developed an effective answer. 'Pakistan is home,' he would say to anyone who brought it up.

He did miss Boston, and enjoyed reminiscing whenever he got half a chance. A treasured memory was the morning drive to the hospital, the Charles River on his left and the Back Bay townhouses on his right as he motored down Storrow Drive. Outsize French windows would be ablaze in the morning sun and joggers and bicyclists would be swarming the running track that hugged the riverbank.

Powerful associations flooded this memory. The anticipation of a tall latte and almond biscotti from the Starbucks on Cambridge Street or a fresh copy of *The Boston Globe* picked up at the corner. And the familiar smile of Whitney, his favourite nurse, who used to be on White 12 but had worked her way through a diploma in emergency nursing to join the helicopter crew of Medford Air Emergency.

But the recollections had become less and less frequent. Just weeks shy of forty, Asad was a career professional, over-committed at both home and work and had little time to spare for thinking about the past, no matter how pleasant. There was too much happening all the time, in all the corners of his life. It was hard enough keeping up with the present. Recalling the past had become an indulgence and thinking about the future seemed irrelevant. If anything mattered, it was the here and now.

His bedside alarm clock went off at 6:30 am but Asad barely stirred. His wife reached over to turn it off. It was a familiar sequence that Seemi performed almost without thinking. Asad seldom needed the alarm to wake him up—except when he had taken an emergency call in the early hours. Seemi had learned to quickly turn the alarm off and let him sleep another few minutes whenever that happened. It was either that, or put up with an insufferable morning grouch.

Six-thirty was the usual summer time for Seemi to get up as well. She first changed the baby, then got dressed herself. After saying her prayers, she went downstairs to unlock the house and let the maid in, before settling in front of the television with a cup of steaming coffee and a fresh newspaper.

She had her own Boston memories. After several years watching *Good Morning America* every weekday morning without fail, she had become addicted to American television at breakfast. Satellite TV had allowed her to preserve this habit in Pakistan. Karachi was ten hours ahead of Boston, so her mornings now coincided with *The Late-Night Show with David Letterman*, but as far as Seemi was concerned, this was a trivial difference.

She was just thinking about going back upstairs to wake Asad when he breezed into the kitchen, working his tie and smelling strongly of after-shave. He poured himself a glass of orange juice and sat down next to her. It was unusual for Asad to wake up on his own when he'd been disturbed during the night. If he did, it usually meant something was on his mind. Seemi knew better than to ask. She suspected he was worrying about one of his patients, and asking would only annoy him. Like most men, Asad enjoyed being mothered by his wife, but not when he was anxious about work. Seemi knew he would forego breakfast as well.

The television droned on in the background. Letterman was grilling a good-looking guest who smiled coyly and played with her ringlets. She delivered a deadpan punch line and the audience erupted in laughter.

Asad stood up, collected his car keys, and kissed Seemi on the nose, as was his goodbye habit. He was out of the house without a word.

The morning drive in Karachi was nothing like coasting on Storrow, but it hadn't taken Asad long to get used to it and it rarely bothered him now. Dreadful road manners were part of the traffic landscape in Karachi. Vehicles changed lanes without warning, motorcyclists zigzagged in and out, camel and donkey carts fought for road space, rickshaws spewed carbon and sulfur fumes, jaywalkers kept popping up from nowhere, and beggars, beggars and more beggars congregated at every traffic light. Asad had rapidly learned the standard escape from this onslaught—cocoon yourself in an air-conditioned sedan and turn up the volume on the audio deck.

There were many work-related worries to occupy his mind. Research grants and academic promotion were chronic anxieties, the burdensome lot of any physician with a university appointment. There was also a full teaching schedule for medical students and residents that had begun to make him feel overextended, and he had been meaning to talk to his boss about it. There were always the usual worries at home—Seemi had fought with the maid, they had run out of diesel for the back-up generator, one of the toilets was blocked, or the antisocial neighbours had spilled refuse on their lawn yet again. But those were reserved for the afternoon drive back.

By the time Asad turned into the manicured landscape of Avicenna University Hospital, Dr Farida's call about the twenty-eight-year-old man in a coma was foremost in his mind. It was 7:28 am on the dashboard clock.

From the parking lot, Asad called Farida on his cell phone and asked how the new admission was doing. Farida reported that the patient had been intubated and put on a ventilator. He was still in coma and had been moved to the ICU, Bed 9. A spinal tap had been done and results were awaited.

Family members were anxious to meet the attending neurologist. Farida wanted to know when Asad would be coming to do patient rounds. 'Seven forty-five,' he said, as he rushed off to his office, hoping to answer a few emails before joining the neurology team for the morning routine.

Ward rounds in teaching hospitals are a nuanced exercise with a complex sociology. Patients are seen to by a team comprising of medical students and doctors who are at various levels of training and accomplishment. The hierarchy is etched in stone. At the head of the team is the attending physician, who might as well be a military chief of staff. The chain of command flows down from the attending physician to senior and junior residents—doctors who had finished medical school and are now in advanced training and downward thence to medical students, who are regarded as barely human. Everyone vies for the attending's attention and approval, and it sets the tone for how the other group members interact with each other.

Asad's team was anchored by his senior resident Farida Ansari, who was in the final year of specialty training as a neurologist and whom Asad considered one of his protégés. She had been a solid performer throughout her residency program and was quickly maturing into an astute and devoted specialist. Farida was assisted by two junior residents who were a year out of medical school and had just started to become familiar with their neurology duties.

At the beginning of most months, a group of medical students was also assigned to the team. This month the team had been joined by a party of four—three boys and a girl. They had only been around a couple of days and Asad hadn't seen enough of them to form an opinion yet. First impressions, however, were positive. Their body language was attentive. Asad thought they seemed eager and interested.

As he walked down the main corridor of the neurology ward, Asad found the team already assembled and waiting. The residents wore long white coats and had a self-assured manner. The four medical students stood around them looking awkward and uneasy in their waist-length white jackets, their pockets overflowing with stethoscopes, pens, small books and papers. Everyone greeted Asad as he approached the group, the amount of pep in their voices inversely related to their seniority.

There had only been the three admissions last night, Farida informed Asad. Two were stable and were well enough to be having breakfast; they had been placed in the general ward, which housed the not so sick. Asad was anxious to see the ICU case. With brisk steps and a sense of purpose, everyone marched down the corridor.

At the ICU's entrance, Farida punched in her security code and the doors swung open. Asad entered first, followed by Farida and the rest of the team. The ICU was a large hall about the size of a tennis court. Down the centre ran a long, cluttered workbench. An officious-looking receptionist busily handled papers and worked the phones at one end of the bench. There were five beds on either side, removed from the central space and housed in a recessed cubicle. Each bed was surrounded by a ventilator and a trolley laid out with tubes, masks, gloves and syringes. Doctors, nurses and nurses' aides moved around the ICU, stepping in and out of the cubicles.

All ten beds were occupied, which was the norm, because these were the ten best-equipped ICU beds serving Karachi's sixteen million. Asad's team walked over to the far end of the hall and assembled around Bed 9. A sign outside the cubicle gave the patient's name as Zafar and listed his seven-digit medical record number; no last name was written. Below the patient's name, 'Dr Asad Mirza—Attending' was scrawled in black marker.

From a nearby chart rack, Farida pulled out a blue ring-binder with an oversized '9' on the cover. She handed it to Kamran, one of the students who had spent the night on-call with her in the hospital. He was now required to make a detailed presentation about the case.

Kamran began fumbling with the chart as he tried to locate the notes he had made earlier that morning. He looked casual and sloppy. Competition with fellow students was fierce, and it made his classmates secretly happy to see that he certainly wasn't scoring any points with Dr Mirza.

While Kamran turned the chart upside down, Asad's mind wandered and he began absent-mindedly scanning the ICU. His eyes fell on a feeble-looking infant across the hall, lying hooked up to a breathing tube and two IV lines. Family members were huddled around the baby. A woman, almost certainly the mother, was sobbing quietly and being comforted by a man and another woman. Asad couldn't help thinking of his own little baby at home, six-month old Mariam. He could not imagine a more darling creature on the face of the planet. What would happen if Mariam were ever sick like the little infant on Bed 4? It was simply unimaginable.

After blundering for what must have been at least half a minute, Kamran finally managed to get his act together, and announced as much by clearing his throat in a noisy off-putting way. It caught Asad's attention immediately.

'This twenty-eight-year-old man previously in good health,' began Kamran, 'was admitted last night with a two-day history of mental status changes and fever.' He went on to give details about the rest of the medical history, including the social background and the measures undertaken for this patient in the hospital. As Kamran spoke, Asad emphasised the main points in his mind. The patient had started acting oddly two nights ago and his behaviour had become progressively worse. He had been violent at one point when he slapped his mother. Soon afterward, he had become drowsy, rapidly progressing to a comatose state.

Kamran informed the group that the man was an unmarried tailor who had recently opened his own shop. He smoked cigarettes occasionally and lived with his parents. Family members had vehemently denied that he had any involvement with drugs or alcohol. After a brief pause, Kamran read out the patient's routine blood test results, which were all normal.

It was time for the examination.

As Kamran wrapped up his presentation, Asad moved closer to the bed and pulled on a pair of gloves. Zafar lay motionless, except for the breathing movements of his chest wall, which rose and fell in synchrony with the periodic hissing noises made by the mechanical breathing machine. A multi-coloured tangle of wires descended from a cardiac monitor anchored to the wall above his head; the wires disappeared beneath a white sheet that covered the patient up to his nipples.

The monitor, which looked like an astronaut's helmet, noiselessly traced out the ECG and gave to-the-minute readings of blood pressure, heart rate and blood oxygen level. A clear plastic tube ran through the patient's mouth, secured in place with adhesive tape that was tightly wrapped around the face. The tube was hooked up to a series of flexible ducts that connected Zafar's lungs to the ventilator. His eyes were closed and his forehead unwrinkled. If one saw just the upper part of the face, he looked serene and comfortable. But the breathing tube had pushed his tongue to one side and was forcing it to stick out from a corner of the mouth. The effect was grotesque.

Asad began the examination by making a mental note of the monitor display, which was giving normal readings. He then bent forward and, putting his mouth up against the patient's right ear, loudly yelled 'ZAFAR!' He didn't expect a response, but like any obsessive physician he always insisted on going through the standard sequence of examination steps.

Next came the pinching of the nipples. It was an ugly part of the examination but it was necessary in people who were comatose. The idea was to inflict enough pain to see if you could get the patient to produce a response, any response—an eyelid flicker, a faint grimace, a straightening of the arms, anything. Asad held the patient's right nipple between his thumb and forefinger and squeezed hard, but the man did not stir. He proceeded to do the same to the left nipple; again, nothing. No discernible reaction to a proper and brutal nipple pinch meant the patient was in a very deep coma and might even be brain-dead. To confirm his suspicions, Asad asked for a flashlight. A nurse quickly handed him one. He held Zafar's eyelids open and aimed the light beam at each eye in turn. It was as he expected: pupils big as saucers and fixed in place, and with a hazy, glassy appearance. Asad held the patient's head in both hands and gently rotated it from side to side. The eyes remained fixed in their sockets, like those of a doll. He decided he had seen enough.

Putting all the facts together, he concluded it was most likely a severe case of encephalitis, an overwhelming infection of the brain. Quite probably, a virus was responsible. In Asad's clinical assessment, Zafar was probably brain-dead, although the examination would have to be repeated later in the day before that conclusion could be definitively reached. While Zafar's heart was beating for now, it was just a matter of time before that, too, stopped working.

But Asad wasn't completely comfortable with the diagnosis. The commonest cause of encephalitis was *Herpes simplex* virus, which didn't usually kill within two days. And the aggressive behaviour displayed by the patient earlier in the illness still bothered him; it was not a common feature of viral encephalitis. It would be useful to have more diagnostic information.

'Do we have the spinal fluid results?' Asad asked, looking straight at Kamran.

Some medical students never get used to the spotlight. Kamran was one of them. He felt his throat tighten. He knew that he should have looked up the test results before assembling for rounds, but he hadn't—and he felt nervous about saying as much. Sensing his hesitation, one of the other medical students, a smartly dressed young woman with twinkling eyes and striking looks, walked over to a nearby computer terminal and started hacking at the keyboard.

Within seconds, she was calling out the results. 'Protein 114, glucose 62, white cells 9, 80 per cent lymphos,' she read stridently while staring at the screen. Then, turning towards Asad, she announced with unmistakable triumph, 'Looks like viral encephalitis.'

Asad returned the young woman's gaze and continued the conversation. Whatever hopes the other students may have had of competing for their teacher's attention now fizzled away.

'I think you're right, but let us think it through. What else could it be?' he asked, hoping to stimulate and sharpen the students' diagnostic acumen.

Like a spry lioness lying in wait and ready to pounce, the clever young girl had been hoping for exactly this kind of opportunity. 'Well, it could be a massive stroke of course but the symptoms started gradually, and besides, the negative MRI scan rules it out. It could be a metabolic or toxic encephalopathy, but the Chem 7 and LFTs are fine and the tox screen is negative as well. It could be meningitis, but the CSF pleocytosis is modest, and anyway, he's far too obtunded. I think cerebral malaria is another possibility, but there was nothing on the blood smear and the history seems too short. So, all things considered, I'd say it's a case of viral encephalitis.'

Asad was blown away. It was rare to come across a medical student who could reason through a difficult case like a seasoned expert, and rarer still for the person to be so attractive and confident. But he wasn't about to show his appreciation right away. He believed in being tight-lipped with praise for students, otherwise it quickly went to their heads. It would be enough to just ask her name.

'Yes, I agree. What's your name?'

'Nadia,' she said, trying to sound as matter-of-fact as possible but overjoyed on the inside to receive the personal attention. A positive interaction this early in the rotation usually laid the foundations for being awarded a top grade by the supervisor.

Asad turned towards Farida. 'Clinically, he's brain-dead. Let's get an EEG and re-examine him in six hours before we complete the formalities.' Farida nodded and made a note on her clipboard.

One of the students asked what it meant to be 'brain-dead,' and Asad led the team to a nearby whiteboard and began explaining the concept. He was in his element when teaching neurology and stressed important points with exaggerated hand gestures that had become his trademark. The students and the junior residents listened intently. Farida gamely went along as well, but this was all old hat for her and after a few minutes, she became fidgety. There were other patients to be seen, a whole day's work to be done. She wished Asad would quickly talk to Zafar's family members, who desperately needed to be told the details.

They were waiting in the hallway outside. As the team emerged from the ICU's double-doors, one of them, a middle-aged man with salt and pepper hair, stepped forward to shake Asad's hand. Asad greeted him solemnly and asked the man if he was the father. No, he was the uncle, but he was speaking on behalf of the whole family. The man pointed to the father, who was sitting by himself on a bench down the hall, staring at the wall in front of him. Two women, both probably in their early twenties, stood next to the uncle. They were introduced as the patient's sisters. All three looked like they had been through a sleepless night. Farida had already apprised them of the serious nature of the case. They had also been in and out of the ICU through the night and had talked to the nurses. Restless for information but fearing the worst, they remained desperate for any sliver of hope.

'I'm sorry,' Asad began, 'I wish I had good news to share with you, but I don't.' He had done this so many times, but delivering bad news to families never got any easier. It was, to him, the hardest part of the physician's job, especially if the news was so unexpected and untimely as in the case of this twenty-eight-year-old man struck down by a lethal brain infection that had came out of nowhere.

'Zafar has encephalitis,' Asad continued. 'I'm afraid he's not doing well. I don't think...'

One of the sisters interrupted. 'What do you mean doctor sahib? Is he going to be OK?'

'Right now, our examination shows no signs of brain activity in Zafar. That's a bad sign, a very bad sign. I'm sorry to be blunt about this, but I don't think he's going to make it.'

Both sisters burst in tears. The students and residents quietly stood behind Asad. It was a difficult moment for everyone.

Brain death was a very thorny issue. Since the deceased's heart was still pumping, useful organs like the liver and kidneys could be removed from his body. You couldn't pick a worse time to bring it up with the family, but it could be life-saving for someone else and had to be done. You also had to come to terms with disconnecting the ventilator, or 'pulling the plug'.

Asad decided he would wait until after the EEG was done and the neurological examination had been repeated before discussing the implications with the family. He shook the uncle's hand and lightly squeezed his shoulder, and began to walk away.

Zafar's uncle would not let go. 'What kind of brain infection, doctor sahib? Why can't it be treated?'

'It's a virus. We did start treatment as soon as he came in, but sometimes the infection is just overwhelming.'

The uncle was desperate. He pleaded for some explanation. 'How did he get this virus, doctor sahib? He's such a nice boy, never hurt a soul. Why him?'

'We don't know,' said Asad, trying to sound professional but unable to hide the tone of defeat in his voice. 'It's just one those things, you could say it was bad luck. I'm sorry, I know that's not very comforting, but I think that's what it really was, pure bad luck.'

'It's Allah's will,' one of the sisters said, speaking through her sobs. 'It's what Allah wanted. Who are we to question it?' She buried her face in her hands, shaking and crying.

Asad shook hands with the uncle for a third time and walked ahead. The rest of the team followed quietly.

Three

What an annoying time for the cell phone to start buzzing.

He had initially resolved to keep it switched off at prayer times. But naturally that would let others know whenever he was incapacitated by dialogue with Allah, and in this business providing any unnecessary information was a very, very stupid idea. So he had settled for simply turning it to silent vibration mode.

Unfortunately, trying to ignore a flashing and vibrating cell phone, was easier said than done. Especially for a man like Malik Feysal, who found it impossible to ignore things around him. Nevertheless, the five daily prayer times could not be avoided, and some solution was needed. As with most things for Malik, this too was a wrenching struggle, but he had finally worked out his system.

Scooping water into his palms, he continued with the ablution ritual. Three splashes on the face; the cheeks and chin rubbed gently, wet fingers pushed inside and behind the ears.

His cell phone lay a short distance away. Malik let it tremble quietly for a full minute, while he went through the rest of the symbolic purification that would prepare him for an audience with his God. At last, he looked at the number to see who was calling. It was familiar.

'Where have you been?' said an urgent voice. 'Shehadeh is dead.'

Malik fell completely still as he processed the news. Salah Shehadeh was the leader of the military wing of Hamas, the Islamic organisation behind violent resistance in the Occupied Territories.

'What happened?' asked Malik. 'Was it Mossad?'

'No, Shin Bet, you fool. It was a Gaza strip operation.'

They didn't know how to talk, these operatives from the Intefada. But they sat in the political centre of the Middle East and were privy to Israeli-American cross-talk. Some, like the man now on the phone, who Malik knew from a previous campaign, also had a reputation for passing on useful details. Malik had learned to ignore the bad manners while he stayed tuned for important nuggets.

'OK, so what happened?' he asked.

'An F-16 dropped a bomb in Daraj. Fell straight on top of Shehadeh's house. Leila is also dead. There were at least six children. Others are dead too. Many wounded.'

'How do you know this? Is there a message out?'

'No, you fool. It's on CNN.'

Ah, the lovely manners. Malik felt a flash of annoyance but bit his tongue. He had consumed Stephen Covey's *The Seven Habits of Highly Effective People* more assiduously than any corporate executive. Never, ever losing your temper was one of the core rules he had long ago adopted.

In a tone of ratcheting impatience, the caller continued.

'I have a message for you, Malik. We heard of your new assignment. Relax, I don't want to know anything about it. We just want you to get it done. You have to succeed, Malik. You must. You have to pull it off. You just have to. Everyone is counting on you.'

It wasn't uncommon that news about an emerging operation would leak beyond the inner circle. Seamlessly, Malik slipped into his practiced denial mode. 'What assignment?' he deadpanned. 'There's no assignment.'

'Fuck that. You hear what I'm saying? You've got to pull it off, brother. We're hearing this could be really big. Don't fuck it up. May Allah protect you and give you victory.'

Malik tried to restate his denial, but the caller had hung up. He thought of calling back, but knew it was pointless. Deny anything too strongly and you only draw attention to it. He did want to find out more about Shehadeh's murder but clearly, it would be more pleasant to simply watch CNN.

Prayer time beckoned. Malik completed the cleansing ritual and rolled out his prayer mat. He stood facing westward, in the direction of Mecca, ready and willing to make Islam's holiest city the epicenter of his imagination. As his hands rose ceremonially, his thumbs flicked the ear lobes on both sides. His mind had cleared of distractions and the idea of the greatness of God and the supremacy of God's word seized him.

Whenever he prayed, Malik was always careful to keep the picture out of his sights. He was capable of intense concentration, but the picture was the one thing that could interfere with his meditation. It was displayed prominently on one of the walls. Malik had been careful to pick a location that kept it behind his back when he prayed.

Nearly two feet wide and three feet long, it was a laminated poster depicting the attacks of September 11. The production quality was excellent, with vivid colours and fine, high-resolution detail.

The photograph had been taken at 9:03 am, the precise moment when United Airlines flight 175 flew into the South Tower of the World Trade Center complex in downtown Manhattan. A large ball of fire surrounded the skyscraper, erupting from the point of impact. Next to it, smoke billowed from the North Tower, which had been hit moments earlier by American Airlines flight 11. Helpless and wounded, the two towers stood abandoned against a spotless blue sky.

Malik was a man frequently on the move, and he was careful to take the picture with him wherever he relocated. It gave him clarity and kept his thoughts aligned with the ethos of the Network. His outlook was straightforward and pragmatic. America came to wield unprecedented power during the twentieth century, and in both the acquisition and the exercise of that power, made a host of enemies. It had been the American century, but by the end of it, the whole world had a litany of complaints against the United States. The galling irony was that American misbehaviour around the world contradicted American's own ideals at home. Grievances were as numerous and varied as the peoples of the world. In one form or another, they were all expressions of the high-handedness of American foreign policy and its disregard for weaker nations.

Nations everywhere were angry at America, but people in the Muslim world were especially ticked off. To many Muslim youth, America's generous support for Israel was enough to justify the label of evil empire. In line with the Network's beliefs and formulations, Malik had other complaints against America too. An obsession with sex, the parading of flesh, and the unquestioned devotion to hedonistic consumerism were the big ones. To Malik, it was all prurient and nauseating.

But it was in the US-Israeli alliance that the Satanic menace of America hit home. Malik saw it as the single biggest threat to the thing he held most dear, his Islamic faith and all the cultural and inspirational values that came with it.

In this, he was one of many.

Malik had not always been of this frame of mind. The child of Pakistani parents, by an odd coincidence he was born a citizen of the United States. Still, he grew up in Karachi and it was well into his teenage years when he finally grasped the significance of the strange blue booklet that had his picture in it. He began dreaming of going away to America, of a new and hopeful future in the land of plenty. But forces in his life soon steered him elsewhere.

His home had always been a tense and sober place. Malik once had a younger brother who had choked himself to death as an infant after inhaling a button that the boy had picked up from his mother's sewing. After that his parents tried three more times for another son, and ended up with three girls, all of whom had survived and were now of marriageable age. The looming costs of their weddings and dowries hung heavy, one of the unspoken burdens of the house.

The other crushing burden was the marriage of Malik's own parents, which had never recovered from the father having overstated his means to wed the mother. The story was a staple of the household chatter, and Malik's father had long ago accepted he would never be allowed to forget it. The marriage proposal, delivered through the time-honoured route of an influential matriarchal figure who happened to be socially acquainted with both families, had claimed that Malik's father was an executive officer with the State Bank of Pakistan, the government's exchequer. It later turned out that he was substantially less—a State Bank employee, which certainly carried its own measure of prestige, but merely an administrative clerk overseeing low-volume accounts and transactions. Far from being an executive, he was not even in managerial grade, and his actual income was a fraction of what had been asserted. For Malik's mother, the only comfort was that the lie had been inspired by her striking looks and coquettish charm, which had utterly ensnared her suitor.

When the deception was finally revealed, it was already months into the marriage, and by then his mother was pregnant with Malik. In Western society, they would have split up long ago, but in the multiple religious, social, cultural and economic pressures of Pakistani society, they stayed put and vented their frustrations by pursuing enduring campaigns of bitterness and resentment against each other. They had condemned themselves to a lifetime of misery.

For Malik's father, the high point of his employment with the bank came early. Accounting records were being upgraded into the digital age, and Malik's father was selected as part of a team that would be sent to New York for a six-week training course in computer operations. Desperate to make amends with his aggrieved wife, he arranged for her to accompany him. Her pregnancy was in the final trimester, but a trip to America was the stuff of dreams and she jumped at the chance. Two weeks into the stay, she went into labour and delivered Malik. His father didn't know any better but all the members of his party advised him to obtain an American passport for the child. It would make his life, they said.

Back in Pakistan, the passport was placed in a drawer reserved for house valuables, and forgotten. It was taken out once, when Malik was five, and a renewal was due. He had faint memories of that visit to the American consulate in Karachi. A beautiful lawn with rich, green lushness he had never seen, a large reflecting pool of crystal water, white people in strange uniforms and an atmosphere so quiet, you felt that you had to speak in whispers. It felt a world apart from the bustle and chaos of the streets outside. All Malik wanted to do was run around and play, but his parents' stern looks and stiff demeanour told him he would be better off sitting quietly by their side.

A great constant in Malik's childhood had been devotion to Islam. Both his parents practiced all the articles of faith—the five daily prayers, fasting during Ramadan, frequent recitation from the Quran—even as they despised each other and plotted to make the other unhappy. Malik grew up with Islam as a way of life that was the most unchallengeable truth.

His sisters would be taught at home, but Malik was sent to school. He was a clever child, and it had stoked his father's ambitions that his son would become a doctor. At the same time, his parents indulged their spiritual ambitions for Malik by enrolling him in a madrassa near their home, where he went every afternoon after school to memorise the Quran and receive theological instruction.

Attendance at the madrassa continued for three years before Malik's father reluctantly withdrew him. It was interfering with schoolwork, and much as the father wanted his son to be steeped in the teachings of Islam, above everything else he wanted to one day acclaim him as a doctor of medicine. With a medical degree and a passport to America, his son's life would be set. It would be a life better than his own. Who knows, if all went well, he could even sponsor the family and get them all Green Cards.

At the age of seventeen, Malik was in his final year of high school. He took up preparations for the medical college admissions exam, but his heart wasn't in it. There was uncertainty about what he wanted from life, and he didn't want to end up an anonymous banking clerk like his dad. These were defining times in Pakistani society and polity. In neighbouring Afghanistan, the Mujahideen were fighting to drive out invading Soviet troops, while in Pakistan a military dictator named Zia-ul-Haq was moving full-throttle to implement the strictest interpretations of Islamic shariah law.

Malik's family lived in one of Karachi's middle-income suburbs, and every few days he would go to his local mosque to attend prayers with the congregation. One day after the sunset prayers of *maghrib*, two young men came over and sat next to him.

'*As-salaam-walaikum*, brother,' one of them began. His face was warm and kind, the tone polite and decorous. Malik was put immediately at ease.

'Are you regular in your prayers, brother?' the soft-spoken man continued. 'Forgive me, but we see you at the mosque only from time to time. Praise be to Allah, it is our duty to do all the five daily prayers.'

The approach had been casual and nonchalant. It was an effective opening line that was used by Muslim groups everywhere as they sought to engage recruits and increase their numbers.

Malik's natural response was guilt. Sure, he missed prayers every now and then. He used to be regular but lately had become lax. He felt ashamed. Sensing his discomfort, the two men made their move. A long discussion about duty to Allah and the rewards of Paradise followed. Malik listened intently and stayed with his new friends until late into the night.

He began attending the mosque regularly. A few days later, he was introduced to other members of the group. They were mostly young men around the same age as him, although there were two or three who seemed older, probably in their mid-twenties.

He began staying back at the mosque after prayer time to join the group in *zikr*, the act of discussion and remembrance of Allah. They would talk about the greatness of Allah and the glory of

Islam, and what they would do to anything or anyone that tried to come in the way of Islam's supremacy. Malik was easily moved. He felt passions being unlocked, forces of outlook and attitude being unleashed that he did not know he possessed.

After precisely one month, during which he had begun to cohesively integrate within the group, Malik was invited to attend a *dars*, a formal lecture by a Muslim scholar. It was a large gathering, numbering in the hundreds, in a makeshift tent outside one of Karachi's famous mosques. The topic was jihad, the Islamic concept of holy war. Malik was transfixed. He returned hungry to read and learn more about the structure and history of his religion. His activities picked up pace. He began attending one or two *dars* sessions every week, and started reading on his own to keep up.

Dialogue within his immediate group also moved apace. The group leader directed them to study pamphlets and other literature from Islamic revivalist movements. Political debate was also introduced. Soon, they had familiarised themselves with the works of the Egyptian scholar Sayyid Qutb and the Pakistani thinker Abul Ala Mawdudi. They would meet other groups and participate in seminars. The Palestinian struggle, the Israeli lobby in the United States, the Saudi royal family, Indian armed forces in Kashmir—it was all dissected and debated. Malik's parents became concerned about the intensity of his involvement, but he would remind them it was all in the way of Allah, which rendered them speechless. Around this time, Malik also managed to scrape through the medical college test and landed a spot in medical school.

In those days, student unrest was common throughout Pakistan. University and college campuses were hotbeds of political movements. At Malik's medical school, classes were irregular and school was frequently closed. It was also a time when the ISI,

Pakistan's infamous secret service, was coming into its own. They had infiltrated all centres of higher education in the country and were looking for smart young men with militant outlooks who could join Afghan Mujahideen in their jihad against the Soviet Union.

A meeting was set up by the leader of Malik's local mosque group. Malik spent three hours with the ISI scouts and impressed them with his keenness, focus and commitment. He came across as driven and passionate, but with a certain degree of insight.

One week later he was in Jalalabad alongside Mujahideen troops learning to booby trap armoured Soviet vehicles.

Malik took to it like a natural and never looked back.

After a few weeks, he returned to Karachi and spun a tale to his family. He attended medical school very sketchily, eventually dropping out and never earning his degree.

Now, years after the Soviets had finally retreated from Afghanistan, Malik found himself lavishly funded by obscure sources that he chose never to question. Tasks were conveyed through intermediaries, the work involving covert assignments intended to further the cause of Islam. Malik had earned an impeccable reputation from his days in the Afghan jihad. He was revered a grandmaster at tactics and logistics—a highly prized individual.

The work could not be done openly. It violated laws made by man and ran the risk of trouble with the police, the legal authorities, and the United Nations as well as dominant world governments, especially those in the Western world who were openly hostile to Islam and the Muslim way of life. This qualified the occupation as jihad—and that needed no further justification. A true Muslim surrendered himself to upholding and safeguarding the Islamic faith, which was constantly under threat from Satanic intrigue.

Malik Feysal had become the very embodiment of this doctrine. He was an operative in the service of Allah.

Approaching the end of prayer, Malik ran his hands lightly over his face, begging God's forgiveness for sins he may have committed, and strength for fighting Satan's darkness and evil. As he got up and folded his prayer mat, the 9/11 poster caught his eye. There was a downpour, and the ceiling in his apartment had sprung a small leak that was dripping onto the picture's plastic coating. Wiping the drops off with his sleeve, he went over recent events in his mind.

Two days earlier, on his weekly surveillance check at the tailoring shop, Malik had found it closed for the first time. There had been no sign of Zafar. His instructions were to check every other day for a week, and then daily. If the subject went missing at any point, a confirmatory check had to be done the following day. Yesterday Malik had staked out the shop again; it remained closed. A handwritten note had been pasted over the pull-down metal shutters. It said that the proprietor had been taken ill and the shop would reopen very soon.

Had they already scored a hit? This was only the first week of surveillance. The plan now called for a phone call to Zafar's house.

Rains hadn't lashed Karachi like this in years. Most of the low-lying localities were submerged, some waist-deep. Water stood on major roads and stalled cars everywhere. Near-chaotic at the best of times, Karachi's unforgiving traffic had disintegrated into anarchy. The lights had stopped working and the police just stood around looking dazed and overwhelmed. Rain invariably had this paralysing effect on Karachi. Unlike most of the subcontinent, the monsoon in Karachi was usually light, and some years it was absent altogether. The city had never bothered to prepare itself for the torrential downpours that came only once every few years or so.

From his tenth-floor apartment overlooking Empress Market, Malik surveyed the streets of downtown Karachi. Traffic still snarled in every direction, but the rain had eased off a bit and the smell of fried munchkins now wafted up from the sidewalks below. Malik punched in Zafar's home number on his cell phone. After a couple of rings, a young male voice answered. It was Zafar's brother.

'*Salaam-walaikum*, is Zafar Majeed home?' asked Malik, disguising his voice with a strong nasal twang.

After a brief pause, the voice at the other end answered. 'Zafar... no, he's...he's been taken to the hospital. Who is this please?'

Malik had rehearsed all this in advance. 'Oh, I'm sorry to hear that,' he said, fronting according to plan. 'I'm calling on behalf of a garments company and we wanted to see if Zafar could do some contract work for us. Any idea when he might be getting released from the hospital? I hope he gets better soon.'

'No idea...I don't know,' the young man managed to say. He was terribly distracted, having just heard from his sister that the specialist doctor had not sounded hopeful about their brother. 'Maybe next week? You'll have to call back.'

Malik could kill to find out the details of Zafar's illness, but he was too disciplined to do anything that could look unusual or out of the ordinary.

'Yes, of course,' he said gently in a signing off-tone. 'I pray he gets better soon.'

Had the patient become wild and crazy, as had been predicted? Malik was itching to know. And how serious was the illness?

Hopefully it would take his life. It needed to be a lethal, devastating illness, if all their efforts were going to be worth anything.

This kind of work resulted in the loss of innocent lives, but Malik had rationalised it. Once in Kandahar, in treacherous territory surrounded by the mountains of southern Afghanistan, he had arranged explosives for a group of Taliban fighters who used them to blow up vehicles belonging to the United Nations and the World Food Program. Some aid workers had been killed too. To Malik, the explosions were an act of jihad, and if bystanders lost their lives, it was a necessary sacrifice. They were *shaheed*s, martyrs to Allah who were guaranteed Paradise. It was the same with the people who had died in the nightclub bombing in Bali, where Malik had been involved in reconnaissance and target selection. He reasoned they were better off dead. Who knows what sinful lives they had been leading? Malik gave them an opportunity to die in the holy cause of Islam. Their souls had been saved. He had done them a favour.

Four

It was well into the afternoon by the time Asad could even think of lunch. After finishing rounds in the ICU, his team had seen two new admissions in the general ward and then visited the private ward where another new admission awaited. There were a number of other patients who had been admitted in the previous few days and were in various stages of recovery or diagnostic investigation; they were each seen to as well.

Morning rounds were part of any busy doctor's workday. They were sometimes a cakewalk, but more often they were demanding and intense. It all depended on how sick your patients were, and how much effort was needed to diagnose their ailments and make reasoned judgments about the best treatment. When Asad emerged from the last room on the list—a woman in her forties who had been fainting without explanation and was undergoing tests to see if these were epileptic fits—he had begun to feel quite drained.

The end of patient ward rounds provided a natural break in the day. Asad's habit was to gather the whole team in one spot and go over the major issues that had come up during the course of the morning. It was an opportunity to reinforce all the key orders and instructions to his staff. Not that he really felt the need with a competent and trusted resident like Farida, but it had become a compulsion. This was also the time when Asad would chat a bit with the students, give them a chance to ask questions, and invite them to make comments if they wished to.

The private wing was the newest part of the hospital. It had been built for an elite clientele who could afford to pay for five-star luxury. There were three splendidly furnished floors with teak-paneled walls, and a cavernous lobby that had been thoughtfully decorated with tropical plants, plush sofas, colourful, abstract murals, and a water fountain in the centre, carved in pink marble. The high-paying patients were typically the last stop on Asad's rounds, and this lobby had become his favourite place to gather the team before disbanding.

Everyone stepped off the elevator and followed their attending to a set of sofas in one corner. Asad turned to Farida and together the two checked off things to be done while the junior residents and the students watched and listened. Asad reminded her to do a brain death examination on their new admission in the ICU and arrange for a meeting with the family afterwards. Farida nodded. The students asked a few questions, and Asad answered them patiently. He found himself repeating some of the things he had already mentioned during rounds, but that was all right. He had once been a medical student too, and he knew very well how a medical student's attention span was easily tested by a busy morning's rounds.

Karachi's midday heat felt like a blast from a furnace as Asad emerged from the lobby's icy air-conditioning. It had rained heavily yesterday but today the sun burned down mercilessly and the heat was back. The private wing was set apart from the rest of the hospital and one had to walk across a sprawling lawn to get back to the main buildings. Farida set off towards the main hospital, heading to her duties in the ICU. The students trudged off in the direction of the medical school buildings—Nadia headed for the library, the others to the cafeteria.

Lunch was on Asad's mind, too. There were two eating places, one in the hospital and another in the medical school, but both tended to be crowded and busy. Like most of his colleagues, Asad preferred the doctors' lounge. The menu was limited but the ambience was relaxing and he enjoyed the repartee that dominated the lounge's atmosphere at mealtime.

The place was in full swing when Asad entered. It was a long though rather narrow room, with tables laid out in two long and crooked rows. Food was served from the far end of the room, across from where Asad had entered. Behind the food service, a wide plate glass window looked out onto a pleasing landscape of manicured grass, trimmed bushes, and a small lake circled by palm trees. The doctors' lounge was usually the preserve of attending physicians—consultants like Asad who had admitting privileges at the hospital as well as teaching appointments on the faculty of the attached medical school. Sometimes the residents used it too. It had been built after years of insistent demand from the hospital's senior doctors. They had waged a trenchant campaign with the hospital administration for a place where they could relax and eat meals without running into patients and their families. Commissioned almost three years ago, it had quickly become the favourite haunt for most of the staff physicians, and had also acquired a reputation as a good spot to sample hospital gossip. Everyone looked forward to spending time there and enjoying conversation with friends and colleagues.

Asad chose from a selection of salads and cold meats and waited in line to pay. A hum of chatter covered the room. All tables were occupied, but a few scattered chairs were vacant. People were eating and talking, laughing and arguing. There was a large plasma screen TV in one corner, tuned, as it usually was unless an international cricket match was in progress, to one of the 24-hour news channels. Hillary Clinton appeared to be giving a press briefing to a crowd of reporters. The channel was either CNN or BBC, Asad couldn't tell from this distance.

A group of his friends spotted Asad and waved him over. Taking the empty chair, he nodded greetings to the three others at the table, each an attending doctor who, like Asad, had gone to the United States for medical specialisation and returned home to Pakistan within the last few years. Asad knew them all well. They were around the same age—late thirties—and often sat together enjoying each other's company. One of them, an endocrinologist named Bilal Kureshi, was actually Asad's classmate from medical school and they went back a long way. The other two were Aziz Kamal, an orthopedic surgeon who had trained in Omaha, and Omar Javed, who had trained for two years as a pediatrician in New York City before changing his mind and becoming a pathologist from the University of North Carolina at Chapel Hill.

Few issues these days excited Pakistanis like world politics, especially the role played by America and the forces associated with their beloved religion, Islam. Asad guessed the conversation around most tables was this very topic, or something closely related.

'Just look at that bitch Hillary,' his friend Bilal said, nodding towards the large TV screen. 'I can't believe she goes about her life with a straight face. She caught her husband fornicating and didn't leave him. And she calls herself a champion for women's issues? What a hypocrite.'

'I didn't think she'd accept the post of secretary of state after all that,' Asad said, referring to the bitter battle between Hillary

Clinton and Barack Obama during the Democratic primaries, in which the two candidates had sparred like sworn enemies.

Aziz Kamal was itching to speak. 'A woman like Hillary wouldn't be where she is if she went about turning down something like that,' he said, with a mouthful of chicken biryani. 'Just look at her. She'd sell her own mother to get ahead. This means nothing to her.'

Asad wasn't sure what Aziz meant, and asked him to explain. He was well aware of Aziz's strong views against American foreign policy, especially the wars in Iraq and Afghanistan, but he wasn't clear if his colleague was admiring the US secretary of state or criticising her.

'American politicians are all vermin,' replied Aziz. 'They have two simple goals—get oil and crush Muslims. They're not concerned about anything else. A bitch like Hillary will do whatever it takes to grab whatever scraps of power she can. She'll go ahead and screw the world and it won't even register on the radar screen of her conscience. Assuming she has a conscience at all.'

The words were uttered with an edge but everyone took them in stride, nodding lightly and getting on with lunch. Deep down, all of them, even Asad, felt aggrieved by America's overreach around the world although not everyone was willing to acknowledge it so openly. To a degree, all four doctors at the table shared a common discomfort about the United States. This was partly why they had passed up a life of material comforts in America and come back to roll up their sleeves in the struggles of Pakistan.

Almost to a person, Pakistani medical graduates who went to the United States for further study eventually opted to get Green Cards and become immigrants in America's melting pot. That the group at this table had foregone America's well known rewards in favour of returning home made them a unique minority. There could be compelling reasons to return to Pakistan—the obligation to care for aging and disabled parents was probably the most forceful—but even that wasn't enough to make people give up the attractive salaries for medical professionals in the United States. Pakistani doctors didn't move back from America unless there had been something negative about their American experience.

The negative part in Aziz's American experience had to do with his extreme sensitivity towards any adverse comments about Islam and Muslims. He came from a conservative household where devout beliefs had been encouraged and nurtured. Professional ambition brought him to America, and his natural work ethic helped him flourish as a surgeon. But exposed to grand temptations like liquor and extramarital sex, he became even more closely wedded to Islamic ideology. Outside of work, he had spent nearly all his time exclusively with other Muslims, meeting only people who were regular attendees at Omaha's Islamic Center.

A few months after 9/11, Aziz sold his thriving orthopaedics practice and left Omaha for Karachi. He had been unable to stomach what he felt was subtle vilification of Muslims in American media and society. At least that was the public story. The private story, everyone suspected, was more sinister, and they were right. In the wake of 9/11, Omaha's Islamic Center was one of many mosques across America that the FBI had placed under surveillance. As one of the mosque's prominent members, Aziz had been brought in for questioning. They grilled him about his background and asked private questions about personal activities and the nature of his beliefs. No charges were filed but Dr Aziz Kamal, orthopaedic surgeon, proud American immigrant and even prouder Muslim, couldn't get over the harassment. Confused and embittered, he felt it would be impossible to find happiness in America and decided to return to Pakistan.

The TV screen changed to a new picture. Hillary was gone, replaced by a comely blonde delivering a news update. The anchor was familiar and Asad realised they had been watching CNN. The sound was turned low and couldn't be heard over the lounge chatter. News snippets ran on a red ticker across the bottom of the screen. Everyone at the table had a good view and for a while they watched and ate in silence.

The scene switched again. On screen now was a hapless-looking man dressed in combat fatigues, kneeling on the floor and looking despondent. Behind him stood three men wearing headbands inscribed with Arabic, their faces concealed behind black *niqab*s. It was a story that had been in the news for the last few days and was now common knowledge. Militants in Pakistan's lawless tribal area had taken a Pakistani soldier hostage. There were no demands, only repeated threats that the hostage would be beheaded as punishment for Pakistan's alliance with America and its tacit support for the wars in Iraq and Afghanistan. Yesterday, the militants had finally done it. You couldn't see it on TV, but the video was on the Internet.

This time it was Omar Javed who broke the silence. 'Did you guys hear about the beheading?' he asked. 'Really disgusting. Really very barbaric and disgusting. Nothing in the world could justify doing that to a human being. What is this world coming to?'

Asad and Bilal gravely nodded, finding it impossible to disagree. Aziz felt differently about the issue, but found it uncomfortable to share his thoughts and kept his tongue in check.

'This is really beyond all limits,' Omar spoke again, seeking to generate some discussion. As a pathologist whose day was spent among dead bodies and organs, he had a taste for the macabre, and was the only one of the four to have downloaded the video.

It was grotesque but it was also riveting, and Omar had played it several times.

Asad decided he had had enough. Suggesting that they talk about something else, he tried steering the conversation towards cricket, usually a failsafe topic. Omar ignored him.

'These people aren't Muslims,' Omar persisted. 'How can they do this? They're giving Muslims all over the world a bad name. This is not what Islam teaches us.'

Of the four men at the table, Omar had been the least enthusiastic about returning to Pakistan. He had embraced life in America with the insight that it was a country where he could cultivate liberal sensibilities. Not long after arriving in New York, he had found his way into a cultural niche, espousing left-liberal causes, subscribing to *The New Yorker* and *The New Republic*, and shopping at ethnic food stores in Greenwich Village. He would listen to National Public Radio, watch nothing but Public Television, and made valiant attempts to become a connoisseur of fine wines.

In the second year of his pediatric residency, Omar met a medical student named Linda and followed her to Chapel Hill. A youthful American brunette, she shared Omar's tastes in virtually everything from movies and magazines to zucchini bread and oral sex, and soon became his live-in girlfriend. The move to Chapel Hill required Omar to give up his fond dream of becoming a pediatrician and change career tracks to start a new residency in pathology, which was the only program at the University of North Carolina Medical Center that had a mid-term opening that year. Omar was in love and considered it a trivial price to pay.

He was back in Pakistan now because he was an only child and, after his father died of a heart attack, his mother had been left alone with advancing Parkinson's disease. Returning to Pakistan was easier than he had imagined. A few months earlier, Linda had left him for a Brazilian dentist. In the emotional turmoil, his father's death and the helplessness of his lonely and crippled mother overwhelmed him. The job opening at Avicenna University Hospital in Karachi had been a godsend.

Now married to a distant cousin, with whom he had an adorable eight-month old girl, Omar had become a devoted family man and was utterly at home in the role. Though he barely kept up with the prayers and rituals, he still considered himself a believer and a Muslim. Those days in the United States had been another life. Omar recalled them warmly for the most part, except the break-up with Linda, which was heart-wrenching, and there was something in him that said perhaps he would never get over it.

Aziz knew Omar to be sympathetic to America and American causes, and he tended to dismiss this attitude as naivety. He had met Omar only about a year ago, when Omar had started his job at the hospital. Both men sensed they held opposing views of life, but still managed to be cordial, interacting together almost daily as medical colleagues. Once, while being lectured by Aziz that Al-Qaeda was nothing but a propagandist American fabrication, Omar had tried to counter-argue by referring to CNN, which Aziz had found laughable and he had said as much. Ever since then, he had been reluctant to engage Omar on religion and politics. But now Omar was making judgmental remarks about who could be considered a Muslim, and it was too much for Aziz.

'It's not for you or anyone else to judge who is a Muslim and who isn't,' Aziz said in a measured, even voice, looking straight at Omar. He had put down his fork and was bent forward, pressing down on the table with the flat palms of his hands.

'Come on, Aziz. You can't chop an innocent man's head off and be a true Muslim. It's as simple as that.'

'Well, you obviously don't know this,' snapped Aziz, sounding irritated, 'but this is the preferred Islamic method of dealing with your enemies. It's in our history.'

'Doesn't make it right,' Omar muttered quietly.

Aziz dropped his head and began picking at the food on his plate. His body language suggested he had decided to drop it. Asad and Bilal looked at each other, exchanging glances in relief. They had both been thinking of excuses to leave the table, had the argument picked up.

A shrill sound broke the table's tense silence. Asad's pager was beeping with a message from Farida: Family meeting, ICU 9, 2 pm. 'Sorry, I gotta go,' he said, excusing himself from the gathering.

Heading towards the ICU, he rehearsed what he would say to Zafar's family. Breaking bad news was something Asad felt he would never become good at. It wasn't the sort of thing you ever got used to.

Five

When rounds broke up, Farida had decided to return to the ICU to perform Bed 9's brain death examination. On the way, she stopped at the sandwich stand next to the outpatient clinics and bought a chicken roll, eating as she walked. The sky was overcast but there was also a breeze, hinting against rain. Gardeners tended to the sprawling grounds. Visitors sat on benches or along the lakeside, looking out on to tranquil water. Here and there, patients in white hospital dress were pushed along slowly in wheelchairs, an IV pole or a catheter bag attached.

It had long occurred to doctors that when patients—particularly young patients—died and were buried, some perfectly good organs got buried with them. Brain death became an important concept once surgical advances made it possible to transplant organs from one human being to another. Experience had shown that there were many situations—a devastating head injury or a massive stroke, for example—in which all brain function was irreversibly lost even though the heart continued to beat. In these circumstances, continuous blood circulation could keep the rest of the body alive for a while, even up to a few days, provided the person was connected to a breathing machine.

Eventually laws were passed to make brain death (properly diagnosed by two independent physicians in accordance with specified medical guidelines) equivalent to death, and the science and practice of human organ transplantation was born.

Once brain death became an accepted medical definition, it was clear that the usefulness of the idea was not just limited to organ transplantation needs. If someone were diagnosed as being brain dead, that provided an obvious rationale for discontinuing medical care. This helped curtail costly expenses associated with futile medical care, and mitigated the anguish that came from medical treatment that had been needlessly dragged out. For medical personnel and patients' families alike, the diagnosis of brain death brought closure in a grave medical situation that threatened to drag on without benefit to anyone.

This had been Asad's intent in seeking a diagnosis of brain death on Zafar Majeed. Care in the ICU was expensive, typically the most expensive part of a hospital stay in terms of daily charges, and even in an impoverished economy like Pakistan's, could cost the equivalent of several hundred dollars a day, enough to cripple the average family in a handful of days. Asad considered it his duty to decide if all this expenditure was going to be worth anything, especially for a family like Zafar's, who from all available evidence appeared to have modest means. Farida understood this reasoning well. She had spent enough hours on rounds with Asad to understand his thinking on a number of complex matters, and had decided to adopt his philosophy on the issue of efficiently diagnosing brain death to minimise futile care.

Two nurses were haggling about the best time for a tea break when Farida marched into the ICU. Nodding them a quick hello, she strode towards Bed 9, where Zafar lay. She had her trademark air of intent and purpose that had won her the respect not only of colleagues and superiors but, importantly, of the nursing staff as well. It was common knowledge among the residents that if the nurses didn't like you—if they caught you being lazy on the job, found you lying to cover yourself or, sin of sins, showing arrogance—they could make your life a living hell. For Farida this was a non-issue. She always meant business, and everyone knew it.

The nurse assigned to Zafar's case stiffened the moment she saw the senior neurology resident walk up. Farida had called ahead and the nurse stood ready with everything needed to carry out a brain death examination.

While Zafar lay motionless, the ventilator at his bedside kept up its rhythmic hiss, blowing a precisely controlled sixteen-breaths-per-minute into his lungs. An IV line curled around Zafar's arm, ending in a fine bore catheter that disappeared under the skin. Another larger bore IV lay just above the collarbone, sutured to the skin against the side of the neck and securely lodged in Zafar's jugular vein. A monitor above the bed sombrely displayed the heart rhythm, blood pressure and blood oxygen—all deceptively normal.

Farida began her evaluation with a review of the nursing charts to make sure Zafar wasn't receiving any tranquilisers or sedating drugs, as their effects would interfere with the examination's findings. Satisfied that he wasn't, she then slipped on a pair of disposable gloves and approached the bed from Zafar's right side.

Bending forward towards his ear, she screamed out his name with enough decibels to wake even the soundest sleeper. This was the opening drill of the brain death assessment. Alarming as it would have been to an outside observer, in the ICU it surprised no one. Farida continued with the remainder of the examination, performing each step deliberately and meticulously. She wasn't one for shortcuts and always approached clinical examinations diligently, performing every procedure according to strict protocol, never missing a step and never altering the sequence. Through it all, Zafar remained immobile.

All of this was as expected. Zafar's young brain had been destroyed by a mysterious and rapid illness—most likely a viral infection, though one couldn't be sure—and had irreversibly ceased to function. It only remained for Farida to determine if Zafar would be able to generate any breathing effort. This was the most troubling part of the examination, because it required disconnecting the ventilator while observing for visible signs of breathing.

With a brisk twisting motion, Farida pulled at the ventilator attachment. Warm, moist air spewed out as the coils of ventilator duct broke free from the endotracheal tube sticking out of Zafar's mouth. Handing the ventilator duct to Zafar's nurse, Farida fixed all her attention on the patient's chest and face as she searched for any effort at breathing. A minute passed by without any trace of movement. The ventilator kept up its steady hiss, blowing hot air into nothing. In the background, the rest of the ICU remained busy as ever.

Farida glanced up at the monitor and saw that Zafar's heart rate had slowed from 80 beats per minute to 60. She decided to wait a little more. After ninety seconds off the ventilator, Zafar's heart rate had crept down to fifty-two. He hadn't moved a muscle or made any effort to breathe whatsoever. Farida motioned to the nurse, who reattached the ventilator tubing to Zafar's airways. The heart rate started to climb up again. The examination was over.

Zafar's brain had been put through its paces and produced no detectable function. He was brain dead. His heart was still pumping warm blood to the organs, but it was just a matter of time before that too would come to a halt. Zafar wasn't coming back. He was dead.

Life as a chief resident was so crushingly busy, you had little time to reflect on the tragic circumstances of your patients. There was so much you had to be responsible for—patients and their families were being cared for in all corners of the hospital, and the cruel reality of Murphy's Law was that anything could go wrong at anytime. Complications and catastrophes erupted in the emergency room, ICU, ward, and clinic without warning, and had to be tackled with urgency, skill and precision. It was the chief resident who directly anchored this crisis management.

Farida was a natural in this role. She had been raised in a conservative household and educated at Karachi's famous Parsi school for girls where any kind of leisure was considered frivolous and the values of hard work and pragmatism were drilled into your bones. She had approached medical school with remarkable single-mindedness and graduated with many honours.

Being an only child, her parents denied her permission to leave Pakistan for higher training. In typical fashion, Farida allowed herself to brood over it for exactly one day, and then flung herself into the neurology training position at Avicenna, where colleagues and supervisors had come to regard her work ethic as legendary.

As she peeled off her gloves and prepared to wash her hands, Farida noticed Nadia standing in one corner of the cubicle. Nadia, who had never been involved in declaring someone brain dead, was shadowing Farida like a second skin, intent on observing every detail. She had followed Farida to the ICU and slipped in right behind her. This reflected interest and eagerness to learn, and Farida made a mental note to put in a special recommendation to Asad when it came time to mark the medical students' grades. While she quickly jotted a note in Zafar's chart to document the examination findings, Farida nodded towards Nadia and asked the young student if she had any questions.

Nadia wanted to know about the significance of rocking the head from side to side, something she had come across in textbooks but had struggled to understand. Farida patiently explained everything, going over the brainstem pathways that were responsible for eye movements and for transmitting information about balance and posture. Depending on which way the head moved, and whether the patient was awake or in coma, the eyes could go one way or the other. If the brain was dead, the eyes did nothing at all and just remained fixed in the head, drifting passively in the same direction that the head rolled. You had to know the exact brain circuits underlying the process to be able to predict and interpret the response, which was essential for measuring brainstem function. It was a common point of confusion for students, but once Farida had gone through it with her, Nadia grasped it clearly.

Stepping out of Zafar's cubicle, Farida asked the ICU reception clerk if Bed 9's family was in the waiting area. She was told that they were.

'Please ask them to come and wait in the seminar room,' said Farida. A small anteroom meant for tutorials and student teaching, the ICU's seminar room also doubled as a meeting room where doctors could communicate with patients' families. More often than not, developments in the ICU were bad, even lethal news, and the seminar room hung heavy with the pall of grief.

'We have to call Dr Mirza,' Farida said as she walked towards a computer terminal and began typing, sending her boss a brief message on his pager through the local network.

Within minutes, Asad was in the ICU. Zafar's family is waiting, he was told. He directed an enquiring look towards Farida, who nodded in return. 'Brain dead,' she said.

'What an unfortunate case,' Asad responded. Having noticed Nadia next to Farida, he now addressed them both. 'How are his family members doing? Shall we give them more time?'

'We need to move on this, Dr Mirza,' said Farida efficiently.

'I think they've had time to adjust. They've known what's coming ever since we did rounds. I know they're expecting to hear the worst. Besides, we need the bed. There's a young trauma downstairs and there's no other bed in the ICU.'

It was a tight fit in the little room, but comfort was farthest from the minds of everyone squeezed in there. An uncle, younger brother, and a sister represented Zafar's family. Through the anteroom's half-open door, Zafar's mother could be seen standing next to her son's bed, rubbing his forehead lightly, tracing out the ridges of his eyebrows with her fingers. When a nurse's aide had come out and asked the family to assemble inside for a meeting, she had known right away, the way a mother's heart knows, that they had been summoned for the worst. She didn't want anything to do with it, and asked instead just to be allowed next to Zafar's bed. Zafar's father had stayed back too, much preferring to remain at his perch in the waiting area, reciting verses from the Quran.

'I regret very much that I don't have good news to give you,' Asad began. Each time he went through a gut-churning family meeting like this, Asad always thought to himself how ironic it was that nothing in medical training really prepared you for such a demanding task. Once again, he was forced to reflect that this was one of the hardest, if not the absolute hardest, things for a doctor to do. Perhaps the only way you learned how to do it well was to keep doing it, to get firsthand experience that seemingly could be imparted no other way.

But after having grappled with these circumstances scores of times, Asad still felt he was a novice. The same anxious chill welled up inside him each time—the same fear that he might come across as callous or disrespectful, a guilt rooted in failure and helplessness, a dread of getting sucked into a vortex of his own emotions. Perhaps, he thought to himself now, you never got better at it because there was no good way to do it.

Six

A THIRD-FLOOR flat in a congested community of squat, scruffy apartment blocks, at the corner of a helter-skelter traffic intersection approaching lethal levels of noise and air pollution—in Karachi, it didn't get more middle class than this. There was no air-conditioning. A rickety fan pushed warm air around the room.

Malik was hunched behind a stout and busty prostitute, pounding into her as she crouched on all fours. This was how he kept himself sane and regulated the pressure level of his furious mind. It was easily rationalised because there were explicit accommodations for male sexual urges. Not for nothing were you permitted to maintain four concurrent wives and have sexual intercourse with concubines, should you have any.

He was working towards a climax but the girl, who offered nothing to the act beyond being a physical receptacle for Malik's hardness, was bored and indifferent. When Malik's cell phone rang, she casually reached out and looked at the display. Craning her neck, she handed the phone to Malik, who saw the caller's name and immediately lost his erection.

Pushing the girl away, he answered the phone. It was Hamza,

asking for details on the index case. Malik had none, and Hamza let loose with a volley of insults and obscenities. He was incredulous. What imbecile had the Network assigned to assist a serious scientific talent like Hamza?

The girl was paid off and Malik got up to wash and bathe. His libido had imploded, and in its place now was a deep, unrelenting anxiety that kept ratcheting further up. He found himself in a situation of which he was not in full command, and his body never took to this well. The mouth had gone dry and his stomach was starting to churn up a storm. He felt hungry but had no appetite. He felt tired, but his restlessness wouldn't let him sit still for a second.

He urgently needed to start feeling in control again, otherwise the physical discomforts would worsen. The temples would throb and his neck would become stiff and sore. And no doubt those dreaded sharp jabs between the shoulder blades, like some agitated bird of prey digging at his back with dagger-like talons, would also return.

Malik's body had been conditioned to generate these visceral reactions whenever things appeared to be slipping. It was a formidable safeguard against error or carelessness.

An amount of uncertainty had crept into this particular assignment, and the alarm bells of his bodily responses had begun to sound. To a degree, some uncertainty had to be accepted in any kind of project management, but uncertainty at the core was like the heinous designs of Satan on man's soul, and could never be allowed to consolidate.

Malik had set his threshold for tolerating uncertainty very low, forcing him to plug all holes in data gathering well before they could became an issue. His instinct, finely tuned like a virtuoso's violin and seasoned to near-perfection through almost a decade of the most secret, high-stakes reconnaissance work, was to smoke out all relevant information from key sources.

Data, data and more data—that was ground rule number one in this line of work. (Ground rule number two being never to proceed on an assumption.) The more you knew about a situation, the greater the chances that you would come out ahead and succeed. The logic was simple and watertight. The success rate for his assignments was expected to be a hundred per cent, give or take nothing.

The adversary wasn't invincible, but it did possess extraordinary and unprecedented strength. Undoubtedly, it would be vanquished, for that was foreordained in the Book of Fate.

Allah had chosen this humble servant to be one of the grand instruments for realising that glorious future, and Malik knew he couldn't afford to screw it up. His great and awesome responsibility was to make it happen.

Just do it, as it said in the Nike ad campaign. Malik couldn't get over the irony that he was able to identify so closely with the motto of something he abhorred to the core, an American corporate behemoth.

Right now the order of business was to confirm the fate of Zafar Majeed. Was the man dead? And if so, was it an illness of the brain that killed him? These were the questions.

The answer—which Malik yearned would be 'yes' to both—lay somewhere out there, in one of Karachi's hospitals, wherever Zafar's family had taken him. It would have been a simple question to ask on the telephone, when Malik had managed to catch Zafar's younger brother on the line, but that risked raising suspicion, and no matter how remote, a risk was a risk. It was a bad place to be—one of the crevices in the earth that led into an infernal abyss called failure.

You never took a risk if you could at all help it. That was the whole point of all the preparation, to get you to a place where risk was unnecessary, even irrelevant.

But of course sometimes you had to, though not before the particular set of circumstances had been story-boarded, or illustrated as a flow-chart, or clarified through some other illuminating graphic, and scrutinised from all viewpoints.

If you had analysed it to death and there was no other way to get to your target, well that was the only kind of risk you took. It had to be an acceptable risk, which ultimately depended on how badly you wanted to get something done.

Like right now.

Karachi had several hospitals but the seriously sick invariably got taken to one of the big three—Civil, Crescent, or Avicenna. The first two were state-run mega-infirmaries with nearly two thousand beds each; the quality of care was unpredictable but as charity hospitals they took all comers and remained constantly overrun by the city's indigent and needy.

Avicenna University Hospital was smaller, maybe five hundred beds, tops. A professionally managed, private teaching hospital, it functioned at the level of a good county hospital in the United States. The quality of care was sound and reliable, but the catch was expense—few could afford it.

Malik decided he would telephone Civil and Crescent first, and then Avicenna if necessary, to make the appropriate enquiry. No risk would be incurred and there was a good chance he could learn something important.

There was no record of a Zafar Majeed at either Civil or Crescent, but at Avicenna, Malik found his target.

'He's admitted in the ICU, sir', the switchboard operator said.

She was reading off an iridescent computer display, which listed Zafar Majeed as an occupant of Intensive Care Unit, Bed 9.

Malik asked to be connected through but got a busy signal. A few minutes later, he tried again.

'Avicenna University Hospital, how may I help you?'

'Could you connect me to the ICU please?'

'Just a moment, sir.'

A popular patriotic melody played while Malik waited on hold. His pulse had quickened and he was suddenly aware of his breathing. He was bracing himself to pose as a relative of the patient. Some nervousness was inevitable.

'ICU, hello.'

'Yes, hello, I'm calling to check on the condition of Zafar Majeed. He's one of your patients in the ICU.'

People were forever calling the hospital to check after their loved ones, but official policy forbade the divulging of any medical information on the telephone. To the ICU receptionists and nurses, fielding these calls was sometimes a nuisance, but mostly it was a mindless drill.

Every few months, the head nurse sent a shrill memo to the hospital's Manager of Communications protesting that the switchboard wasn't doing enough to screen these calls. The memos were usually ignored. His switchboard operators were meant to forward calls and not screen them, was how the manager saw it.

'I'm sorry, sir, information about patients cannot be given on the phone.'

Malik made a rapid risk assessment in his mind. His heart was thumping, but he decided he could push a little.

'All right, but please can you just tell me how he's doing? I'm his brother-in-law and we're all worried sick about him. We've been told he's really very sick. Is he still in dange…'

The receptionist cut in. 'Can't tell you on the phone, sir. We can only communicate with the family in person. I'm sorry.'

Malik said thanks and hung up.

That was as far as he would allow himself to go. A small concern appeared in his constantly self-scrutinising mind that he might already have gone too far. Was there a chance the phone call might be remembered and get relayed to members of Zafar's family? He reasoned that it would not, because the hospital must be getting such calls all the time. That's right, it would hardly have been noticed.

The thought relaxed Malik and allowed him to exhale. He felt his pulse ease.

The call to Avicenna had been a good, productive move. More data was needed but still, critical information had been gained. The subject was in the ICU at Avicenna, which meant, at the very least, that he had been taken dangerously ill. He was probably dying. That's what happened to most people in an ICU.

But of course that would be an assumption, and assumption was the ultimate basis of all screw-ups. The disastrous operation with anthrax, hastily cobbled together in those hectic days following 9/11, could not be forgotten. The legwork had been spotty and the lethal dose of spores fundamentally miscalculated, which had led to an unworkable plan founded on faulty assumptions. There was no question of taking a casual approach this time around. Was it a brain disease raging in Zafar, as they had projected? That was still unanswered. Malik couldn't report back to his associate just yet. Not before the scouting was complete.

Allah had no patience for incomplete work, nor did the Network.

Ramzi Yousef's pathetic example was a lesson for all. In 1993, he had stuffed six-hundred kilos of urea, nitroglycerin and other explosive chemicals into a Ryder van and exploded it in the underground garage of Tower One of the World Trade Center in Manhattan. Far from causing the skyscraper to collapse—as was predicted in the operational plan—the bomb proved little more than a nuisance. Only six people died, and the building was reopened within days.

The calculations had been based on assumptions about the building's foundations and steel frame, all of which turned out to be wrong. Even the cyanide gas that Ramzi had hoped would massively release from the explosion, ended up consumed in the combustion because the wrong ratios of aluminum and magnesium azides had been used.

It was sloppy reconnaissance and stupid execution.

And Allah had no patience for it. Nor did the Network.

Malik had no plans to be another Ramzi Yousef. A past master of scouting, Malik also understood that in this kind of work if you allowed yourself to believe you were good, you might as well be dead. No two situations were the same, and events had to be analysed and re-analysed from multiple angles constantly, so there would be no blind spots left.

And this new project was different, far more demanding and treacherous than anything he had previously been involved in. Malik understood the importance of biological warfare, which he felt was certain to be the terrorism of the future. After 9/11, conventional explosives were passé. They had become too difficult and too risky in any setting, either in airplanes and airports, or in bridges, malls, parks, stadiums or other public settings. The idea of a nuclear explosion was still attractive, but the logistics were formidable and in any case all attempts to obtain a functioning nuclear device had failed. A few senior Network figures had advocated making one from scratch, but uranium enrichment required the resources of a sophisticated country, and constructing an implosion plutonium bomb was even more arduous. Some people in the Network were taken with the idea of a 'dirty' bomb in which a small conventional explosion was used to spread radioactivity, but Malik had read up on the physics and knew it wouldn't cause much damage and was basically a dead end.

That left biological weapons. The technology was fundamentally different, the approach completely new. But as the anthrax embarrassment had clearly shown, it had to be done with the utmost precision, understanding, and diligence or you ended up with a fizzle. Malik had known from the outset that anthrax would not work. The mechanics of anthrax spores spilling out from a postal envelope were simply not lethal enough. The LD50 was quite high—you needed to reach sensitive internal areas deep within the lungs, and the spore dust would inevitably get diluted in ambient air and ventilation systems. Malik's biting critique of the anthrax affair had found an influential audience within the Network, and convinced the decision-makers that he was the man who could get it done right.

And now here he was, in the thick of it. Zafar Majeed lay in the ICU, probably dying, probably with a brain that was fried, pickled and rotting. Malik reminded himself of the need for discipline. Remembering Ramzi's sorry example and the pathetic anthrax fiasco helped. The most urgent need was to get all the necessary data—and some more besides, if one could—without endangering the project in any way.

There was no way around it. He was going to have to visit Avicenna.

The hospital's layout was familiar to him from previous visits. Around this time last year, shortly before he had begun his current assignment, one of Malik's aunts had developed jaundice. Her liver was failing, and she was admitted to Avicenna, spending nearly a week in the ICU before her kidneys also failed and she succumbed. A bad case of hepatitis, the doctors said. A virus had wiped out all her liver cells, and irreversible complications had set in. Strange, Malik thought, that it was a virus, considering the inventive new project he was handed just a few days afterward. The irony was inescapable.

He had never been close to that particular aunt. His mother, in fact, had been estranged from her for years over a petty family dispute that had long since been forgotten, although the emotional distance persisted. But the aunt was childless and had an invalid for a husband, who was stuck in a wheelchair following a stroke. So the responsibility for guiding her through the medical system fell naturally to Malik, her nephew, who had a family reputation for knowing something about everything and had even attended a few years of medical school before doing well for himself with—what?—no one in the family was quite sure. Malik was off-assignment those days and he performed the role, reluctantly but faithfully, becoming the family spokesperson and going over his aunt's prognosis every day with the medical and nursing staff. It became a bonding event because his mother also forgot old squabbles and the family rallied together.

Stationed in the waiting area next to the ICU for hours at a time, Malik had picked up a good sense of the place, its rhythms and regulations. Allah's motives in putting him through that experience, baffling at the time, were now crystal clear. It had obviously been preparation for what he was now required to do.

As an extra precaution, he decided not to take his car and got on the bus instead. For good measure, he set out towards an area of the city that was in the opposite direction from the hospital, changing buses twice to follow a zigzag route. About an hour later, he finally got on the route that took him straight to the hospital.

It was well after six o'clock when he walked through the hospital's main gates. Karachi was having a full monsoon this year and the hospital's imposing concrete façade was damp from two straight days of nearly uninterrupted rain. It had stopped raining today but the skies were still heavy and overcast. In the distance, Malik could see a brilliant rim of red and gold staining the horizon where the sun was about to set.

As usual, the hospital's gates produced a cacophony of sights and sounds. This was during visiting hours, and people of all ages were walking through. Vendors stood outside, hawking fruit juices and spicy chickpea salad from pushcarts. Cars were lined up at the gates, waiting to collect a parking token before being cleared to go inside. A driver in one of the cars was forcefully arguing some point with a uniformed security official. Whatever the dispute's finer points, it was having little impact with the guard, who just kept shaking his head. With a rifle slung over one shoulder and a starched blue and beige uniform smartly draped over his tall frame, he cut a commanding and authoritative figure, and it appeared to be pushing the poor driver round the bend.

Malik entered with the crowd. He was simply dressed in a powder blue shalwar kameez, white prayer cap, and rubber sandals. As he walked, a string of prayer beads swung noticeably in one hand; in the other hand, he was clutching a pocket-sized copy of the Quran. A small dropper-bottle of Artificial Tears, a harmless saltwater solution recommended by doctors to keep the eyes moist, sat snugly in his pocket. Malik had bought it at a pharmacy thinking it might come in handy if he was required to show grief.

He had come to Avicenna with the specific aim of covertly sniffing out the medical details of Zafar Majeed. The situation required a clever plan with minimal or no risk, that combined stealth with a high likelihood of quality information retrieval. An idea had come to him, and he had finalised the details in his head before setting out.

The ICU was on the top floor of a five-storey redbrick tower located in the centre of the hospital complex. It was a short, quick walk from the main gates, but Malik decided to get there by taking a leisurely and circuitous stroll, walking two laps of the hospital's perimeter and then cutting across the long courtyard in front of the X-ray suites before finally arriving at the elevators for the central tower.

He wanted to look sombre and melancholy, to give the impression that he was the sad relative of some desperately sick and dying patient; in fact, with the solemn prayer cap, a gloomy facial expression, and religious artefacts in both hands, he looked positively funereal. His mind was in overdrive, hyper-alert and hyper-vigilant, as he scanned—unobtrusively—all around him and tried to eavesdrop on anything that made a sound.

The plan called for spending some time in the ICU waiting room where patients' families gathered to keep watch and wait for any scrap of information from the ICU staff. It was a fraternal setting where people found themselves sharing a common predicament in an enclosed space; it was natural that there should be a culture of camaraderie. Malik had experienced it himself in the long hours he had spent here during his aunt's hospitalisation last year. In this place, families commiserated with each other, exchanged stories, bonded. Conversations were struck up all the time, popular topics being doctors, particularly their reputations and their bedside manners, as well as the patients themselves, and what they used to be like and how they were full of goodness and warmth before ghastly maladies had caught up with them.

Just a few hours in the waiting room, and Malik was confident he'd know everyone's story.

Everyone's, including Zafar Majeed's.

When Malik had been here last year, one of the elevators had been out of order throughout. Now, however, all four lifts were working. Two were reserved for transferring patients while the other two carried general traffic.

Malik got on one of the general elevators along with what appeared to be at least two other families. One of the families also included small children—a boy and two girls who laughed and playfully pushed each other, jostling for the best position from where to make a run for it the moment the elevator doors opened. They were headed, no doubt, for obstetrics on the second floor where the kids would be welcoming a new cousin perhaps, or maybe a new brother or sister in their lives. The other group looked wretched and distraught, likely saddled by the burden of some terrible illness in one of their own, their dearly loved kith and kin.

Not many people were present when Malik walked into the ICU waiting room. There must have been no more than a dozen or so, mostly women, with nearly half the seats empty. It was close to *maghrib*, the time for the sunset prayer, and the menfolk were probably at the hospital's mosque.

Malik took a seat in the corner, away from where most of the people were gathered. Aiming to attract little or no attention, he opened his Quran to a random point and appeared to be reading, while also quietly worrying the prayer beads.

For a fleeting moment he felt guilty about missing the *maghrib* prayer himself, but he was quick to rationalise it by thinking of the momentous nature of his current task, which surely superseded God's other commandments.

Maghrib could wait; this could not.

The waiting room was shaped like a long corridor, its walls lined with built-in seats covered in withering upholstery. In the centre of the room stood a pair of low tables that were cluttered with newspapers and magazines that had been thumbed through and lay strewn across. Through a long window that stretched the length of the room on the far wall, Malik could see anyone going into or coming out of the ICU. Behind him was an ornate wooden screen that overlooked the hospital's main courtyard and through which the dying light of day now filtered in.

After a few minutes, the men began returning, and the place soon filled up. A heavyset man with a trim moustache and friendly eyes took the seat next to Malik's. Other men joined the women who were with them, or took whatever vacant seat they could find.

Through the long window, Malik noticed a patient being wheeled towards the ICU. The face was hard to make out but it appeared to be an elderly woman. A group of doctors in surgical scrubs—they might have been paramedics or nurses even—were running along with the bed and one of the doctors held a mask to the woman's face through which he was giving her artificial breaths by squeezing a large rubber balloon.

'Looks like she's going to be put on the breathing machine,' the man sitting next to Malik said. He had cocked his head and was looking at Malik as he spoke.

Malik was delighted to make conversation. He recited a Quranic verse in Arabic, then said, 'May Allah grant her a full recovery, *ameen*.'

The man continued. 'They wheeled my mother in yesterday, just like that. They were giving her breaths through the mask. When they took her inside, they put a tube in her throat and hooked her up to the breathing machine. I can't bear to see her like that.'

'I'm very sorry, I hope she gets better. What happened?'

'It's such a shock. She had lunch with us yesterday, then complained she was having a headache. She hardly ever gets headaches, but we thought it was nothing—just a headache you know. Who would have thought? Then she just collapsed. Barely had stepped away from the table. Just fell over, collapsed in a heap.'

'That's terrible.'

'Brain haemorrhage, Dr Mirza said. He's the best. Have you heard of him? Dr Asad Mirza? He's been really nice, seems very competent. He said her condition's very serious but it's early to say and there's a small chance she could still pull through.'

The man now sat forward in his seat and turned towards Malik. 'Brother,' he implored, 'you look like a nice, pious man. Will you please pray for my mother? I don't want to lose her.' He sounded on the verge of tears.

'Patience, my brother. May Allah have mercy on us all,' said Malik, following it up with another verse from the Quran.

A man who's been here since yesterday and he likes to talk, Malik thought. The conversation needed to be prolonged. This was a good time to use Artificial Tears. Malik excused himself to go to the toilet, just a short distance down the corridor. Once inside a stall, he took the dropper-bottle out of a side pocket and squeezed two drops into each eye.

After a couple of minutes, he was back in the waiting room. He had barely been able to sit down before the man started talking again.

'That family over there,' he said, looking towards two women in long black coats and headscarves and a man wearing a crumpled shalwar kameez, all sitting together in the distant corner, 'their patient is also under Dr Mirza's care. Came in late last night, some mysterious brain illness they say.'

Malik froze.

Then he immediately relaxed, hoping he hadn't betrayed how this bit of information had just electrified him. Was it Zafar Majeed this man was referring to? Malik desperately hoped it was. He would be able to confirm Case 1, their first hit, right according to plan.

While Malik pondered what to say, the man blurted, 'But how insensitive of me.' He had noticed the tears welled up in Malik's eyes. 'I hope your patient isn't too sick,' he said.

'We don't know,' replied Malik, in a low, hoarse voice, trying to sound like someone who had been weeping quietly with grief. 'It's my aunt, her liver's not working. Our hopes are with Allah, He can do miracles.'

'Undoubtedly,' the man concurred, and then fell quiet. Malik became quiet too, looking down at his lap and worrying his prayer beads, as he contemplated his next move.

A loud female voice interrupted his thoughts.

'Family of Zafar Majeed...Majeed family please,' a nurse had stuck her head in through the door and was calling out to the people gathered in the waiting room. Malik shot furtive glances around. The two women and the man that his neighbour had just pointed out, now stood up and walked towards the nurse, who pushed a clipboard towards them. She was saying something Malik couldn't quite make out.

The man in the group took the clipboard and wrote on it,

apparently affixing his signature. With a couple of quick nods, he handed it back to the nurse. All four of them then stepped out into the corridor, where Zafar's attendants started walking alongside a stretcher carrying a human form that was covered from head to toe—a corpse. The women sobbed and held each other as they walked. The man, stoic and impassive, marched in resignation. Malik tracked them through the long window as the procession drifted down the corridor, headed for the elevators.

He said a silent prayer for Zafar Majeed, who was a martyr. Unwilling, but a martyr nonetheless to the cause of Allah. What greater fate could there be? Oh, the pleasures that awaited Zafar Majeed in Paradise.

Malik spent several more minutes making idle chatter with the voluble man sitting next to him, before saying a polite goodbye. Outside the hospital gate, he flagged a cab and got into the backseat. As the hospital buildings receded behind him, he took out his cell phone and sent a text message to his associate.

Before long, he was back in his apartment, a modest walk-up comprising two small rooms. One of them contained his prayer rug and a set of folded quilts that he used as a mattress. This room also contained a small portmanteau. It was a cricket kitbag really, purchased years ago, repaired many times, and outfitted with a side pouch that was a snug fit for the laptop. This valise was more or less a permanent home for Malik's clothes, comb and toothbrush (he hadn't shaved in years), which he took everywhere he was sent and out of which, for all purposes and intents, he lived.

The other room, the one with the 9/11 poster that he held as sacred, was a workroom where Malik spent most of his time whenever he was in the flat. It contained a steel filing cabinet, a strongbox stuffed to capacity with cash, a large worktable and, hanging just above the table, a cluttered corkboard that was the busiest thing in the room by a distance.

In one corner of the board was an oversized facsimile of the Last Sermon, the venerated address delivered by Prophet Muhammad on the occasion of his last pilgrimage to Mecca, just a few months before his death in 532 CE.

'O People,' it began. 'Lend me an attentive ear, for I know not whether after this year I shall be amongst you again.'

Malik had memorised it, but he still put it up wherever he set up shop. It was an old, faded copy that had been folded and unfolded, over and over again. Key phrases were underlined. *Beware of Satan, Remember one day you will appear before Allah, Do not stray from the path of righteousness.*

In the other corner hung a calendar diary showing pictures of famous mosques from around the Islamic world, one for each month. July's image was a fetching elevation of Emam mosque's blue-tiled mosaic dome, posing grandly against the backdrop of the city of Esfahan, once the jewel of ancient Persia, now a tourist stop in modern Iran.

Sandwiched between the Last Sermon and the calendar diary was the list, which had been carefully organised as a long table with four columns and several rows. In the first row were the names, in the second were age and gender and in the third, addresses. Rows 4 through 20 were a grid of open spaces, some of which had been filled with checkmarks to document the results of ongoing surveillance.

The first name on the list was Zafar Majeed. Malik stepped forward and crossed it out.

Seven

Ayesha Anjum was a thirty-something housewife with three kids, a lower middle class life, and dreams to match.

One recent morning, she awoke with a strange feeling. The night before, she had gone to bed with a mild body ache. She thought she might be coming down with the flu and had checked her temperature, but there was no fever. In the morning, she had woken up feeling strange and jumpy.

Ayesha was the sole workhorse of a busy household that also comprised a set of aging parents-in-law, in addition to a demanding and unfriendly husband and the three kids. As the daughter-in-law, her husband's parents were Ayesha's responsibility. Her father-in-law had a ticker crippled from three heart attacks and it had left him with a pulse so feeble he could barely walk the few feet from his bed to the bathroom door without losing his breath. On a bad day, a simple act like putting on his shirt could leave him panting like a marathoner. Her mother-in-law, for her part, was blind from years of diabetes, utterly rejecting the concept of dietary discipline and refusing to take any allopathic medicines, to all of which she had given a blanket label of 'Western poison.'

And though the mother-in-law at least wasn't a physical cripple, with her salty tongue and exceptional talent for inflicting verbal torment, Ayesha sometimes wished she were.

Her husband of thirteen years was no help. His job as a sanitation inspector with the City Water Board brought in barely enough to keep their heads bobbing just above the Third World definition of a poverty line. Being the sole breadwinner, and before that, an only son invested with a disproportionate ego by an indulgent mother, he expected his wife to wait on him, hand and foot. But in return he offered little affection and no mercy.

A petty, capricious, and vastly insecure man, it was not unknown for him to whack Ayesha on the face for even minor infractions in housework, like leaving his trousers un-pressed or over-brewing the tea. He often released frustrations picked up at the workplace by letting out steam on Ayesha, usually by disapproving of her cooking or by passing cutting remarks about her appearance.

There was no comfort to be found in her marriage, but there was no escape from it either. Ayesha had come to both resent and fear her husband but she also felt obliged for the roof he had put over her head and for his monthly salary, which provided for her and her children.

Naturally, the children were her life.

A girl aged nine and two boys aged six and five, they worshipped their mother, and she worshipped their future. Ayesha's own upbringing had been modest and mostly miserable, and now, her personal fate was sealed within the confines of an awful marriage. She was sustained only by the desperate hope that her children would see a better life than she had. She was determined to get them a decent education even if it killed her.

Even on holidays she was frequently up before dawn but this was a weekday, a workday for her husband and a school day for the kids, and she was up early with the anxiety that always comes from a homemaker's concern to see the morning through without a hitch.

Except that the anxiety this morning was a little more than usual.

Ayesha couldn't explain it. Her muscles ached, and she felt uneasy about something—or was it nothing? She felt uneasy and jittery, but she had no idea what exactly about.

This was a weekday morning, no different from any other. It was before sunrise and everyone was asleep. Soon, loudspeakers from the neighbourhood mosque would broadcast the muezzin's call to *fajr*, the prayer marking daybreak.

'Allah-o-Akbar, Allah-o-Akbar,' it would begin, the grand vocals drifting through darkness, minutes before first light. *Allah is great, the greatest of all. I bear witness that there is no God but Allah. I bear witness that Muhammad is Allah's messenger. Come rush for prayer, come rush for beneficence.*

Ayesha got out of bed and went into the bathroom. When she sat over the toilet, her buttocks felt as if they had received a pummelling through the night. When she stood up, the feeling was worse, and it made her wince with pain. After washing her hands, she splashed water on her face three times to begin the cleansing ritual that would prepare her for prayer.

Bending over the bathroom sink, she felt an ache in her shoulders and upper back, as if the muscles were being kneaded by a brawny masseuse with no idea of his own strength.

She also felt tired, which was distinctly unusual for this hour. With the onerous morning demands of the household, she was always at her most alert this early in the day. She must be coming down with something. It was a very disconcerting thought because her life had no give, and she got no concessions for being sick.

Wasn't it but two, maybe three months ago that she had been running a fever for two days and had to visit the doctor? An hour and a half stolen from the middle of the afternoon, the only time of day when no one usually made demands on her, and it had still caused so much fuss.

She wasn't home when her husband returned from work, and he wouldn't let her hear the end of it. Later that evening he had wanted a back rub but she was helping her daughter with homework and they had had a row, which ended only when he stormed out of the house in a rant. God knows where he went for she never dared ask him.

Her state of mind made it impossible to concentrate on *fajr*, but she moved through the ritual anyway. Head draped in a veil, hands up to her ears, the palms and face looking westward in the direction of Mecca, quietly she whispered 'Allah-o-Akbar' and launched into the sacrament.

Her back hurt when she bent at the waist, and when she knelt and prostrated herself in worship, she felt dizzy and disoriented, as if her head had come unstuck from the rest of her body and was cascading aimlessly down an endless waterfall.

Somehow, she pulled herself together to ready breakfast. While she fried an egg for her husband, her daughter called out wanting help with her hair band.

Inexplicably, her daughter's shrill voice startled Ayesha completely. She was left panting, overcome with a sense of dread she couldn't understand. Before she could gather herself, the egg was overdone. Mercy of mercies, her husband was running late and wolfed it down without a grumble.

Her youngest having turned five, all three children were now attending the same school. It was a fifteen-minute walk from the house—twelve if you took the shortcut past the garbage dump—and to Ayesha it was a ritual approaching religious significance. It was a private school that the family could just about afford, and for Ayesha, the route to the school and back with her children was the equivalent of shepherding them to the Promised Land. It had to be, it was the only bright hope in her life.

As she did every morning except on Sundays, Ayesha led the children out of the house and headed left, down the street. At the corner milk shop, they crossed the intersection and began walking past a row of cheap eateries. Discarded scraps of food and empty soda bottles from the night before littered the sidewalk. Stray dogs patrolled up and down the street, sniffing at the scattered refuse. These shops did their best business late in the day and still had their shutters down.

Traffic was picking up. By noon it would be so busy that you had no choice but to breathe exhaust fumes. This wasn't a rich neighbourhood, and scooters and motorbikes far outnumbered automobiles. Even the cars one saw here were old rusting heaps, never the shiny new Japanese models, SUVs, or European luxury sedans one found in Karachi's posh areas.

Ayesha and the kids stood by the curb at the end of the street and waited for the traffic light to change. Faces scrubbed, hair neatly parted and combed, uniforms starched and pressed with motherly care, book bags and water bottles slung across the shoulder in earnest, the children looked a picture painted by God and kissed by angels.

When the light changed, they followed the crowd to the other side of the street. The school was two blocks further down and when they went past the news stand where their mother sometimes bought the mid-day newspaper on their way home, they began to see the blue archway that towered above the school's entrance.

Approximately twenty minutes earlier, a man who looked about thirty, of average height and nondescript looks other than a runaway beard, had purchased the morning's newspaper from this very news stand, and seated himself at a breakfast table on the roadside restaurant across the street.

Malik had been following this routine exactly for the last three days, now that the second week of surveillance had begun. Peering from behind the newspaper, he noted Ayesha as she walked down the street. In his mind, he checked off one of the open boxes on the grid that was thumbtacked onto the corkboard in his apartment. As per instructions received, he scanned her face, body language and walk for any unusual signs, but saw nothing.

For a moment, he felt she looked pale and sickly, but sunlight interrupted by a row of crooked rooftops was putting her in and out of shadows, and he concluded it must be the light.

Ayesha was having a rough time just walking the short distance from her house to get her children to school. This was something she normally did almost on instinct, automatically and effortlessly, six mornings every week. For some reason today, it was a struggle and getting worse. It wasn't just the flu, she felt sure. Something else was afoot. The body pains were a shade better but her head was in a spin and now her forehead had begun to throb.

And at the margins of her mind, Ayesha kept feeling nervous and unsettled, and she just couldn't explain it.

They were at the gate now. The children let go of her hands, disappearing into a throng of kids drifting down the school's front yard towards a whitewashed row of classrooms.

Ayesha turned around and tried to pull herself together.

Could it be that she was hungry? She usually had tea with a piece of toast before going out with the children, but today she had skipped it. Out of habit, she had made the tea, but poured it down the sink because the thought of taking a sip had made her nauseous. The feeling rose up from deep within her belly and she had an intense urge to throw up that made her recall the first trimester of each of her three pregnancies.

Could it be that she was pregnant? She was certainly having unprotected sexual relations with her husband, yet as soon as the question came to her, she knew it to be absurd.

She'd had her tubes tied. How could she forget something so unforgettable, so personal and close to her sense of self?

On a hot October morning, one year after the birth of her youngest, she had taken the bus to the family planning centre behind the city government hospital in Civil Lines. Now that she thought about it, the memory became crystal clear. Thirty long minutes she had queued to arrange an appointment as the sun baked the earth around her and the women waiting in line jostled for whatever little shade could be brokered from the branches of an old banyan tree, rising from the street just outside the centre's gate.

The appointment was for two days later at ten in the morning, and she had arrived at the centre nearly three-quarters of an hour ahead, after a shower and on an empty stomach, as directed.

She had been asked to remove everything—especially the underclothes, she recalled being told—and was then injected with a light anaesthetic as she lay uncomfortably on a cold and hard table with her legs pulled apart and her feet in stirrups. The procedure itself was a blur. A needle had been pushed under the skin near her belly button and, after what had seemed to her an eternity but in reality was just a few minutes, her belly had started to swell as it became distended with pumped carbon dioxide.

That was the last thing she remembered before waking up in a recovery bed and seeing Razia, her next-door neighbour who had come to fetch her, by her side.

She was a good woman, Razia—Ayesha's one friend in the world. Oh, she could be annoying in her own special way; Razia's grandfather had once served on the personal staff of the Nizam of Hyderabad, and self-important remarks about her family's oh-so-illustrious background were a finely honed skill that often got under Ayesha's skin, but Ayesha was fond of her. Razia was mostly a cheerful and agreeable woman, a resource and a confidante, and the most natural (indeed, the only) choice for baby-sitter.

The sight of the red sandstone Abu Bakar mosque jolted Ayesha from her thoughts. A distinctive landmark, the mosque was located on an interconnecting street that led to Jinnah Road, one of the city's main thoroughfares.

That Ayesha was now standing in front of it, meant she was headed in the wrong direction.

After seeing off the children, she must have kept on walking straight ahead instead of turning around and going back towards her house. What was wrong with her today? She had never lost her way like this, not on such a familiar route. She prided herself on her sense of direction. It was one of her strengths, even her husband acknowledged that. She turned around and began hurrying back towards her home, with mounting anxiety and unease that—for some perplexing reason—she was not her normal self.

It was a great exertion, but somehow she made it back to her house. Instead of the usual fifteen minutes, it had taken her twice as long, and once again, on the way she had taken a wrong turn and walked aimlessly for several minutes before realising what she had done.

The convoluted route meant she had not gone past Malik again. He would definitely have noted something was wrong with her if she had—she was almost tottering now—and he would have made a different entry for that day on the surveillance grid in his workroom.

Malik waited patiently for nearly an hour before giving up the stakeout. She must have gone ahead to run some errands, he reasoned. Based on the available data, it was premature to reach any other conclusion. He would be back at one o'clock to log in his second observation for the day, when Ayesha came to collect the kids from school.

Back at her doorstep, Ayesha fumbled with the keys as she tried to let herself in. Her husband would have already left for work and very shortly, the demands from her mother-in-law and father-in-law would begin.

She felt like her body was shattering into little pieces and she just couldn't bear the thought of going through the taxing work routine that inevitably filled her day. Her head kept feeling empty and chaotically adrift, as if it were plunging through a void. Her thoughts felt muddled and confused, beset by some thick and mysterious cloudy mist that was falling like a heavy blanket on her mind. Her arms felt like they had been wrung out, and her legs were like jelly, with barely the strength to support her. She had a feeble sense of foreboding, a feeling that she was helplessly looking devastation in the eye. Her consciousness twisting in fear and pain, it gently struck her that she was living a nightmare.

As soon as she heard the front door, Ayesha's mother-in-law started calling out for her. The father-in-law needed to be assisted to the toilet. Where in Allah's name had that woman been? She was already fifteen minutes late. Any longer, and the poor old fellow, demented and wasting, would soil himself. What an unmentionable disaster that would be.

But where was Ayesha? Surely she had come back in, the front door had opened and shut. 'Ayesha! Ayesha!' the old woman hollered. Why wasn't she answering?

At the very edge of her awareness, Ayesha could make out someone was calling her name. Other than that, she was senseless. She had stumbled straight into her room—a short passageway from the front door led directly into it—and collapsed on the floor, unable to think or move.

Having to help her invalid husband to the toilet, a nasty routine that had been firmly established as one of Ayesha's non-negotiable duties, put the mother-in-law in a foul mood. To complicate things, the husband decided to have a large and noisy bowel movement and she stewed in his smells and her own frustrations while she waited for him to finish.

What was that devil of a daughter-in-law up to? Where was she slacking off this time? As soon as she helped her husband back to bed, the mother-in-law stepped out looking for Ayesha. Because she was functionally blind, she rarely ventured out of her room on her own; she was furious at being inconvenienced and felt a strong urge to give Ayesha a physical beating. It was something she had never done but extreme situations demanded extreme measures, and there had to be a first time for everything. Tightly, she grabbed on to her walking stick as she thought about how she would teach this girl a lesson.

Feeling her way down the hall, the cranky old woman checked first in the kitchen, then in the small living area that also doubled as the family dining room. As she moved across the rooms, she kept swishing her stick back and forth. She kept calling out for Ayesha, but heard nothing.

Finally, she made her way into her son's bedroom; the largest room in the house, it was shared by her son, his wife and their youngest.

Her stick fell on a human form and she heard Ayesha let out a moan. The mother-in-law bent down and felt around. She could tell that Ayesha was on her side and seemed to be breathing rapidly. Grabbing hold of an arm, she squeezed and shook it, but the girl still wouldn't talk. Reaching towards her face, she could feel perspiration on Ayesha's forehead, her hair flat against her sweaty scalp.

What was wrong with this girl? Was she sick? That just won't do, because who's going to do all the chores, all the work of the house? These were the mother-in-law's first thoughts about the situation at hand. She felt panic. Fuming and confused, the old woman swung with the stick and caught Ayesha's flank with a thud.

She heard Ayesha retch, followed soon by faint vapours of bile and acid, the unmistakable stench of human vomit.

There was no point asking her husband to help; a bed-bound invalid, he could barely support his own weight. She would have to ask a neighbour. Gingerly feeling her way, she stepped out and crossed the narrow alley to the house right across, and began rapping the door hard with her stick.

'Razia, Razia,' she yelled, 'come quick, something's happened to Ayesha.'

It was a small house, and within no time, Razia was at the door. She sensed an emergency right away because Ayesha's mother-in-law almost never ventured out by herself. The alarming tone and urgent knocks at the door unmistakably signalled trouble.

Razia helped the old woman back to her house and found Ayesha's form lying in a pool of vomit on the bedroom floor. She had the presence of mind to feel for a pulse at the wrist, which she found to be feeble and rapid. The body also felt warm to the touch. With a wet towel from the bathroom, Razia wiped her friend's face clean and turned her around to lie flat on her back. She began slapping her face, gently at first, then a couple of times quite vigorously, and kept calling Ayesha's name.

Ayesha opened her eyes weakly and mumbled some incomprehensible sounds, but that was as far as she got. It was clear to Razia that Ayesha was gravely ill.

Their underprivileged houses didn't have telephone lines but there was a public telephone at the corner of the street, where Razia now went to call her husband. The payphone was already being used, with another couple of men waiting in line. Razia pleaded it was an emergency and the men quickly obliged.

Razia's husband worked in the mailroom at the headquarters of a private bank downtown, and it was several minutes before he could be located. When he finally came on line, Razia asked him to get hold of Ayesha's husband at the Water Board.

'Ayesha seems terribly ill, he needs to come home and get her to a doctor.' She made sure she impressed on her husband how serious it was. 'She's unconscious and is probably also running a fever,' Razia told her husband. 'If you can't get hold of him, you need to come and take her yourself. She looks really very sick, I'm so worried.'

ꙮ

Karachi's Water Board was an archaic bureaucratic enterprise where work moved at a glacial pace, if at all. When the phone call came, Saleem Anjum was idly sipping tea and reading a newspaper.

On hearing of his wife's sudden illness, his first reaction was surprise. Why, he had left her just fine as a fiddle this morning. This quickly gave way to annoyance and irritation at having to disrupt his workday. Even worse, the thought of all those expenses that were invariably incurred on medical care began to gnaw at him.

Razia's husband had conveyed every bit of the urgency of his wife's message, and Saleem quickly decided that he had no choice but to get back home and attend to the situation. He thanked his neighbour for the call and took permission from his supervisor to take the rest of the day off on account of a family emergency.

Approximately an hour later, Saleem got off at the bus stop and turned the corner into the narrow street leading to his modest house. He was greeted at the door by Razia, who urged him to get Ayesha to a hospital immediately. She also offered to collect the children from school and keep checking in on his parents until Ayesha recovered, for which Saleem was genuinely grateful.

With a mixture of denial and a habitual disregard for Ayesha's genuine needs, Saleem suspected that the situation wasn't really as bad as it was being made out to be. He walked in to find Ayesha lying flat on the floor with her head propped up on a pillow.

Eyes half open, mouth crusted with remnants of dried vomit, she looked vacant and lifeless. Saleem's natural instinct was to try and give her a drink of water, but when he pulled her up and brought a glass near her lips, Ayesha's eyes sprang open with a start.

It took Saleem completely by shock. Her head rocked sideways, and her whole body was racked with spasms. The haunted expression on her face reminded Saleem of that girl in the movie—what was it, *Exorcist* or something?—that had played in Karachi for an entire year and he had seen it twice, fascinated by the idea of a girl's soul being possessed by Satan.

After careful thought, Saleem decided to seek help from Baba Sikander. There was no point going to state-run hospitals like Civil or Crescent, one never got proper attention there and even if you did, it was only going to be from medical students or junior doctors who were clueless anyway.

And private hospitals like Avicenna were simply out of the question. It would cost a lifetime's savings and if Ayesha had some incurable disease that nobody could fix, then all that money for what? It would be a damn shame.

༄༅

Baba Sikander was a fakir but, by local standards, a rich one. A brooding personality dominated by overgrown locks and flowing robes, he cultivated a spiritual disposition and claimed to be a servant of God devoted to faith healing.

Only fifty rupees for the first session, and thereafter whatever was commanded by divine inspiration.

Saleem found that price far more reasonable than the two hundred rupees Ayesha had outrageously spent at the doctor's, a couple of months ago for some minor flu thing.

With a talent for exploiting the gullible and vulnerable, and no conscience to speak of, Baba Sikander commanded a strong following among Karachi's wretched and desolate masses. Charlatans like him flourished in societies like this, where life at the edge of poverty helped sustain a culture of superstition. Baba was famous in the locality for solving people's problems through his mystical powers. Marital friction and domestic disputes were his specialty, but he also welcomed the sick and diseased.

The more desperate, the better because desperation meant gullibility and poor judgment.

Wives went to him to have spells of loyalty and obedience cast on errant or unfaithful husbands. Mothers-in-law went to regain control over newlywed sons who were forgetting Mama and becoming unduly charmed by their brides. Men went in search of recipes for virility and sexual prowess, or in hope of quick riches. Childless couples came seeking fertility; the aged and infirm came for the elixir of life.

Baba was, simply put, a natural refuge for the hopeless and disconsolate who had no one else to turn to and who could not resist being offered hope at a bargain price, even if somewhere deep inside, they knew it to be false.

It was common knowledge that Baba, who lived in comfortable quarters not too far away from Ayesha and Saleem's place, didn't do house calls. He did not go to the doomed, the doomed had to come to him.

Saleem got hold of a taxi and, with the help of the taxi driver, bundled his unconscious wife into the backseat and drove off to see Baba. He was relieved to learn that the mystic was in, and felt honoured when he was called in for an audience without too much of a wait.

Baba was seated cross-legged on a low stool in the middle of a darkened room overflowing with smoke and fumes from burning incense. Two attendants hovered nearby. No one else was around; mid-morning was typically a quiet time at Baba's, where the traffic really picked up after sunset and remained steady until the early hours.

Entering with soft steps and a sense of awe that seemed to come automatically, Saleem greeted Baba with a respectful salaam. The fakir did not respond, choosing instead to keep his head down and rock his body gently back and forth.

One of the attendants motioned to Saleem to sit at the floor near Baba's feet; the other quietly asked for fifty rupees, which Saleem promptly handed over. The opening transaction complete, the attendant motioned towards Baba with an open palm, the signal for Saleem to speak his need.

Ayesha's sudden illness was described, in a tone of suitable humility. Baba kept up a nasal hum while Saleem talked. After pausing for effect, he spoke in grave and solemn tones, asking for the sick woman to be brought in.

Young women who had lost control of their senses were uncommon clients at Baba's, but it was a trade secret that they were a special treat.

The attendants got up and walked out to get the client. Saleem followed behind them. Soon they were back in, both attendants carrying Ayesha's limp form towards Baba. One of them had hooked his arms under Ayesha's and had his hands pressed up against her breasts, producing what he anticipated were the first of many thrills for the day. The other man had his arms under her knees, and was getting aroused feeling the soft flesh of her thighs.

They placed Ayesha down on a rug in front of Baba. Her head was towards Baba and her body lay stretched out before him.

Saleem stood obediently by, waiting for Baba to work his magic and revive his wife so everything could be normal again.

As the woman was brought closer, Baba's nasal hum got louder and louder until it became a rhythmic chanting. It sounded vaguely like Quranic Arabic, which gave Saleem ever greater confidence that this mystic knew what he was doing.

Without looking up, Baba motioned to one of his attendants, who asked Saleem to step out. Baba's policy called for all clients, and most particularly young women, to be dealt with in private. To make sure they would be left undisturbed, any accompanying family members were usually handed an assignment requiring several hours to accomplish.

In a dramatic and weighty voice, Baba ordered Saleem to boil a lock of Ayesha's hair for four hours in the blood of a dozen pigeons sacrificed in the room that Ayesha normally slept in. One of the attendants, in a swift and practiced motion that had obviously been performed many times, stepped forward and snipped a small piece of Ayesha's hair and handed it to Saleem. It would keep him busy for a while.

The moment Saleem left, Baba stretched out a hand and shook Ayesha by the shoulder.

When she didn't respond, he pinched her cheek and slapped her.

Still, nothing.

He checked to make sure she was breathing, and she was. From where he was seated, Baba had a good eyeful of cleavage peeping out from Ayesha's shirt. He slipped his hand into her neckline and rubbed it over one of her breasts, fingering the nipple and squeezing the soft flesh. He felt himself get hard as he did so.

Ayesha remained unconscious. Her hair was matted with perspiration and flecks of dried secretions covered her mouth, but in an otherwise attractive and well-proportioned woman, these were minor inconveniences.

The two attendants positioned themselves to stand guard at the entrance. Their turn would come soon. Baba got up from his stool and walked around to stand between Ayesha's legs. They were already spread out, but Baba knelt down and pried them further apart with his knees.

He never wore any undergarment, and his penis was pushing out rock-stiff from under his robes. Intensely aroused and breathing hard, he undid Ayesha's drawstring trousers with one hand and grabbed at her genitals with the other, pushing a finger into the vaginal orifice.

She was clean-shaven, which was common Muslim practice. She was also dry as a bone, as Baba had expected. Pulling up his robes, Baba slobbered gobs of spit into the palm of his hand and rubbed it generously over his penis. Suitably lubricated, he penetrated Ayesha, falling on top of her as he began thrusting. Soon, he was in trance-like ecstasy.

The sudden private intrusion produced a stirring in Ayesha.

She let out some unintelligible groans and tried to flutter her eyes open, but Baba was too excited to notice. Neither did his attendants see it; they had to stand watch for outsiders, with strict orders not to turn around. Baba could sense his climax building. For heightened pleasure, he pushed a hand under Ayesha's buttocks and began fingering her anus.

Momentarily startled out of her stupor, Ayesha woke to the fear and panic of a woman who has just discovered her own rape.

A strange man, his smelly head buried into the side of her neck, was assaulting her from back and front. Mind aflame in chaos, Ayesha reacted with animal instinct and caught hold of Baba's ear between her teeth. Without mercy, she bit down hard and lacerated the cartilage as blood effused and mixed with Ayesha's saliva and oral secretions.

Baba's scream was loud enough to be heard by passers-by in the street.

His attendants thought he had been stabbed with a knife. They turned around to find Baba clutching a bleeding ear and smacking Ayesha repeatedly on the face and chest as he mouthed obscenities loud enough to wake the dead. He had pulled out of Ayesha now and his penis, soft and shrivelled, hung limply.

His assistants ran towards Baba but he was seething in shock and pushed them away.

As he stood up and stepped away from the woman, Baba gave Ayesha a vigorous kick in the ribs. Her body shook like a flaccid, lifeless dummy. One of the attendants bent down and realised she wasn't breathing. He checked for a pulse but there was none.

Ayesha Anjum was dead.

Eight

The traffic light changed again.

It had already gone through three cycles yet she hadn't been able to get through. No one stayed in lane, no one had any patience and everybody wanted to get through right away—the joys of vehicular traffic in urban jungles in the Third World.

Except that this was worse. A major flyover project was under construction on the main thoroughfare leading to Avicenna Hospital, and it had backed up traffic on the road that Nadia always took on her way to the hospital each morning.

This last time she almost made it through the traffic light—only for a beggar to come in front of her car at the worst moment, just as the light turned from green to red yet again. She had half a mind to run him over, but he was on crutches and looked pretty decrepit. But she quickly did the mental math—who knew if he was for real?

Beggars were an infuriating nuisance in Karachi. Despite giving the appearance of absolute poverty, they attracted little sympathy. Most of them were professional alms seekers, able-bodied men and women who had perfected the art of begging and faking physical handicap to the point where it had become a way of life. Credit where credit is due, it was clever enough to provide a reasonable livelihood.

Nadia felt no generosity towards them, not when they obstructed traffic at a busy crossroads, and not when they threatened to make her late for the morning's clinical case conference. In sheer frustration, she slammed down hard on the steering and let the car horn blare rudely.

Few things mattered to her more than punctuality, something inherited from her father, an affluent banker who had always impressed upon his three girls the values of thoroughness, diligence and respect for time. If you respected time, you respected others, and it was only through respecting others that you ultimately respected yourself. These values had taken her father, born into a family with modest means, to executive vice-president at the country's leading multinational bank.

Nadia had picked up the lesson easily. She had inherited much of her father's personality, most particularly his obsessive streak and attention to detail. She was furious at the situation she now found herself in, because in the little universe of Nadia's medical student life, this was no ordinary morning.

It was the fourth and final week of her neurology rotation, and her last chance to make a lasting impression on Dr Asad Mirza, who was fast becoming her role model, and seemed headed towards being an outright idol. As one of the top students in her class, Nadia set herself exacting academic standards and was determined to secure the best possible grade from this rotation, as from any other. But this rotation was more special than the others. She had taken a deep and immediate liking to the field of neurology, and by the second week of the rotation was almost certain she would choose it as her future area of medical specialisation. Her attraction to neurology had a lot to do with the subject matter—the brain and its diseases were complex and challenging, and tended to draw the best medical minds—but it also had a good deal to do with Asad, who had really turned out to be as likable as the student grapevine said he was. He was devoted to his patients and also took a genuine interest in teaching students, which was a lot more than one could say for many of the other attending physicians, most of whom had little time for students and tended to be short with patients and their families.

Six months ago, at the start of her final year at Avicenna University Medical School, Nadia had gone over the course options and rotation schedules for the coming year with great care and detail. The neurology rotation was important to her and she wanted to make sure she went through it at a time when the teaching duties were assigned to Asad, the perennial students' favourite. Now that she had finally come into contact with his casual, affable bearing and the obvious professional ability that he wore with quiet confidence, she had been charmed at many levels.

The light was still red but at least crawling through three cycles had put her at the front of the pack, ready to speed off at the next change. Another beggar crossed in front of her, an almswoman in what appeared to be late middle-age, unwashed and dressed in filthy rags. Looking every bit the part, Nadia reflected cynically. While Nadia gunned her engine, the woman walked around and tapped on the window as she begged for charity.

'In the name of Allah, *beti*, give this poor woman some money to eat. I have not eaten for three days,' she said.

Could've fooled me, thought Nadia, taking note of the woman's generous frame and bulging love handles.

'I have no one in this world, no one,' the woman went on. 'Allah has given you so much, share a little with this poor woman *beti*, you will be rewarded many times over. *Beti*, *beti*, please. In the name of Allah.'

This was standard fare for any major traffic intersection in Karachi. Most people had become immune to the emotional blackmail, but every now and then someone caved in and doled out anything from five to fifty rupees, which was ultimately responsible for keeping the begging culture alive. In this swarming city of fifteen million, at any given time there were enough motorists giving in and sustaining virtually an army of beggars.

Nadia too found herself moved by the old woman's entreaty, but she steeled herself to look straight ahead and ignore her. She was aware that the statistical odds of this beggar being a professional deceiver were overwhelming. There were other better and more reliable avenues for charity.

Nadia didn't have to dwell on this too long because the light changed. With a clear road ahead of her, she floored the gas and took off in a flash. Minutes later, she was turning into the students' parking lot at Avicenna. Pushing sloppily into the first available spot, she gathered her books and stethoscope under one arm as she struggled to slip on her white coat and tried to lock her car at the same time, all in one frantic movement. She was running late for the morning conference and it consumed all her thoughts.

From the viewpoint of the neurology rotation, it was quite a big deal, actually. At eight o' clock every Friday morning, Karachi's neurologists and neurosurgeons gathered to discuss interesting and challenging cases. The city's three main hospitals, Civil, Crescent and Avicenna, took turns hosting the meeting. This week it was Avicenna's turn. It was a very popular and useful meeting and all the concerned professionals attended faithfully to exchange opinions and advice on challenging patients whose illnesses were difficult to diagnose or whose symptoms were not responding to treatment.

As was often true of medical meetings of this nature, this morning's conference too was steeped in tradition and dominated by a profound hierarchy. At Avicenna, a seminar room down the hall from the neurology ward was always used. Seating was classroom-style, accommodating fifty people comfortably. Students sat in the back rows, residents were in the middle, and members of the teaching faculty occupied two rows in the front. On most occasions, there were a few empty chairs left, but sometimes there was standing room only, and it was understood that those lowest in academic rank would be the ones left standing.

Once the meeting was called to order, the air hung thick with authority. An unwritten rule said that faculty members could speak at will, but residents and students would generally not speak unless they were spoken to. Even amongst the faculty, a certain pecking order prevailed, with older members commanding more awe than younger ones like Asad. The oldest professors, crusted, irritable and well into their sixties, sat on a lofty perch at the top of the hierarchy—although Asad had been doing his bit in trying to soften the elitism and get everybody to lighten up. Every now and then, he would challenge an older colleague's clinical opinion or diagnostic reasoning. This usually did not go down well.

Unwritten rules were one thing, but the meeting was meant to be a learning exercise for everyone, so the official line was that students and residents could raise their hand and ask a question if they wanted to. In actual practice, only the brave and adventurous managed to build up the nerve to do so. If your question was deemed stupid or irrelevant, it drew cynical shakes of the head and moans of dismay from the faculty. The effect was to make you feel so demoralised you felt like killing yourself.

The usual order of business consisted of case presentations lasting ten to fifteen minutes, each followed by a short discussion.

Presentations were made by residents, after which the attending overseeing the case would get up and moderate the Q&A. Typically, three or four cases could be accommodated in the hour-long meeting.

This morning's proceedings were already underway when Nadia walked in. All eyes turned on her. This was not the kind of meeting you could walk into so late. She felt deep embarrassment, which quickly turned to anger at the unexpected traffic mess she had run into on the way.

Asad was sitting in the front row and Nadia caught his eye as he glanced towards the door. 'S-O-R-R-Y,' she mouthed silently, and Asad gave her a friendly smile. Her main goal for attending this meeting being the need to score points with Asad, this pleasant gesture immediately put her at ease.

A neurosurgery resident from Crescent Hospital was presenting the first case. Taking a seat in the back row, Nadia quickly read off the details projected up on the screen. A twenty-six-year-old woman had been having headaches for a month and had finally been brought to the hospital after suffering an epileptic fit. A brain scan had been done.

The room went dark as an MRI scan of the brain appeared on the screen. Nadia quickly looked it over to see if she could pick out the problem. She recognised an abnormal spot in the back region of the brain that might have been a brain tumour. The speaker confirmed that it was. They had done a biopsy and diagnosed a low-grade astrocytoma. The lights came back on again. One of the doctors from Crescent got up and invited opinions from the audience on how best to treat the case. Someone suggested the tumour should be radiated with strong X-rays to make it disappear, which was one of the standard approaches to cancer. There was a brief discussion, all fairly technical. Nadia realised she could follow almost everything that was said, and it pleased her no end.

The next presentation was by the neurology team from Civil Hospital. Civil was Karachi's largest public hospital, and therefore the busiest. It was the primary refuge for the city's destitute and insolvent multitudes, and it tended to attract the weirdest cases. Two weeks earlier at this conference, the neurologists from Civil had reported on a young girl who had acquired malaria that had spread to the brain. Despite their best efforts with the most aggressive therapy, the woman had died. Nadia had read about this condition—cerebral malaria—in her books, where it had been mentioned almost as a medical curiosity. With its unusual combination of symptoms leading to a rare and lethal diagnosis, that case history had absorbed her, and she had been rapidly reading up on her neurology books ever since, trying to master as much of the subject matter as she possibly could.

As the presenting doctor now stepped up to the podium, she expected to hear about some other, equally unusual, case.

'A thirty-eight-year-old man, who had otherwise been in good health, was seen in our emergency room with confusion and agitation,' the resident from Civil Hospital began.

A thin sliver of sunlight filtered through broken Venetian blinds in the conference room window, lighting up a thin horizontal strip on the wall across. The door opened and another student entered, to the predictable disapproving stares of the front row. It was Kamran, Nadia's classmate and also groupmate in the neurology rotation. He walked towards the back row sheepishly and took the empty chair next to Nadia's. Nadia nodded a quick greeting then turned her attention back to the speaker.

The presenter continued. 'He had been well until one day earlier when his wife noted odd behaviour. He was having difficulty opening the door to his house and she noted that he was trying to turn the lock with his pen instead of his usual set of keys. Later, in the evening, he became quiet and withdrawn and ate very little, which was very unusual because he was normally a jovial and talkative person, apparently. The next day his wife noted he had fever. He was also very irritable. At some point there was an altercation between them and he became very abusive.'

Sudden confusion and fever...had been in good health otherwise... sounds like central nervous system infection, Nadia thought to herself. It reminded her of the young man she had seen in her first week on neurology, the one who had become brain dead in a day. Dr Mirza had diagnosed him with viral encephalitis but no one was really sure.

Her thoughts were interrupted by a heavy authoritarian voice.

'The altercation and abuse—was that unusual?' One of the senior professors, a white-haired man with a gruff demeanour, wanted to know. 'I mean, if the husband and wife had a troubled relationship, the abusive altercation might not be so out of character.'

'No, sir, we understand it was quite out of character,' the presenter responded. 'His wife says he never uses bad language and it was a shock for her. Later that day she offered him water to drink and at that point he just went berserk...'

'Meaning what, exactly?' the same professor asked, a touch more aggressively this time. '"Berserk" is not a neurological term.'

Needlessly interrupting a junior doctor like this was par for the course at this meeting. Kept the trainees in their place, the thinking went.

'Yes, sir, I was just about to explain,' said the young physician, defensively. 'When he was offered water, he became very agitated and started screaming and clutching his throat. His wife tried to soothe him but he lunged out and hit her in the mouth. That was when she called her brother and they brought him to our emergency room. It was a serious blow. In fact, she had to be seen as a patient as well, because her teeth had been knocked loose.'

This was sounding eerily familiar, thought Nadia. The agitation and violent behaviour made it sound even more like that case she had seen earlier in the ICU. She remembered Asad mentioning that it was unusual for someone with viral encephalitis to become aggressive and use violent force. But other features of this case certainly suggested a diagnosis of encephalitis. She wondered if violence and aggression were so unusual in patients with viral encephalitis, how was it that this case had it too? Nadia couldn't reason through it any further. She wanted to know more details about this patient. Were there any particular physical signs? And what was the hospital course? What happened, then?

As if on cue, a professor seated in the front row asked for details of the neurological examination.

The speaker was standing at a podium on an elevated stage. A laptop computer lay open in front of him, which he was tapping periodically. The wall behind the podium was dominated by the Avicenna Hospital logo; underneath it was a fiberglass blackboard that ran the full length of the wall. In one corner of the stage, across from the podium and obscuring the far side of the blackboard, stood a tall white screen on which slides were being shown from the speaker's laptop which was hooked up to a multimedia projector.

'Yes, sir,' the speaker continued, as he tapped on his laptop and a new slide appeared on the screen. 'Our patient was an ill-looking man of average height and build. Pulse was 104, blood pressure 160/100, respiratory rate 22 per minute. The neck was supple and there was no rash. He kept mumbling nonsense and wouldn't follow any commands. There was no gaze preference. All four limbs were being moved symmetrically and without obvious weakness, and both plantar reflexes were downgoing.'

Not very helpful, thought Nadia. The examination details had not provided any particularly revealing clues about the diagnosis.

The speaker tapped on his laptop again and flashed a new slide. At the top of the slide in large, bold letters was the heading 'Investigations.' He read off the salient points. 'Routine bloodwork including CBC, Chem 7 and LFTs were normal. An EEG showed diffuse slowing, mostly delta range, but no asymmetry. Brain MRI was normal. A spinal tap revealed normal opening pressure, protein 88, glucose 64, WBC 0 and RBC 4, all well within acceptable limits. PCR for *Herpes simplex* virus was also negative.'

Strangely similar to that other case—what was his name? Zafar something or other, Nadia thought once again. The initial symptoms suggested viral encephalitis, then there was an unexplained episode of violence and aggression, and no diagnostic clues were forthcoming from the special investigations. The similarities, it seemed to her, were unmistakable. But she was a mere medical student, and realised that she lacked the depth of specialised knowledge and the clinical experience to understand the significance of this new case. Could she be reading too much into it? She kept wondering.

Hoping to detect some hint of the puzzlement that she was feeling, Nadia tried to look at Asad's face. He was seated several rows ahead of her, though, and all she got was a view of the back of his head. The earliest signs of a bald patch, she couldn't help noticing.

The speaker appeared to be wrapping up his narrative. 'We intubated him and made a provisional diagnosis of viral encephalitis. Spinal fluid was normal, which of course can sometimes be seen in encephalitis. Empirical treatment was started with acyclovir, but our patient remained in coma and did not respond. The second day of admission, he lost all brainstem reflexes, and later that day he went into cardiac arrest. His relatives had already been explained that he had become brain dead, so CPR was not attempted. Death was declared at 5:40 pm on admission day two.'

A man whom Nadia had not seen before now got up from his seat in the second row and walked on to the stage. He appeared to be in his late forties and had the collected manner of an experienced attending physician. Nadia guessed he was one of the senior neurologists from Civil who had been supervising the case. Standing next to the podium, the man asked for the lights to be brought back on, and then invited the audience for questions and comments.

Asad stood up to offer the first comment. 'Thank you for sharing this case, Dr Azeem,' he began. 'I find it very interesting because we saw a similar case recently where the diagnosis seemed to be encephalitis, but the patient had displayed some physical aggression that didn't seem to fit into the typical picture of viral encephalitis. And just like your patient, his illness was also very rapid and he was brain dead by the second day of admission.'

There was usually some background chatter during Q&A time, but Asad's comment had grabbed everyone's attention, most of all Dr Azeem's. One otherwise healthy young man dead after two days without a clear diagnosis was quizzical enough for this audience. Now to be told of a recent similar case, it was almost the equivalent of lightning striking twice. A hush fell over the room as everyone became deeply interested in this exchange.

'That's very interesting,' said Dr Azeem. 'We were struck by the aggression too, especially since it was provoked by water. Was that true of your case as well, Dr Mirza?'

'It could be,' replied Asad, 'but I'm not sure. I mean, he did attack his mother when she offered him a glass of water, but he'd apparently been acting strange and paranoid even before that. I'm not sure if his violence was a reaction to the water, or if it was just the natural progression of his paranoia.'

All eyes turned towards Dr Azeem.

'Well, I've certainly seen enough cases of rabies at Civil,' he said, 'to tell you that the violent response evoked in our patient resembled the hydrophobia reported in rabies patients. But this case wasn't rabies. Our patient had no history of a dog bite. You can't get rabies without the bite of a rabid animal. In fact, he didn't have any contact with animals at all. We probed this in detail with his wife and relatives. Was that true of your patient as well, Dr Mirza?'

'Yes, it was,' said Asad. 'We did consider rabies as part of the differential diagnosis, but dismissed it once we confirmed that there had been no dog bite. In fact, no contact with animals at all, as you said.'

Nadia was following with rapt attention. She recalled Asad having mentioned something about doing a brain biopsy on Zafar's case, but it was never done because he died so soon. She thought it would be a safe question to ask now. Her intellectual curiosity had been strongly aroused by the exchange. She may have come to this meeting with the aim of just looking good and getting brownie points, but a genuine desire to properly interpret the meaning of these two cases had now taken over.

The moment she put up her hand, Dr Azeem noticed and motioned towards her.

'Could a brain biopsy have helped in this situation?' Nadia asked. It was a sophisticated question from someone whose voice was not known to this audience, and many people turned around to look at this young woman in the back row.

'Excellent question,' said Dr Azeem. 'A brain biopsy can reveal important features in encephalitis, and I do think it may have given us some diagnostic clues that were not forthcoming from the other less invasive tests. But his illness was overwhelming. We did think about it, but couldn't arrange for it in time.'

Asad felt the need to explain the point further. 'All the same,' he said, 'it's important for the residents and students to know that a biopsy of the brain wouldn't have changed the outcome for either case. Only one kind of encephalitis is curable, the type caused by *Herpes simplex*, and both patients were given that treatment anyway. We can't be sure what kind of encephalitis they had but I think it can be safely concluded that it wasn't herpetic.'

'You can't even be sure they had the same illness,' the gruff professor from the front row interjected. 'Two uncommon cases don't make an epidemic, you know.'

Asad nodded in his direction, but didn't say anything. After a brief awkward pause, he said, 'We need to move along now. There are other cases to discuss.'

Nadia couldn't concentrate on the rest of the meeting. She made up her mind to go see Asad in his office the very next day to follow up on this discussion. Perhaps she could even get him to help her write about these cases as a scientific report that could be published in one of the professional neurology journals. An article published in the world's scientific literature—it was the ultimate medical student dream. And to be mentored by this young teacher she had taken a liking to...

Her head began to swim. Her mind wandered.

Nine

Three topics in Pakistan—Islam, cricket, and the state of the nation—had always been fail-safe conversation starters. To this list could now be added America and American foreign policy. George W Bush, the American invasion of Iraq, the war in Afghanistan, the election of Barack Obama, the Jewish Lobby, the political calculations of Republicans and Democrats—it had all become table chatter that nobody ever tired of.

America, in other words, was the topic of the day, every day. In more tranquil times most people would recognise, at the most, the name of the American president. During the Bush years, even cabinet officers such as Rumsfeld, Cheney, Powell and Rice had become widely known. People who couldn't name the mayor of Karachi could rattle off the membership of Bush's National Security Council. Fathers who didn't remember all the names of even their own children, displayed subtle familiarity with the US Senate. Daschle, Frist, Leahy, Lugar and Lieberman the Jew—they had become recognisable names in Karachi's streets.

There was supposed to be institutionalised democracy in the United States. Presidential elections were held every four years and there were always two viable candidates representing the major political parties. The will of the American people prevailed. It had been happening for over two hundred years, ever since America's founding fathers promulgated their famed constitution and launched a republic in 1776.

But in Pakistan, few took it seriously. Not that they were not interested. Quite the reverse, in fact, because American politics was followed here more closely than even many items of local news. It was rather that in Pakistan everyone thought they had America figured out. They saw through its urges and motivations, its desires and desperations. The outcome of all politics in America was foreordained, the voting a charade to keep up appearances. There was a hardly a soul in Pakistan who could be convinced otherwise.

Poor John Kerry. He had been a fool for even trying. An hour in the drawing rooms of Lahore and Karachi, and they would've talked him out of it. You don't stand a chance, buddy. Bush and the boys are doing with the world as they please; they're not going to let a liberal softie like you get in their way. Elections are to be manipulated, democracy is a sham. Once a cynical, marginalised view, now this belief had become mainstream.

The aficionados—and there were so many connoisseurs of world politics here—couldn't get enough of it. They spoke knowledgeably on the central issues of US foreign policy and presidential politics—the 'battleground' states, the divisive issues of gay marriage and abortion rights, the different media outlets that shamelessly tilted liberal or conservative. But they saw these as feigned contrivances designed for convenient consumption by a gullible American public. The real drama was being played out behind the scenes, orchestrated to perfection by crafty political operatives and their unforgiving conspiratorial masters in the military-industrial complex.

When the Obama campaign gathered momentum, this know-it-all Pakistani attitude was caught off guard. People became confused how an omnipotent nation founded and controlled by white people could permit a black man to come so far. Was it really true that Obama had spent his childhood in a Muslim household in Indonesia, that his middle name was Hussain, that his father had been a Muslim from Kenya? Many found these questions and their factual, verifiable answers disorienting. The immediate reaction was to dismiss the possibility of an Obama presidency altogether.

Then the moment finally arrived when CNN called the election. Pakistanis had followed the coverage like it was a cricket match with India. Street children could tell you that Wolf Blitzer was the anchor and it was Ohio's twenty electoral votes that carried Obama across the threshold. Pakistan's countless armchair politicians scrambled to adjust to this incredible new reality. Within hours, they had processed and digested it into a freshly spun narrative. Obama was the 'token' black—a quota appointment designed to convey an impression of inclusivity and tolerance but who in reality was just a tool in the hands of the invincible white establishment. His Muslim background was just a ruse to charm and disarm the Muslim world. Just watch, the connoisseurs said, not an iota of US foreign policy will change.

For America had certainly crossed over to the other side of the moral divide and was exploiting humanity without respect or remorse. Like the rest of the world, Pakistanis too noted these developments with mounting anger, frustration and helplessness. They needed some mechanism to assimilate this, some convenient way to absorb these unpleasant realities. A popular rationalisation emerged that this was the fate of all empires before the end finally came, and surely all this sabre-rattling and war-mongering signalled the coming demise of the great American monster.

How stupid of them to have gone into Afghanistan. Didn't their leaders and policymakers know it had already swallowed two great powers whole? That this was the one place in the world where great powers went to die?

Had they learned nothing from the hiding they had in Vietnam and from all the misplaced American adventurism in Iraq? Neither country had been a threat to the US. Yet in Vietnam they used chemical warfare against a meek and vulnerable Asian race and left their homeland ravaged. Now Iraq, a nation within the fold of Muslim brotherhood, had been bled to near-total exhaustion from years of crippling sanctions while it sat defenceless on huge deposits of oil. All the fuss about weapons of mass destruction had been followed with cynical detachment in Pakistan. Colin Powell and the State Department had fooled few people here, if at all.

The term 'neocon' had been swiftly absorbed into the vernacular, and it was readily bandied about as a term of derision. People equated it with Satanic intent to subvert the world. It was supposed to be like the Nazis under Hitler, except this was worse because the neocons were more powerful, with access to thousands of thermonuclear bombs that could blow up the planet with the touch of a button. And more evil and dangerous, because unlike the Nazis whose wickedness was manifest, the neocons were the devil you could not readily see. They were masters of deceit, claiming to abhor only extremist and militant Islam but all the while working against the entire world of Islam as the one great enemy. Whether this was true or not, the feeling was nevertheless firmly entrenched as the conventional wisdom in Pakistan's collective mind. The neocons mouthed irksome shibboleths like 'Muslims hate our freedom,' which people felt was nothing but vacuous rhetoric because they knew perfectly well that Muslims hated America's policies, not its freedom. Who hated freedom?

Anger and depression had become the prevalent emotions. There was deep rage at America's blind support for the Jews of Israel against the Muslims of Palestine, and abiding depression at the paralysis of over one billion Muslims who couldn't do anything about it. Pakistanis understood the power of faith and the religious word, and in a perverse way, the American-Israeli bond was also deeply satisfying. There was a biblical injunction to protect the land of Israel and prepare it for the Second Coming of Christ, and America was following it to the letter. This essentially reduced America's Israel policy to a fundamentalist Christian obsession, something everyone in Pakistan, itself the land of passionate religious obsessions, felt they could easily relate to.

This was one of the more curious things about Pakistan—that the great forces influencing societies globally couldn't find a foothold here. Elsewhere in the world, political disputes threw nations into chaos and economic deprivation moved masses to revolt. For some reason, Pakistan was different. Here political ideologies inflamed passions only in armchair conversations, and crushing hunger and abject poverty were not regarded enough of a bother to get worked up over.

Derogatory cartoons in Danish newspapers demonstrated that it was really blasphemy against the prophet of Allah and desecration of any of the symbols of Islam, that could momentously unlock the vast energies trapped inside the Muslim mind. Blasphemy was punishable by death from hanging, and sacrilege of the Quran could cause the population to detonate like a depth charge.

Michael Moore was celebrated as a hero. Few Pakistanis had been exposed to Americans caricaturing their own government, and the spectacle of this overweight white man with working-class features lumbering around wearing a baseball cap pulled low over his eyes, more American in flavour than probably even GI Joe, with whom you found yourself so completely in agreement, was intoxicating. Moore had become bigger than many other American icons, with the possible exception of Muhammad Ali. Pirated copies of the *Fahrenheit 9/11* DVD traded like pornography. Everyone had settled on their favourite scenes from the film, and they discussed them with friends and strangers alike. 'Was it all just a dream?' The film's opening line, spoken as a voiceover with images from Bush's 2000 presidential victory, had become a catchphrase. Even those who did not speak English knew what you meant when you said that.

The wars in Iraq and Afghanistan were being followed through 24-hour television news channels. Those without TV sets listened intently to BBC radio. Enthusiasts had mastered the websites, and they exchanged opinions and chatted with political junkies from the US and other parts of the world. Local news sources had never been taken seriously by Pakistanis, the inevitable endpoint of decades-long media control by the state. A range of private round-the-clock Urdu news channels had emerged and acquired some independent credibility, but they were regarded as informal sources of news. Al-Jazeera English was understood by only a few, who rated it highly. The original Al-Jazeera channel, although broadly admired and acclaimed, wasn't understood at all because Pakistanis did not speak Arabic, the result of a very complex inoculation of Islam into the Indian subcontinent. So the Al-Jazeera stations were hardly watched, except when channel-flipping, when out of deference you tended to linger on them just a moment longer.

It was common knowledge that watching Fox News Network was an effective means to make your blood pressure surge. Everyone still watched. Many were addicted. Part of the reason was to indulge the perverse human craving for self-inflicted pain, but the bigger reason was that it made you feel secure you were keeping up with what Uncle Sam Satan and his nefarious disciples were thinking and planning. Pakistanis saw it as a window into the neocon mind.

Whether true or not, it was a perception that produced intense voyeuristic excitement. For many Pakistanis, Fox also validated their worst suspicions about the Anglo-Saxon race. The same peoples who had plundered the wealth of Asia and Africa through the British empire, who had driven native populations in America and Australia to near-extinction, and had come up with the shocking scheme of apartheid down south in the African continent, were the peoples who were now staging the grotesque global vaudeville of American hegemony with—so the thinking went—Islam and its followers firmly in their gun sights.

Superficially this mindset may have seemed like paranoia, but it was actually the collective product of a highly indulgent ego. If the mightiest nation in the history of civilisation had designs on you, surely that meant you were a pretty important nation yourself? Pakistanis would never openly claim theirs was a country of any importance; it made you sound naïve and gullible, and your own compatriots would be the first people to hoot you down.

But who doesn't want to believe in their own potency? So talk about an impending American invasion of Pakistan had been innovated as an indirect trick, an absurd way of having your cake and eating it too, that Pakistanis frequently brought up to feel good about themselves. It implied a special significance for Pakistan that may or may not have existed. This was feel-good patriotism, Pakistani-style.

Media news coverage from the standard sources was bad enough, it was really the unsaid event—the horrific tragedies that no one spoke about but which everyone knew were happening—that were exercising Muslims in Pakistan and elsewhere. Multitudes of innocent Muslim children had perished under economic sanctions imposed on Iraq after the First Gulf War in 1991. In the West Bank and Gaza, Palestinian youth were daily treated like cattle and gunned down at little provocation. After twin bombings of two American embassies in Africa, American airpower had destroyed a pharmaceutical plant in Sudan, claiming it was a factory for chemical weapons. No apology had been forthcoming; instead, rabid media outlets like Fox kept going out of their way to justify the excesses. Hatred of American overreach was ballooning into a worldwide pandemic. In Muslim countries like Pakistan it was felt strongly by virtually everybody.

ꙮ

At a roadside café in downtown Karachi, the breakfast crowd was starting to gather. They were all men. Some of them were visitors from outside the city, here for trade or business. Others were locals who probably worked in the vicinity, and for one reason or another found it convenient to get breakfast here rather than in their own homes.

At 8:30 am rush hour traffic was at a peak, the thoroughfares overcrowded with smoke-spewing vehicles, the sidewalks alive and pulsating with urban hustle and bustle. Scooters and motorcycles overflowed on the roads, jostling for space with yellow passenger buses and ramshackle donkey carts whose drivers looked as bedraggled and beaten as their beasts. Drab Suzuki vans carried schoolchildren spilling out the back, and an aging collection of Toyotas and Hondas muddled along, with the odd BMW and Mercedes sticking out like noblemen in a crowd of peasants.

Noise of all kinds dominated everything. There was the roar and sputter of motorcycle engines, the hiss and belch of overcrowded buses, the honk and hoot of car horns. Mixed in with countless human conversations and the occasional braying donkey, it created a cacophonic din.

The café was makeshift. A kitchen shack wedged into the side of a decayed and abandoned building, run by a besieged cook who doubled as the cashier, and by an unexcitable waiter who looked like he had seen and done everything there was to see and do and had no further desire to do any more. Several feeble-looking tables surrounded by equally fragile chairs occupied a large portion of the sidewalk in front of the shack, on which customers sat oblivious to pedestrian traffic. The pedestrians, for their part, nonchalantly side-stepped the tables as if they were walking around a natural obstacle, like a tree.

The spot was several blocks from his apartment, buried in one of the canyons within the concrete maze of downtown Karachi. The surroundings were depressing. Most of the buildings were in various states of decay, with peeling paint and leaking drainpipes, and refuse littered the streets. Malik preferred it because he felt anonymous here. He was careful not to become a regular, coming only on infrequent days when he felt like the indulgence of a greasy omelet rich in onions and cumin seed, to be consumed with fried, flaky flatbread and washed down with the *doodh-patti* tea of Karachi's streets, that was really milk and sugar flavoured with tea.

Casually dressed in a rumpled shalwar kameez, he bent over his table and scrutinised the newspaper stretched out in front of him. His attention was divided between the usual inflammatory headlines about the war in Afghanistan that were being served up as daily fodder, and a nearby table from where he was picking up snatches of colourful conversation. Despite the ambient noise, he could clearly make out two voices. Without looking up, Malik allowed himself to listen in.

'Bush may have left the White House but he will not be forgotten. He is going to have a bad end.'

'Musharraf too, man. He may have escaped from Pakistan but he is going to have a bad end, too. He got the whole country bent over and sodomised by the big American prick. Motherfucker will burn in hell.'

'Tony Blair is also going to have a bad end.'

'You bet.'

'Hey, did you hear that Bush once had a camera pushed up his ass for medical examination and they found Musharraf in there.'

The voices erupted in guffaws. The joke creased Malik's lips with a smile too. After their laughter died down, the two men fell quiet for a while.

'I tell you, Pakistan is next,' one of the men started again. 'After finishing off Iraq and Afghanistan, they're coming straight here.'

'You got that right. They want our nukes. Ours and Iran's—these American bastards are hell bent on coming after us.'

'They'll stop at nothing. Cocksuckers.'

'America is going to have a bad end.'

'You got that right.'

Indeed, thought Malik, as he turned his attention back to the newspaper. The eavesdropping had kindled his spirits and angry emotions welled up from somewhere deep inside. America would pay dearly for its sins. It would come to regret every scrap of support meted out to the Jews of Israel, every warrior of Allah tortured at Guantanamo Bay, every Muslim harassed under the Patriot Act. And the children. Innocent life, soft and chaste like kittens, goodness itself—how they have been slaughtered, in Palestine, in Iraq and Afghanistan, like cattle.

America will pay for each and every act of injustice. Malik was going to see to that.

The front page wasn't holding his attention anymore. As he turned the paper over to the back page, the unflappable waiter plopped breakfast in front of him. A delicious aroma of onion omelet and warm, fried flatbread overpowered his senses. Folding the paper and putting it aside, he began taking mouthfuls.

As he ate, he looked around idly. The men at the neighbouring table stood up, paid the waiter, and walked off in the direction of the bus stop located down the street. Malik turned around to take in the activity around him. An overweight man with a droopy walrus moustache had set up a vibrant little display of pills and potions, around which a small crowd was beginning to gather. Malik guessed that the man was hawking cures to all kinds of sexual inadequacy.

Closer to where he sat, two women modestly clad in traditional *hijab* were trying to cross the street. Munching away on his breakfast, Malik watched them negotiate oncoming traffic. Courtesy was a commodity unknown on Karachi's roads, and even though the women stood at the bank of a pedestrian crossing, the stripes were faded and the river of traffic barely registered their presence. Both women stood fidgeting, wondering when to make a move. Eventually they stepped into the path of an oncoming taxi, which came to a screeching stop inches away. Malik heard the driver shout profanities.

The waiter was back with *doodh-patti*. Having polished off the omelet, Malik was ready for the sugary cup of piping-hot tea and began sipping it with quiet pleasure. Most Karachi dwellers had yet to begin their workday, but even by this relatively early hour, it had already been a busy day for him.

Following routine, he had been up at 5:30 am to offer the *fajr* prayer at daybreak. This was also the best period to find an uncrowded Internet café, and catch up on email. Malik maintained five email accounts at a time, which he rotated according to a complex algorithm generated by a computer program. There had been eleven new messages today. One of these was from a discussion thread on jihad that he had been following passively. Six others were updates and FYIs from different quarters and did not need a response.

Dealing with the remaining four, however, consumed close to two hours. It wouldn't normally take this long, but today was the second Friday of the month, the day of the monthly resetting of the Network's communication code. Malik had to decipher the messages by working backwards from an elaborate set of rules based on the sequence of Arabic letters in selected verses from the Quran. Even after years in the job, he had still not mastered it. Decoding messages was the one thing in this line of work he hadn't taken naturally to.

One of the most important emails was from the Oceania chapter asking for help with reconnaissance on a plot to blow up Sydney Harbor Bridge. The chapter leader was citing what he called Malik's excellent work in Bali as justification, but he was clearly unaware that the man he was seeking had been fully involved in the Karachi project for well over a year. He would soon be told to look elsewhere.

Another email was from Central Command asking for an update on finances, and a set of enquiries on when the Karachi project could be expected to activate the Boston pathway. This one was simple—finances were in good shape, and the Boston pathway could be activated within three months. Things were going well.

The remaining emails were from his partner, Hamza Kadri. He was running short on supplies of ammonium disinfectant and phosphate-buffered saline. There was also a reminder that the ultracentrifuge was acting up and could Malik make sure that it was serviced within the week or else the whole project would be ruined. A typically dramatic yet effective communication, thought Malik. He opened up his work log and made notes to attend to Hamza's needs.

Slurping noises broke the bubble of his thoughts. The *doodh-patti* tea had been drained, and Malik caught himself absent-mindedly lapping away at the margins of the cup. Out of the corner of his eye, he saw the cool dude waiter approaching. As he swung by, Malik placed a fifty-rupee note in his palm, enough for the meal and a generous gratuity. Cool dude tried to smile but it came off as something of a smirk. What a loser, thought Malik, but on the other hand also a creature of Allah, and who are we to question the wisdom of His acts?

Malik was irritated by the thought of what a touchy and excitable prima donna Hamza was, constantly threatening that the project was in imminent danger of total collapse.

Hamza's most annoying habit was his penchant for going overboard, for constantly overstating his case just to make sure his needs were followed up. Malik knew it well, but even over the course of a year, it hadn't become any easier to deal with. Hamza acted more like a moody film star than a scientist. Tending to him had been a terrific challenge, exercising Malik frequently, occasionally pushing him to the brink and keeping him from blowing his stack only through the monumental self-control developed in his years with the Network.

It was fourteen months ago, but the meeting in which Malik had first received details of his Karachi assignment was still a fresh memory.

'This person will try your patience,' his contact node had said, as the two sat sipping black tea in Felafel Stall, just down the road from Umayyad Mosque in the heart of old Damascus.

'Understood, Brother. I am up to it.' It was an almost perfunctory response.

'You cannot afford to be overconfident, Brother Malik. Hamza is very good at his work, but he has been selected for the work, not his behaviour. He can be moody and demanding.'

The contact node, a seasoned veteran, wasn't one to put stress on personal frailties. Malik had been with him last year during chapter meetings in London and Cairo, and had partnered him during post-event media monitoring after the US embassy bombing in 1998 in Dar-es-Salaam. He knew the man to be an expert hand, utterly professional at all times. The insistent mention of Hamza's whimsical constitution had alerted Malik that a serious challenge was afoot.

Subsequent experience with the Karachi project had proved his suspicions. Hamza was supposed to be a gifted scientist, and of Pakistani origin to boot, which had raised expectations for the chemistry between them, but he tended to be petulant and churlish and changed moods so frequently, Malik sometimes felt the Karachi project was like a bad marriage to a spouse who was suffering from perpetual PMS.

But the perseverance and restraint, the hardship and the hand-holding, was all beginning to pay off.

Hamza was certainly a pain, but he had also proved himself a genius. Malik stood up, twisted his paper into a roll, and began walking towards the bus stop.

TEN

PHLEBOTOMY HAS TO be one of the worst jobs in a hospital. There may be worse ways to earn a living—it was probably better than being a janitor whose workday revolves around only dirt and refuse, and certainly better than being a nurses' aide who wipes excrement from buttock creases—but not much better.

The assignment involves drawing blood from patients for laboratory tests ordered by doctors. Nobody likes to have a needle stuck in them. They try to wriggle out of it, complain and fidget, make faces, and bitch and moan afterwards. Sometimes they'll just let you hear it, swearing at you with venom like you were a tormentor practiced in the art of torture. It is horrible to be reviled like this, especially when you mean well. You're only trying to help these people. Why don't they get it, these animals?

At 2:40 am early on a Friday morning, these were the thoughts of the night-duty phlebotomist at Avicenna University Hospital. He hated his job. It was his tenth year doing this, and there were no prospects.

In the beginning, back when he had started drawing blood samples from patients, he had felt important enough. But that was nearly a decade ago, and the feeling soon lapsed. Three years before that, he had joined Avicenna as an errand boy in the medical laboratory. His workday used to be full of being told to do this and do that, all the time. There was no respect from anyone. It had started promisingly enough, with all the novelty that came from getting a job in a big and famous organisation, but after a few months of do-this, do-that, go-here, go-there, it wore thin. There was no respite, no break.

At the same time, he was constantly exposed to the phlebotomists in the lab, and they began to appeal to him. They wore white coats and one or two would even put a tie on. They got to act officiously, telling patients to push out their arm, make a tight fist, look the other way. They got to touch young women. People responded to them by doing what they were told. It was the extent of his worldview, and it became his ambition to become a phlebotomist himself.

He picked up the trade on the job. With care and deference, he learned to expose the veins, tie the tourniquet just so, hold the needle with the bevel facing upwards, slide it through to pierce the skin, and pull back on the plunger to suck out the frothy dark red liquid from human veins. He felt pride at mastering something that not just anyone could do.

When one of the older phlebotomists retired after thirty-two years of service, he received his first (and only) promotion. It should have given him pause, that the man he was replacing had not advanced in the job in over three decades. But that was easily overlooked in the heady rush of donning a white coat and putting on a tie, telling people what to do, holding the wrists of young women just so and squeezing their forearms as he tapped the veins to make them prominent.

He now worked in eight-hour shifts, sharing the schedule with two other phlebotomists. This month he was on the night shift, 11 pm to 7 am. It was the worst aspect of a job that was nasty to begin with.

As the frustrated phlebotomist returned from a round of blood-drawings in the obstetrics ward, hoping to doze off for a while in the staff lounge next to the ICU, his beeper went off again. It was never a pleasant sound, but now in the quiet of the night, the shrill tune sounded especially revolting. Unhooking it from his belt, he upturned the pager's LCD display. '*Come to ER*,' it said. Sour-tempered and disagreeable, eyes heavy and burning from being forced to stay awake, he descended the two flights of stairs that ended at the emergency room's back entrance.

The ER wore a quiet, almost deserted look, which was not unusual for the dead of night. A tart young receptionist decked in cheap make-up was manning the front desk, looking the very picture of idleness as she applied nail-polish while a heavily thumbed copy of *Cosmopolitan* lay upturned next to her. As he entered through the automatic sliding door, she looked up and motioned him towards the acute bay, the six-bedded hall reserved for serious emergencies. A single slip of paper waited for him in the specimen collection tray.

Just one person to be bled—a relief. With any luck, this one would be in a coma or something. From his perspective, that was the best way for a patient to be. People didn't bicker about needle pricks if they were unconscious.

Only one of the six beds was occupied. He could make out a large, middle-aged man with a beard, face covered by an oxygen mask, a monitor over the bed displaying ECG, pulse, breathing rate. A nurse stood next to the bed, making notes on a clipboard.

He walked up to the patient and shook him lightly by the shoulder. No response.

'He's unconscious', the nurse said flatly. She had finished writing. Hanging the clipboard at the foot of the bed, she turned around and walked away. The phlebotomist was left alone with the patient in the acute bay.

As was standard practice, he looked at the name on the paper slip in his hand, and matched it with the plastic identification tag on the patient's wrist: Sikander, Baba—Medical Record No. 129-63-29. He had the right man. As he looked the patient over, trying to decide the best spot from where to draw blood, he noticed a large, ugly scab on the right ear. Covered with flecks of crusted blood, the margins of the wound looked like teeth marks. A wave of repulsion washed over him. He quietly pushed the syringe into a vein and began collecting a sample of blood, trying not to look at the wound on the ear. It was disgusting.

The other beeper that went off around 2:40 am was Nadia's.

It had been a quiet night for her and she was asleep in the women doctor's call room. Medical students did not have an official place to sleep during night duty, but the doctors' call rooms had two sets of bunk beds and there was usually space for a student or two. Tonight, Nadia shared the room with Dr Farida, her supervising neurology resident.

This was Nadia's last night on duty in her neurology rotation. Tomorrow morning, she would be joining the gastroenterology service, and would be taught about diseases of the liver and digestive system. She was sad to be leaving neurology, a month-long experience that she had enjoyed immensely. Nadia was a careful girl, too cautious to commit to anything prematurely, but with each passing day she felt convinced that in the specialty of neurology she had indeed found her true calling.

Rubbing her eyes, she strained to read the lighted beeper display in the dark. '*Call 7033. Farida*'.

Farida picked up at the first ring. 'Yes, Dr Farida?' Nadia croaked the words out, fighting back sleep.

'Nadia, there's a patient in the ER who may be coming to neurology. I'm stuck here in the private ward with a seizure case. Can you go down and take care of it? I may be busy here for a while.'

'Uh, sure. I'll go right away. Any idea what it is?'

'Someone in a coma, apparently, but I don't have the details. Check with the ER supervisor, he'll fill you in. Call me when you've seen him and we'll go over the treatment plan.'

Fully awake now, Nadia sat up and straightened her hair. After checking the time on her wristwatch, she got up to brush her teeth and use the toilet. Processing a sick admission typically took two, two and a half hours. She was certainly done sleeping for the night.

The request from Farida implied great confidence in the abilities of this bright young medical student, who was still a few months away from finishing medical school. It put Nadia in a buoyant mood, but it also made her anxious at the sense of responsibility. Entering the ER from the back entrance, she passed the phlebotomist on his way out, a portable tray loaded with blood-filled specimen bottles swinging in his hand. Stiff and self-conscious, he nodded at Nadia as they crossed, but she barely noticed. Her mind was on the ER supervisor, whom she had spotted through the glass doors washing his hands at a sink.

She had just made it past the entrance when he called out to her. 'Hey, are you the medical student Farida said she'd be sending for the new admission?'

As she listened to the supervisor's briefing, the story transfixed her.

'It's a fifty-six-year-old man', the supervisor began. 'Brought in a few hours earlier, around midnight. Apparently in good health until two days ago, when he began talking strangely. That was followed by some visual hallucinations, imagining he was in a room full of dwarfs or something. The next morning, yesterday, he was found to have a fever, and he became very lethargic. He's supposedly a faith-healer of some kind, has no family to speak of. The history was obtained from a couple of friends who came with him.'

As he talked, the senior doctor edged towards the patient's bed. Nadia walked with him. Standing at the edge of the bed, she took in the vital signs displayed on the overhead monitor. When her gaze drifted downwards, she noticed the ear wound.

'What happened to his ear?'

'It's very strange,' the senior doctor said. 'His friends said he was trying to cure a mad woman of her mental illness but she became delirious and bit him on the ear. The wound looks all right. We've cleaned it and he's been given a dose of antibiotic just to be safe.'

Nadia knew that ear cartilage lacked a good blood supply, so infections of that area healed poorly. 'Perhaps he's septic from an infected ear?' she ventured.

'Doubt it. I think we need to rule out CNS infection. He's in coma now, and the vitals really don't suggest sepsis. He needs a CT scan followed by a spinal tap. Probably should be in the ICU. We've already drawn blood for routine labs and blood cultures.'

A nurse came over and asked Nadia what kind of intravenous fluids she wanted to order. The nurse was just doing her job, but Nadia had never been asked to give doctor's orders before. Anxious to get the patient out of the ER and into a proper hospital bed, the nurse was trying to move things along. She knew Nadia was a medical student—it said so on her ID badge—but for all purposes the student was now functioning as a doctor, and had to be dealt with as such. Nadia tried not to show it, but she was almost dizzy with elation.

'Lets start D5-saline with ten milliequivalents potassium,' she said, speaking effortlessly, as if ordering IV fluids for sick patients was second nature to her. Quickly, she went through a mental checklist of the things that needed to be done. A CT scan of the brain was the most urgent. She filled out the paperwork and handed it to the nurse. Within minutes, the nurse and an aide had Baba hooked up to a portable heart monitor and were wheeling him down the hall towards radiology.

Nadia was keen to get more information about the patient's clinical history. The friends who had accompanied Baba to the hospital were still around. She found them stretched out in the waiting area. They confirmed for her all the clinical details that the ER supervisor had already summarised. Nadia felt a creepy resemblance of this case to the two mysterious cases of suspected encephalitis she had come across earlier—the case of Zafar Majeed, and the case of the thirty-eight-year-old man seen at Civil Hospital who had been discussed at the neurological case conference last week.

Here was a man with a brief history of confusion progressing to coma. It was tempting to ask if this new case was somehow linked with the other two.

Medical students were routinely cautioned against reaching fanciful conclusions about their patients. Nadia was well aware of this admonition, but she brushed it aside now, sensing that she was on to something that could potentially be of great medical interest. She had read inspirational stories of medical geniuses who had relied on intuition and astute clinical observation to uncover novel disease patterns and associations, their bold thinking leading to famous scientific breakthroughs.

Chance favours the prepared mind—it was a timeless dictum. Only last week, during a pharmacology lecture, she had heard one of her professors use it to characterise Alexander Fleming's groundbreaking discovery of antibiotics. Sometime in the early 1920s, Fleming had noticed that bacteria refused to grow in a medium that had been contaminated by a fungus called *Penicillium notatum*. He reasoned that the fungus contained something that had the power to kill bacteria. It was a fantastic possibility, because at the time bacteria reigned supreme—infections were as lethal as cancer and medical science was powerless against them. Fleming purified the active ingredient in the fungus and produced penicillin, which many experts now regard as the single greatest achievement of modern medicine. For his troubles, the good doctor received the Nobel Prize.

Heady thoughts, they were making Nadia's mind reel. All the excitement she felt in last week's case conference had come flooding back. She tried to collect herself. What made the other two cases unusual was their display of violence and agitation shortly before lapsing into coma. Interesting that, in both instances, the violence seemed to have been triggered by the presence of water. Possibly. In the conference, she remembered, someone had raised the question of rabies, but the suggestion had been dismissed because you could only get rabies from a dog bite. Everyone knew that. Neither case had been bitten by a dog. In fact, they had had no contact with animals at all.

A series of questions began sprouting in Nadia's analytical mind. Had there been any frenzied, aggressive behaviour by this new patient? And if so, did it possibly occur as a reaction to water? And what was the significance of the freaky bite on his ear—not an animal bite admittedly but, even more peculiarly, a human one? Who really bit him and why?

Nadia looked straight at the two men as she spoke. 'What exactly was wrong with the woman who bit your friend's ear? And how is she...where is she now?' Her voice was questioning, but confident and direct. The fatigue and sleep debt had vanished.

Both men gave each other knowing looks. They seemed to be saying, 'We knew this was coming.' They had been very nervous about the whole episode surrounding Ayesha Anjum and Baba that had resulted in Ayesha biting Baba's ear just before breathing her last. They had secretly felt Baba had killed her, or at least hastened her death, and if you thought about it, the two things were really not that different. Baba and his men had raped delirious young women before, women who had been brought to Baba the faith healer by unsuspecting relatives. The girls had invariably been too ashamed to talk about it afterwards. Some had been in a genuine stupor and not realised they had been violated. None of them died, at least not in their custody.

Baba had reassured them that Ayesha's death was nothing. She had died because of the fatal illness that her husband had brought her in with. The finessing had worked—until Baba himself was taken ill. Before bringing him to the hospital, Baba's men had decided to tell everything if asked. There were clear human teeth marks on the wound, and a human bite would have to be acknowledged. They would tell all—except for the sexual assault. That would be foolish to divulge for it implicated them as well.

After fidgeting for a few seconds, they began to talk. 'Baba is a great faith healer, you see', one of them began. He was the taller of the two and appeared to be the dominant one, a natural spokesman. After establishing Baba's credentials in the most glowing terms, he told Nadia about the ear bite and the poor woman's sad demise. Baba was blessing her with prayer, he said, when the woman just went wild and took a bite out of his ear. Nadia was dumbfounded.

She asked questions about the woman's condition and illness, and listened to the two men with mounting excitement.

The shorter man asked if Baba was going to be okay. Nadia gave evasive answers. They wouldn't have a diagnosis until some tests had been done. When the attendant persisted, she cut him short.

'Has he shown any signs of agitation or excitement?' she asked.

The two men looked at each other again. Their glances betrayed a rising sense of awe at Nadia's perceptive skills. Once again, it was the spokesman who talked.

'It was yesterday, maybe noontime. He had a fever...his skin was burning. I was wiping his brow with a wet towel, and that woke him up right away. It was very strange. I was dipping the towel in a bowl of water, and when he noticed it, his eyes became wide like this. I'll never forget that look. He smacked the bowl over. It really got him worked up.'

Un-fucking-believable, thought Nadia. What was she dealing with here?

She was on to something, she really was, and she could feel it. She prided herself on having a meticulous and scrutinising mind that wouldn't race to conclusions. Was she making half-baked inferences, letting herself be tricked into thinking something was afoot when in fact it could all be nothing but a series of unconnected, chance occurrences?

She didn't think so.

She was certain this was either a new kind of disease, or a strange new twist on an old one. Dr Mirza would have to be called right away. She couldn't believe she had to leave her neurology rotation and start a different rotation tomorrow.

Un-fucking-believable.

Eleven

While Nadia was talking to Baba's companions, back in the ER the duty nurse was becoming edgy that her patient was being ignored. She wanted him out of her ER, wanted him to get his brain scanned quickly and get his spinal tap done so he could be sent upstairs to the ICU, or wherever it was the neurology team had planned to place him. Her supervisor had called the neurology resident soon enough, only for the resident to pass the job on to a medical student, which was so typical.

She had been told the resident was tied up elsewhere, which was surely plausible, but at four o'clock Baba was the only patient in the ER and, with her first grandchild on the way, the night shift nurse was eager to catch up with her knitting. As far as she was concerned, the neurology resident was just passing the buck. It was just a delaying tactic.

As the nurse considered her options, Baba's heart rate began to drop. She noticed it immediately.

Years of professional experience had trained her ear to the beeping sounds emanating from the cardiac monitor. It was an instinct with emergency room nurses everywhere. Her patient's heart was beating around eighty times a minute, the steady *toot-toot* had been telling her. With just the solitary patient in the ER right now, she could easily keep track of it. Eighty was a good rate, solid and steady. Every now and then, she would also glance up at the monitor and be reassured that the heart rate was hovering in the low eighties, the fluorescent green tracer of the ECG easily visible on the jet black screen.

When the beeping became less frequent, her ears pricked up.

A glance at the monitor confirmed Baba's slowing heartbeat. Sixty-eight...sixty...fifty-four. It was plunging as she watched. When the rate dipped below fifty, the monitor let out a piercing alarm. Everyone heard it.

The ER doctor came running towards Baba and felt his neck for a pulse. The nurse quickly put a stethoscope to his chest and listened for breathing. Hearing nothing, she turned around and shouted at the ER receptionist to call a code.

Within seconds, '*Code Blue, emergency room, Code Blue, emergency room*' was booming over the hospital's loudspeaker system.

Nadia looked through the glass doors of the waiting room and saw the nurse urgently pulling a large red cart towards Baba's bed. The doctor had covered Baba's face with a mask and was forcing air into his mouth by squeezing a rubber bag.

As Nadia rushed back into the ER, she saw two other doctors come in from the back entrance. One of them jumped up on Baba's bed, straddled his chest and, with both hands locked together, began rhythmically pressing down on his breastbone. The other doctor looked at the monitor for a few seconds, then began fiddling with the defibrillator machine sitting on top of the fire engine-red code cart.

CPR—cardiopulmonary resuscitation—held enormous fascination

for medical students. Nadia kept her distance from the commotion, knowing she would be in the way, but she was absorbing every little detail. She marvelled at the clockwork efficiency—skilled physicians were at the bedside within seconds of the code call. Everyone knew the role they had to serve, and they served it well. The team appeared seasoned and drilled. This was the only way to do it, because there was never time to waste in these situations.

CPR was predicated on the biological reality that the human brain could not do without oxygen for even one minute (two minutes, tops). The techniques of CPR—artificial respirations and chest compressions—manually recreated what the heart and lungs normally did: circulate the blood and make it rich in oxygen.

The tracing on the monitor was now a flat line. The heart rate displayed was a bright yellow zero, flashing repeatedly.

Standing at the head of the bed, the ER supervisor uncovered Baba's face and asked the nurse for an intubation set. Sliding a shiny metallic device into the mouth, he pried apart the jaws. By lifting the lower jaw straight up, he had a clear view of the vocal cords, representing the entrance to the windpipe that was his target. The nurse handed him a curved tube of thick, clear plastic, which he pushed down Baba's throat, slipping it over the metallic flange that was pressing down on his tongue and sliding it past the vocal cords into the windpipe.

Baba's airway was now secure. The rubber bag was reattached to the endotracheal tube now sticking out from Baba's mouth. As the bag was squeezed, Baba's chest rose and fell rhythmically.

'Atropine,' one of the doctors shouted, and a dose of atropine was quickly pushed into the IV running in Baba's arm.

The doctor working the defibrillator had smeared some jelly onto the machine's metallic paddles and was preparing to send an electric shock to Baba's heart.

'Clear the bed, clear the bed,' he said loudly.

Placing both paddles on Baba's chest, he pressed a button to deliver the voltage. Baba's body leapt up as if it had been kicked by a mule. All eyes turned to the monitor—still a flat line.

The supervisor felt for the carotid pulse again but shook his head. 'Adrenaline, then shock him again,' he hurriedly said.

A syringe-full of adrenaline was emptied down the IV line. From the defibrillator paddles, another electric shock was delivered, this one at the highest possible voltage. Baba's frame leapt up again, then flopped back down like a rag doll. Nothing changed on the cardiac monitor. The prospects of kickstarting the heart were becoming more remote with each passing second. They had delivered the strongest drugs and shocked the heart twice, but the writing was on the wall.

Death had not been averted. The team's sense of urgency began to ebb away.

The doctor doing the chest compressions motioned to Nadia to come over. The medical student was being invited into the mix, a sure sign that everyone had mentally given up on reviving the patient.

In the tradition of teaching hospitals, the remaining moments of the scenario would now be used as a hands-on learning exercise. Nadia straddled Baba's chest and pressed down with all her might, but she could barely make it move. 'Keep your hands together and elbows straight', the doctor instructed her. Taking the palm of her right hand, he placed it over the lower part of Baba's sternum. Then he took her other hand, and made its heel press down on top of her right hand. Nadia's elbows were still kinked but he pushed them straight. As she pressed down on Baba's chest again, the movement became clearly visible.

The nurse began preparing an adrenaline injection to be pushed straight into the heart, but the ER supervisor motioned her to stop.

With sombre movements, he shone a flashlight into each of Baba's eyes. As expected, the pupils remained fixed and frozen. 'We'll stop the code now,' he said. 'I'm pronouncing this man dead.'

Lifting his arm, he glanced at his wristwatch. 'Time of death, 4:22 am.'

ꕥ

Not far away, in one of Karachi's elite neighbourhoods, the Mirza household was the very picture of peace and stillness. Husband and wife had enjoyed an after-dinner movie on the DVD player and turned in around midnight. The baby was in her crib, snuggled in by stuffed versions of the entire cast of Winnie-the-Pooh. Outside by the gate, an armed security guard dozed off with a repeater shot gun in his lap. It was a hot night. The neighbourhood hummed faintly with the soft whirring of air-conditioners and the chirping of crickets.

Asad was woken up when the telephone rang. His nightstand clock flashed 4:39 am. Nadia was on the line, sounding pressured and edgy. 'Dr Asad, are you awake?' she began. 'This is Nadia. I have something important to tell you.'

By the time he hung up, approximately ten minutes later, Asad and Nadia had agreed on a plan. He could barely contain his excitement.

As Asad brushed his teeth and quickly got dressed, he found himself shaking. He messed up the tie knot twice, before quickly stuffing the tie into a pocket for later retrieval. A hastily scribbled note was left on his wife's nightstand saying he had to leave for the hospital in an emergency.

Before rushing out, he stopped in the basement and went through his toolset, picking out a handheld small circular saw, a large screwdriver, and a compact pair of wire-cutters. The set had been bought impulsively at a Sears store just before he left Boston. He had never been happier with the purchase than he was now.

At five o'clock in the morning, the streets were deserted. Traffic lights blinked yellow. The only creatures to be seen were stray dogs, and the occasional security guard who had ventured outside to interrupt the monotony of his watch.

Within ten minutes, barely half the time it normally took him, Asad screeched to a halt in one of the early bird parking spots at Avicenna University Hospital. As had been agreed, Nadia met him at the top of the stairs leading to the morgue. Per instructions, she had brought along two pairs of plastic gloves, a size eight for him, five for her. They clambered down with swift and speedy steps, breathing hard, hearts thumping, mouths dry.

The morgue was a large chilled chamber accessed through a cavernous space called the autopsy room, which was located off the main hallway in the hospital's basement level. In Islamic practice and Pakistani culture, the injunction was to respect the dead and bury them quickly, so in fact autopsies were never done here. Still, that's what the sign on the door said and that's how everyone referred to it. It had become a storage facility.

The door to the morgue was thick stainless steel, secured by a card-operated lock. A digital display declared the temperature inside: 4.2°C, the interior of a household refrigerator.

'You're sure he's in there?' Asad asked Nadia.

'Positive. His attendants left saying they needed time to make burial arrangements. He was moved here right afterwards. I saw them wheel the body away.'

'You've got the formalin?'

'Yep,' said Nadia, cocking her head towards a white plastic bucket lying on a shelf next to the morgue door.

Asad tried the door but it was locked tight. His mind was frantic. Should he call security? He may have to, but it risked raising suspicion. Hoping against hope, he slid his ID card through the lock. To their delight, a small green light flashed rapidly and the handle gave way.

Their bodies were accustomed to the warm summer air, and the sudden cool of a four-degree chill felt luxuriously pleasant. There were three corpses in the morgue, each laid out on a metal stretcher, covered head to toe with a white sheet, an identification tag tied with brown string to the big toe. White fluorescent lighting gave everything a ghostly appearance.

Asad checked his watch—5:25 am, still another three hours before the morgue staff showed up for work. He went to the stretcher that appeared to have the largest of the three bodies, and upturned the tag: Sikander, Baba—129-63-29.

Nadia dragged the formalin bucket inside. She was starting to feel cold now and pulled her white coat tighter. Asad slipped his gloves on.

After plugging the circular saw into a wall socket, he slid the white sheet off Baba's head. He was glad to see the cadaver's rich locks, which would hide the handiwork well.

With a steady, practiced hand he traced a line around Baba's head using a marking pen, drawing a circumference across his temples, forehead and the back of his head. Then he flipped on the saw and began cutting along the line. As he hit bone, it made a loud jarring sound startling them both. Soon, the pungent smell of burning human tissue filled the air.

'Shouldn't you be wearing goggles?' asked Nadia.

'Ideally,' muttered Asad. 'But this is hardly ideal.'

His face showed utter concentration as, with a measured hand, he continued sawing off the top of Baba's skull. You had to get the depth just so, he remembered from his days doing brain autopsies in Boston when he was training to become a neurologist. Any deeper and you cut into the brain. How that would make his neuropathology professor flip out, he recalled fondly.

After cutting his way all around the skull, Asad put the saw aside and picked up the screwdriver. 'Now comes the tricky part,' he said.

Nadia watched in silence as Asad used the screwdriver to peel away the brain's membranous covering from the inside of the now loose skull flap.

'That's the dura mater,' he said. 'It sticks tightly to the periosteum on the inside of the skull. You have to peel it carefully. Here, you want to try?'

Standing there just dying to be asked, Nadia lunged for the screwdriver. Asad reminded her to put the gloves on first. From the moment he had told her they needed to remove Baba's brain for microscopic study, she had been experiencing an intense rush. The whole thing was just too much. She couldn't believe she had stumbled on to some enigmatic neurological illness and was now engaged in a stealth brain autopsy to figure it out.

Asad hadn't bothered asking anyone's permission because he knew there was no point—the cultural aversion to autopsies was absolute in Muslim societies. He was taking a serious risk by doing something illegal, but the mounting clinical mystery of these deaths had grabbed him. He could lose his job, but his curiosity and the lure of a dramatic medical discovery were overpowering.

Nadia also understood this implicitly; the forbidden nature of the act had amplified her excitement several-fold.

Scraping the dura mater from the skull was hard work, and after a few minutes Nadia's strokes became sluggish and she handed the screwdriver back to Asad. After a couple of quick strokes, the skull flap came free and he put it aside, exposing the pale, veined dural membrane under which lay the brain. Using the wire-cutters, Asad snipped off the membrane.

'Behold the human brain,' he said.

Nadia was mesmerised. The rounded surface of the brain with its pink ridges and convolutions covered in a sparse mesh of thin blue blood vessels stared back at them.

Nadia poked it with her finger.

'It's like soft cheese, very delicate,' Asad said. 'That's why we need the formalin—it denatures all the proteins and makes the brain tissue hard enough to be cut into thin slices for the microscope. Get the bucket ready.'

Placing his left hand under the frontal lobes, Asad lifted the brain from the front end. With the other hand he slipped the wire-cutter into the skull cavity and began snipping at the cranial nerves that tethered the brain to the structures of the face—to the eyes, the facial muscles, the throat and the tongue. As each cranial nerve was cut, the brain became freer and easier to lift up.

Finally, Asad reached under the brain and felt for the brainstem, the stalk at the base of the brain that connected the brain with the spinal cord. He cut right through it.

Nadia held the lid open as Asad scooped up Baba Sikander's brain and dunked it into a bucketful of formaldehyde. Squeezing magic glue onto the skull's cut margins, he stuck the top of Baba's skull back in place. Nadia rearranged Baba's hair around it and wiped the pen marks off with rubbing alcohol.

Baba had lost his brain, but nobody could tell the difference.

'What now?' she asked.

'We have to store the brain for a week.'

'A week!'

'It takes that long for the tissue to be properly prepared. I'll hide it away in my office.'

'That's going to be a long wait. What am I supposed to do until then?'

'The woman who bit his ear—you can try and find out more about her,' said Asad. 'She probably had the same illness and passed it to him through the bite. That's a crucial piece of the puzzle. Any paper we write about this will have to address that part of the history.'

'Do you think it's some weird form of rabies?'

'I don't know. Maybe.'

'I guess we'll know in a week,' said Nadia.

'I hope so,' said Asad.

Twelve

Everything about Hamza Kadri was thin, beginning with his patience.

He had a thin, almost skeletal frame that despite his six feet two inches stature weighed only fifty-eight kilos. His hair, thin to begin with, had started thinning out more rapidly now that he had entered the fifth decade of life. His face was also thin and slender, with thin lips, a thin and pointed nose, and piercing eyes that cast a laser-like glare through thin, narrow slits. Thin, wire-rimmed half-moons complemented the effect admirably. And although clean-shaven now, in graduate student days he had even sported a thin moustache.

He also used to have a thin bank account.

Just managing to meet monthly expenses, he had no investment portfolio to speak of, barring the odd Certificate of Deposit that at any rate would get liquidated within one or two terms, and a humble employer-initiated retirement plan filed away somewhere that he had lost track of. For university-employed scientists like Hamza, accustomed to ignoring personal concerns while they survived from one research grant to the next, it was almost a defining characteristic.

That was an obvious vulnerability the Network had capitalised on. And the changing mindset of Muslims in America—that had been crucial too.

The teal blue display on the PCR machine flashed a series of technical numbers. Hamza stared intently at the digital readout. Indecipherable to a non-professional, to a seasoned scientist like Hamza they were as familiar as his own skin.

The polymerase chain reaction, set for twenty-five cycles, was nearing termination. He checked on the gel apparatus, topping the buffer yet again. Noticing a speck of grit on the machine's shiny *Perkin Elmer* monogram plate, he flicked it off with a finger. Then he fidgeted with his trousers, adjusting them over his hips again. He stuffed in his shirt. Then, noticing a fold that wasn't quite right, he pulled it out and stuffed it in again. Appeased, at least for the moment, he turned his attention back to the laboratory bench, checking the power connections of the gel set-up, pushing in the jack plugs, then pulling them out and pushing them in again.

Hamza had an established case of obsessive-compulsive disorder. It tormented him, but it also made him a meticulous scientist capable of unflagging attention to detail. He consumed Prozac like a staple.

Every now and then, he would run out of his prescription and miss a few doses. The effect would be almost ruinous. He would spend hours checking the locks inside his apartment, and hours more washing and rewashing his hands, hopelessly trying to satisfy an overpowering urge to cleanse them of dirt that existed only in his imagination.

The Prozac, however, worked brilliantly. It didn't eliminate the preoccupations that drove him but, even better, it controlled and channeled them into useful and productive urges.

A soft beeping sound emerged from behind, alerting him that the incubation time for the mutagenesis experiment was up. From a shelf above his head, he pulled out a large leather bound notebook to recheck the next steps in the protocol.

After leafing through a few pages of technical notes and calculations interspersed with scrawled diagrams of bacterial and viral genomes, he was finally at the right spot. As he poured over his notes, his hands kept adjusting the collar and cuffs of his button-down Oxford, and he kept squeezing his toes and pressing them hard into the floor. Reaching down, he pulled at his trousers again.

In a corner of his spacious desk he noticed a haphazard pile of scientific articles that had been downloaded from the Internet, and he arranged and rearranged them several times to make them neat, orderly and perfectly aligned with the edge of the desk.

The experimental protocol was clear: insertion of the intended base-pair into the mutated vector would need to be confirmed by nucleotide sequencing. Hamza was running low on the necessary reagents. Malik had been informed, but the shipment was yet to arrive. He thought about calling Malik and indulging in one of his periodic bouts of cathartic yelling, but the wretched fellow had at least just managed to get the ultracentrifuge working again and, at least for now, was probably best left alone.

Hamza may have spent his career as a university scientist, but the arrangement he now found himself in was an unusual one. It happened nearly two years ago, in the middle of a memorably hot Carolina summer.

By that time, Hamza had been a microbiologist on the Duke University faculty for close to ten years. It had been a highly productive decade that saw him rapidly ascend the academic ladder, garnering some coveted research honours and awards, and building a reputation for accurate experimental observation, technical excellence, and analytical brilliance.

Arriving at Duke as a postdoctoral research fellow, he had risen all the way to become professor of virology, and an acknowledged authority on viral replication. There was no question he was a gifted, highly analytical intellect. Evidently, the Prozac too had worked its magic.

He came to the Network's attention because of a small news item that had made the national press in the United States.

At a meeting of the American Society for Microbiology, eminent virologist Dr Hamza Kadri had walked out in protest in the middle of delivering a plenary lecture. His grievance—that the Society had not provided the option of halal meals for conference delegates—found traction in America's national maelstrom of political correctness, and the story was picked up by wire services.

The Network saw it in thirteen of the nineteen American newspapers they were screening daily. A virologist who was demanding halal meals—it added up nicely.

Two agents with experience in recruitment were dispatched from the Boston cell to Durham. Employment was arranged at an Amoco gas station run by a devout Egyptian family. The two rented an apartment on LaSalle Street, just off the University Road exit on Highway 15, and planned their recruitment strategy.

Dr Kadri was born and educated in Karachi, Pakistan, earning a Master's degree in microbiology from Karachi University. He attended Johns Hopkins University on a Government of Pakistan scholarship, graduating with a PhD in microbiology. His dissertation, 'Molecular diversity of the *Lyssavirus* genus,' was awarded the Wolff Prize, annually given to the best doctoral thesis in the biological sciences at Johns Hopkins.

After a brief stint as a government scientist back in Pakistan, Dr Kadri returned to the United States and became a postdoctoral fellow in virology at Duke University in Durham, North Carolina. Five years later, he received tenure at Duke, and four years after that he became the Susan and Irving Richmond Professor of Virology. All this was public information available on the Duke University website.

The website also mentioned that Dr Kadri had a bibliography of fifty-seven original research articles, almost all in leading journals with high academic impact. He had also written eleven book chapters, eight review articles, and numerous letters to the editor. His book *Essentials of Viral Replication* (co-authored with departmental colleague Dr Horton Lessing) was a popular graduate-level text now in its fifth printing. Some of his research papers were considered seminal contributions to the field of viral genomics and cited widely in the scientific literature. The web page had a link to his current research, which listed ongoing projects in the Kadri laboratory and also provided short profiles of his laboratory staff, which included two postdoctoral fellows (a Korean and an Indian), an American PhD student, and two technologists.

Personal details were hard to come by. Gradually it was gathered that he lived alone in a second-floor apartment a short distance from campus. Meals were mostly pizza, Chinese takeout, or whatever frozen dinners he bought on his fortnightly trips to Kroger's.

There was no socialising to speak of. A couple of times a month he went to the discount movie theatre, always alone. Taste in cinema did not appear very discriminating. Occasionally, he would be seen at *Khyber Pass*, an Indian restaurant in nearby Chapel Hill, either alone or accompanied by someone from his lab.

There was no evidence of a love interest, either straight or gay. His PhD student was a desirable woman with pleasing Southern features who went around in tight cut-offs and thin T-shirts. Hamza had never been seen with her outside of the lab.

Every Friday afternoon, Hamza Kadri drove to a mosque in downtown Durham to participate in the weekly congregational service. He wore a traditional cap and appeared practiced at the prayer motions. A faint mark in the middle of the forehead indicated he was prostrating himself in front of Allah regularly and was in all likelihood observant with most, if not all, the five daily prayers.

The mosque's imam was an Algerian firebrand specialising in vitriolic sermons condemning US leadership and foreign policy. Hamza was seen to nod reflectively along. Many African-American Muslims attended the mosque, along with a few Arabs and a handful of Pakistanis, Bangladeshis, Indians, and Indonesians. Hamza interacted with everyone politely; however, he had not made any stable associations.

There were also rumours about a failed marriage to an American girl; they had divorced after a short while, apparently because she had gone back on an earlier promise to convert to Islam. Hamza's obsessive neurosis could well have contributed, too. There was no evidence of any children.

All these attributes were viewed as strong positives.

For the Network's recruiting scouts, placement at that particular gas station had been a strategically planned move. Hamza drove a Volkswagen Passat whose best days had long passed; as a result, he was a frequent client at the garage, which was convenient to campus. Both Network agents soon struck an acquaintance with him.

Hamza appreciated the extra attention they gave to his car. One of the recruiters was a Saudi, the other an Iraqi, both in their early thirties. They spoke good English but with thick Arab accents. They portrayed themselves as fresh immigrants hoping to get a foothold in a free society and carve out for themselves a small slice of the American dream.

He had sympathy for outsiders trying to make it in America, and felt a paternalistic regard towards them. After about a month, Hamza's natural reserve had eased considerably. The agents engaged in banter with him and exchanged small talk. They began slipping in items found in the *Key Concepts* chapter of the recruitment manual—Zionism, Israel, American hegemony, puppet regimes in the Middle East, global injustice, war, freedom, Hamas, Hezbollah, jihad, and glory of Islam.

Hamza's responses were in the favourable to extremely favourable range. They started joining him for Friday prayers.

One Friday afternoon, after the prayer session had ended, the Network's agents asked Hamza to lunch. There was a nice Chinese restaurant hardly two blocks from the mosque. Few customers were present. They asked the waitress for a quiet booth and got one.

Hamza had no urgent business back in the lab. Sipping hot tea, he began to relax. A convivial atmosphere prevailed. When the menus arrived, they waited for him to order first. He chose seafood, the only category of food that was universally halal and could be consumed freely by the faithful anywhere in the world.

On the recruitment grid, it scored as yet another favourable characteristic.

Hamza insisted on flattening out the dog-eared corners on the menus. After the waitress took them away, he fussed with the plate settings on the table, straightening the cutlery and aligning the plates just so. The recruiters exchanged glances, dismissing it as an academic quirk.

Before long, 9/11 and the global war on terror had been deftly worked into the conversation. Hamza was cautious at first, but with a little encouragement spoke his mind. America was Satan and 9/11 was its just desserts.

'What else did they expect after raping the world for the better part of the century?' he asked with indignation.

'Brother Hamza,' the Saudi man asked, 'What emotions do you feel towards the 9/11 hijackers?'

Hamza's reply was animated. 'How can one feel about them? They stood up to an overpowering presence that has been responsible for injustices against Muslims. They are heroes, heroes and martyrs. Not since Saladin have we been able to bloody a Western power like this.'

If for no other reason, the use of the pronoun 'we' placed this response firmly in the highly favourable category.

Ideology was not the only factor shaping Hamza's opinions. Ever since 9/11, he had felt a general sense of alienation from his university colleagues. A distance had developed. There was no denying it.

With the jingoistic American media reaction to 9/11, he had become very self-conscious about being a Muslim. Perhaps people looked at him differently, or perhaps he was imagining it. But as far as Hamza Kadri was concerned, the end-result was the same—a discomfort at not blending in.

It was an ugly feeling that refused to go away. He had begun to feel helpless and infuriated.

There had also been two specific incidents.

A few months after 9/11, two Malaysian medical students had written to one of his colleagues, an American woman renowned for research on amoebic infections, for a summer experience in her lab. The professor turned them down, saying that with their Muslim-sounding names, she couldn't be sure they weren't terrorists.

Outraged, the students emailed a scathing complaint to the chairman of the department, copying it to all faculty members in microbiology. Hamza was on cordial terms with the offending scientist and was shocked to learn how she had acted. He brought it up with her, but she was remorseless and said she couldn't even be sure if Hamza himself was not a terrorist.

The chairman got involved and smoothed things over, but it left Hamza with a nasty taste.

Then one day, while teaching an undergraduate class on viruses, he became the victim of an insensitive practical joke.

During the middle of his lecture, someone dressed up as Yasser Arafat entered the classroom and sat in the back row. It was an excellent disguise, with a coarse goatee, sunglasses, chequered *kaffiyah*, and flowing white robes.

Hamza tried to ignore the intruder, figuring it was a student playing a prank, but still it unnerved him. There must have been sixty or seventy students in class that day, and once they had spotted the prankster, the place erupted in howls.

He lost control of the class and was forced to abandon his lecture. Humiliated, he threatened to quit teaching the course, but the dean for undergraduate studies persuaded him to continue. Hamza later lodged a formal complaint with the provost's office, but nothing came of it.

Once Hamza had compared the 9/11 hijackers to Saladin—the

conquering Muslim General from the medieval ages—both recruiters decided they had heard as much as they needed to.

Further dialogue would depend on guidance received from the Boston cell. The lunch conversation was cleverly changed to college sports, an invariably safe topic at Duke, even with foreigners.

Later that evening, the agents held a conference call with the head of the Boston cell. Requirements for the position were reviewed. Ample funds were available, but money was the least of their worries. The Network was entering entirely new territory with this venture. Success depended on finding a highly motivated professional with an unconquerable resolve who combined high-grade technical competence with keen scientific insight.

They had been scouting for nine months, during which time four other candidates had been looked at. Each had been discarded without contacting, being found unsuitable for one reason or another based on the background search.

A wait of nine months struck the Boston cell leader as rather apt. It was the duration Allah had chosen for the creation of a human being from fertilised seed. It seemed a fitting length of time for their search to bear fruit.

Hamza Kadri was the first person they would actually be approaching. The basic need was to find an experienced Muslim researcher with special expertise in virology. Hamza fulfilled these requirements well, clearly possessing the appropriate scientific preparation and specialised competence that the project would demand.

Two additional features stood out. One, there was no wife or kids, and no love attachment. (He may have been gay but, purely for pragmatic reasons, that was deemed irrelevant.) Two, his religious views and behaviour had orthodox overtones that were nicely in keeping with the Network's outlook.

At the end of the conference call, it was unanimously decided to proceed with recruiting Hamza for this project that had been developed as a new strategic priority by the Network.

An up-front offer would be made the following week. If he accepted, it was understood he would be dictating his own terms. A generous sum had been set aside for him, and based on rough estimates a sizeable budget awaited the project itself.

He was expected to show reluctance, although both recruiters opined he would eventually come around. The background screen was pretty solid, and their preliminary experience with him had been promising.

If for some reason he rejected the offer outright, they would abandon the approach and reattempt contact after six months. In the meantime, search for new candidates would continue.

The following Friday, Hamza himself suggested lunch. He had rather enjoyed himself with these two Muslim immigrants the last time and had been looking forward to it all week. They went to the same restaurant and opted for the same booth. Instead of shrimp in black bean sauce, Hamza went for fried squid this time. The agents stuck with sweet and sour shrimp.

Hamza had read an article in *The New Yorker* about dissidents plotting against the Saudi royal family, and he'd been hoping to discuss it.

The recruiters had other ideas.

'Fuck the royal family, brother,' the Saudi said. 'We have something important to say to you.'

Having carefully established Hamza's credentials, mindset, and loyalties over the last several weeks, the agents now came out directly with the offer, laying it out in clear and simple terms.

Hamza heard them out. Listening in silence, his gaze kept shifting from one agent to the other. The Saudi man did most of the talking.

Hamza's immediate reaction was incredulity. 'This must be a joke.'

Not in the least, they said. This was solemn and dangerous business, hardly a laughing matter. Was he interested? Would he help them? Would he help his own people and serve the cause of Allah?

Hamza shook his head in disbelief. 'You can't be serious! You guys are nuts!'

'Look at us, Brother Hamza. Have you understood what we're asking of you? We have to be very clear about this.'

'This is crazy. You don't know what you're doing.'

'Maybe you're the one who doesn't know what he's doing, brother.' It was the Iraqi this time.

His voice was calm and soft. 'Serving your American masters while your Muslim brothers and sisters suffer. What kind of a life is that, Brother Hamza? Not a life of dignity or meaning. You toil away for these evil people while your own kind are tortured at the hands of the very power structures people like you are slaving for. Just ask yourself, "Is this a life worth living?"'

Hamza felt disoriented. Not knowing what to say or do, he toyed with his fork, picking at the squid. All appetite had vanished. Frankly, what he was hearing from these two sounded ridiculous. It had to be a practical joke, but he couldn't be sure. These two were certainly putting on a great act.

'This has got to be a joke,' he said out loud. Unmoved, the agents stared back at him. 'This is lunacy,' he continued. 'I don't even think it can be done.'

'That's not your worry, Brother. You just have to give it your best. That's all we're asking for. And in return you will be rewarded well. Great reward will await you in Paradise, which no one can even think of matching. But we will make it good for you in this world, too. You won't regret it.'

'I'm sorry, but I don't want any part of it. I think we'd best forget about all this. It's best that you leave me alone.'

The recruiters decided they had gone as far as they needed to for the day.

The table fell silent. The check was called for and the agents insisted on covering it. Hamza thought they should split it like last time, but he didn't argue. As they were getting up, one of the men reached inside a jacket pocket and pulled out a DVD. He pushed it towards Hamza.

'Take a look at this. It will make things clearer. It's only twenty minutes. Take it home, watch it when you have the time.'

Hamza took the disc but didn't say anything.

The other agent spoke up. 'Please look at the DVD. We'll leave you alone if that's really what you want, Brother Hamza. We'll be out of your life, gone, vanished. Just watch the DVD, OK? And by the way, you're an intelligent man, I'm sure you understand there's no need to talk about this to anyone. That will only lead to trouble. You don't need that, trust me.'

Nice, thought Hamza. A warning.

What insane characters had he got himself mixed up with? They were probably dangerous. Fidgeting nervously, he started edging away, desperate to get rid of the company. No more words were exchanged.

Emerging from the restaurant, they went their separate ways. Hamza headed back to the lab, hoping to sit alone in his office and try and clear his head.

After he had gone, the agents conferred. They were unsure about their chances with Hamza. His curt, almost surly reaction disappointed them.

Still, it was early to reach conclusions. They had never tried recruiting a university professor before; it was probably an overly skeptical breed. At least he had taken the disc, which raised their hopes. Based on his favourable to highly favourable rating on the preliminary screen, they felt quite certain he would watch it.

Hamza returned to the isolation and serenity of his office, his heart was still thumping like a jackhammer and a storm was raging inside his head.

Placing the video on his desk, he just stared at it, half-expecting it would explode like a time bomb. Teresa, his graduate student, had left a set of experimental results on his desk with a series of queries jotted in the margins. He picked up the papers but was unable to concentrate. The conversation in the restaurant kept playing over in his mind.

If nothing else, he would have to see the video. Just to get it out of the way.

'I'm going home,' Hamza announced to his technician, who had popped his head into the office hoping to get a purchase order for supplies approved by his boss. 'Not feeling well,' Hamza added quickly, signing the paper.

Minutes later, he was home and slipping the disc into his DVD player.

Throat parched and mouth dry, he popped open a can of ginger ale and guzzled it down standing in front of the refrigerator.

When the sound of the Quran being read in Arabic emerged from the television, he turned around. On the screen were grainy images of what appeared to be a bombed out street in some Third World country. Young men with faces covered in *kaffiyeh*s were running about, scampering for cover. Bullets were flying. A youth got hit and fell on the road, bleeding from the head. His body convulsed in the middle of the street. A small group of men ran out and hurriedly dragged him into a side alley, as more bullets flew.

The Quranic rendition stopped and a narrator's voice came on. He was speaking in Arabic, but there were English subtitles.

Jews have been occupying Palestine since 1948. They have treated Palestinians as one would not treat animals. They have killed them like dogs. They kill us because we are Muslims, because we believe in Allah, most Merciful, most Beneficent.

Hamza felt a surge of emotion.

The scene switched to a stark, white room with a table and a chair. On the table lay a book. The camera zoomed in on the book. On its cover, underneath a prominent Star of David, were the words *The Protocols of the Elders of Zion*.

The narration and subtitles continued.

They have a plan. They want to control the whole world. In the process, they want to slaughter us for our beliefs.

While the camera continued to focus on the cover of the book, the Star of David faded away and the flag of the United States appeared in its place.

Do not be misled. It is the same old enemy, only the face has changed.

A new scene appeared. Children of all ages—babies, toddlers, preschoolers and older kids—lay on beds littering a decrepit hallway in some impoverished hospital. *Baghdad, 1991.*

Many of the children were maimed. Layers of bandages, some of them blood-soaked, covered several limbs. Faces were disfigured, wailing cries could be heard. The camera focused on a girl of about ten whose eye sockets were empty. Half her face had been burnt. One arm and both her legs had been amputated.

The Arabic voice came on again, then the subtitles.

This is what Americans call 'collateral damage'. Will you just sit and watch while the agents of Satan go about murdering and mutilating our innocent babies?

Hamza couldn't watch anymore.

He pressed a button on the remote control and the screen went blank. Nausea rose from his depths. The more he tried to blot out the wrenching images, the more they kept playing in his mind.

He got up and took two extra Prozacs.

It was about four o'clock in the afternoon. He needed to get distracted, and decided to go for a drive. Rush hour traffic was just starting to pick up on the highway. Although he had never touched a cigarette in his life, he felt an intense urge for a smoke.

A stiff drink would have helped, but being an avowed teetotaller the thought did not enter his mind. Taking slow, deep breaths, he tried to calm himself. An old nervous tic—moving his right elbow in a small, circular motion—was back.

After poking around with the radio settings for a while, he finally settled on Classic 88.9 FM, which was playing tranquil piano tunes.

He drove for over an hour, going south on Interstate 85. Lush green forest swept by. When signs for Atlanta began appearing, he thought he had gone far enough and decided to head back. The fuel tank was also running low.

It was almost seven o'clock when he turned to take the exit for downtown Durham. The sun had gone down. His mind was still in commotion, but at least the drive had helped him lay out the issues he was being faced with.

He was also feeling hungry. A looming McDonald's sign suggested the prospect of a hearty fish fillet sandwich with fries and a Coke. He looked into his wallet—empty.

In need of cash, he turned into Ninth Street and found a bank with a drive-through automatic teller machine.

Rolling down the car window, he reached out to operate the teller. With the press of a button, he withdrew $50 and waited for the cash and his receipt. He stuck the cash into his wallet. Out of habit, he also glanced at the account balance. About to crunch up the little paper slip and toss it, he did a double-take.

He couldn't believe his eyes. He turned the little paper over and back and just kept staring at it. This was absurd. It was nonsense, it just couldn't be.

Thinking it must be an error, Hamza reached out to the automatic teller again and punched buttons asking for his account balance. A little paper slip just like the other one was spewed out. He held it in his hands, riveted.

It was close to the end of the month, and he knew there couldn't have been more than a couple of hundred dollars in his account. But according to the machine, he was suddenly rich.

Convinced a mistake was being made, he parked his car in the bank's lot and flipped out his cell phone. After a short wait, a customer service representative from his bank was on the line. She confirmed what the automatic teller had been showing. After hanging up the phone, Hamza just sat there, incredulous.

For some bewildering reason, his checking account was suddenly richer by exactly two million dollars.

Thirteen

In Hamza's mind, that invitation from the Network was the best thing that could have happened to him. Allah worked in strange and wondrous ways. Hamza steadfastly believed that his faith had rewarded him with a great opportunity to prove his devotion to Islam. He had made a zealous commitment to be up to the challenge.

A few months after meeting the Network's recruiting agents in Durham, Hamza decided to relocate to Karachi. Several factors led to this decision.

He held an orthodox view of Islam and took pride in his religion, culture and people. Although educated as an occidental rationalist, these sentiments were nevertheless part of his innate make-up.

His sense of feeling alien in America had also become acute. Even prior to 9/11, he had understood and accepted that he would probably remain a permanent stranger in American society, but he had not been prepared for this attitude to invade the cocoon of his comfortable university life.

Certainly the money had proved very persuasive.

The two million bucks that had suddenly shown up in his current account in Durham were disguised as a wire-routing error. Through a circuitous and untraceable route they were redirected to a bank in Karachi, ready and waiting for Hamza were he to accept the offer. Two million dollars was far more than he could ever have expected to make from a lifetime in science.

And this was just the signing bonus.

Another million would be due upon successful field-testing, and a fourth million on accomplishment of the project's ultimate goal.

Of course there was the DVD, which brought into sharp focus the whole argument against America. It was a stirring call for jihad against Islam's oppressors, expertly edited from a combination of branded news footage and unauthentic but manipulative private camera work. The English subtitles were sharp, precise, effective. They grabbed you right away, and Hamza had been shaken.

He could not stop thinking about the decades of official terror in Palestine, and about naked and ugly US policy leading to the dehumanisation of Iraq. This was just the beginning. The short film went on to highlight pogroms of Bosnian Muslims at the hands of America's Serbian allies, and alluded to large-scale killing and displacement of Muslims in Afghanistan, Central Asia, and Chechnya.

By invoking abuse and exploitation of the United Nations, America was implicated in affairs even where it was not obviously involved. The Indonesian government's forced expulsion of Muslims from Timor and the UN-mandated American military intervention in Somalia were all detailed and brought up as charges against Uncle Sam, the Crusader-Zionist Satan.

Nor could the lure of the technical challenge be discounted.

The product would have to be odourless and undetectable, and capable of easy delivery and wide dissemination. It would also need to be able to produce an illness that was incurable, untreatable, and swiftly lethal.

Few such entities existed in Nature, and whatever came close was impossible to harness. To satisfy all the specifications demanded by the Network, a designer product would have to be artificially configured. It would test Hamza's know-how and scientific ingenuity to the maximum.

Scientists often liken the process of research and discovery to intrepid geographic exploration. The sweep and majesty of Peary reaching the North Pole, Magellan charting the Pacific, or Livingstone uncovering the heart of Africa—to scientists the act of accomplishing their most challenging discoveries and inventions is no less grand. At the end of the day, using his best skills to find hidden treasure in uncharted waters was, for Hamza, a stimulus like no other.

Once he showed interest in the offer, Hamza had been invited to Boston, flying there over Labor Day weekend to engage in exhaustive discussions with members of the Boston cell.

He went there with many questions, carrying the same hardnosed inquisitive mindset he might have taken to a job interview for an academic post at a university.

Were there ample resources?

Had the logistical and administrative demands been properly understood?

What kind of help would he get?

Did everyone understand there were no guarantees here—not exactly a shot in the dark, but certainly not a sure thing?

Was there a fallback plan?

After two days of debate and dialogue, he agreed to proceed.

The following week he met his department chairman at Duke and submitted a polite letter of resignation. It stated that the emotional and physical needs of his ageing parents were requiring him to return to Pakistan.

What were his professional plans, the chairman wanted to know. Hamza said that some of the top universities in Pakistan had made offers. He was looking at options.

The abrupt departure of such a brilliant and productive microbiologist would be a major blow to the department. His boss had implored Hamza to reconsider.

A substantial salary increment and extra lab space were promised, but lab space held no meaning in the face of ideology, and the salary jump was dwarfed by the deposit waiting for Hamza in Karachi. It was no contest.

The departure had been cordial. His boss threw a farewell party that was widely attended; even the abrasive female colleague who had snubbed Hamza came, and attempted to make an apology of sorts. The chairman gave an affectionate speech, praising Hamza for his scientific productivity and even-tempered demeanour. He offered to hold his position for the next twelve months, should Hamza be able to sort things out with his family in Pakistan and wish to return.

A group of graduate students were also on hand and performed a short lighthearted play, depicting Hamza as a dashing knight dedicated to fighting the forces of scientific error by mercilessly haranguing apprentice scientists at the point of his sword.

It was an instant hit with everyone in the audience, who knew Hamza to be a stickler for data accuracy and something of a hard taskmaster with his graduate students.

The play ended with Hamza getting crowned 'King of Science', to the rousing notes of Beethoven's Fifth Symphony. After the play ended and the actors took a bow, some of them jumped off the makeshift stage and placed an actual crown on Hamza's head as he sat in the front row. Everyone stood and clapped.

'Americans know how to put on a show,' Hamza had told them, smiling broadly from ear to ear, as he tried to keep his emotions from running away. But to feel so wanted would move anybody, and a part of Hamza savoured the moment with moist eyes and goose bumps.

Later that month, Hamza had flown to Istanbul to meet Malik Feysal.

It was their first meeting, and each approached it with enough anxiety and anticipation for the both of them. Malik had never managed a scientist before, and for Hamza of course this was entirely new territory. He had been told he could and should rely on Malik for all logistics, resource management, and material needs.

Malik's mandate was even clearer: do whatever is necessary to get the job done.

The two met at a waterfront café on Kennedy Caddesi overlooking the roiling Bosphorus as it flowed into the Sea of Marmara. It was a very public setting but Hamza, who had no past experience of subterfuge and feared the unknown, had insisted on it.

They recognised each other through pre-communicated subtleties of dress and manner. Malik was a little late, and found Hamza already seated. He had expected an embrace, but Hamza remained sitting and simply offered his hand.

Malik was expecting a real weirdo and he got one. Hamza came across as thin and neurotic, with the eccentric air of one who was a highly touted virus expert all right, but also a prima donna of science with a huge professional ego.

For his part, Hamza hadn't known what to expect. Malik was supposed to be of Pakistani origin, fluent in English, Arabic, and Urdu, fair to middling in Farsi and French, and with a reputation for getting things done. Hamza wasn't sure he saw all that.

Malik, more than anything, appeared sturdy and muscular, hairy as an ape, pragmatic, impatient, and with an ego in operations and logistics to compete with Hamza's in science and discovery.

It was a forced marriage but, thought Hamza, this was probably the best way to do it.

After returning from Boston, one of the books he had begun reading was Richard Rhodes's *The Making of the Atomic Bomb*, hoping to gain inspiration for his devastating new ambitions from the history of the Manhattan Project. That was the scale at which he had begun to think. It wasn't much of a stretch to see himself as Robert Oppenheimer, and this Malik character certainly seemed like a General Leslie Groves. To a crackerjack scientist, the comparisons seemed fitting, even necessary.

Malik took charge of the menu and ordered çig kofte and lakerda. Hamza, unsure if the meat in Turkey was halal, asked for yogurt soup.

As soon as the waiter turned to leave, Hamza reached into a leather briefcase and pulled out a bunch of catalogues merchandising scientific laboratory equipment.

'What's this?' Malik had asked.

'More stuff that I'll be needing.'

He waited for some further elaboration, but Hamza just sat straight and motionless, looking out over the water.

The waiter brought over the appetisers. Hamza asked if the meat was halal, and he was told that it was. Picking at the food, Malik began leafing through the catalogues. Jazzy techno names were on the spines—Promega, Genentech, Genzyme, Biogen, all corporate giants from the world of biotechnology. They were familiar to him from his background preparations. Pages had been flagged in each catalogue. Malik picked one up and began thumbing through it.

'This is just to get the whole thing started.'

'Right,' said Malik.

'I'll need them soon. We won't make any progress until I get the stuff.'

'You'll get it. It's my job to see that you do. Within four weeks.'

'What about customs?'

'I'm on top of it. We've arranged for delivery to Gawadar, where the customs operation is relatively new.'

'Make sure you make the purchases exactly as I've laid it out.'

'That's what I'm here for,' Malik said with a frown, finding it difficult to hide his irritation.

'What's the update on Karachi?' Hamza asked.

Malik had come prepared. He was deeply conscious of his responsibility; everything was riding on getting things absolutely right. Hamza was coming across as a royal prick, but Malik understood that this microbiology professor from America would require a great deal of assistance and resources to make the most of his intellect and talent.

The stakes were impossibly high, and Malik was determined to see the project through.

Substantial advance groundwork had been accomplished in Karachi, he informed Hamza. A company called Jamaluddin Pharma Co had been created and registered with the Karachi Chamber of Commerce and Industries. Its mission statement waxed eloquent about quality assurance of locally manufactured pharmaceutical products in Pakistan. It would be fronting for the real work.

A small abandoned factory had been purchased in Korangi, one of Karachi's industrial estates. The plant was once used for manufacturing portable fans, but the partners had fought over a misunderstanding and the enterprise had gone out of business. It occupied an area about the size of a tennis court, and comprised two floors plus a basement.

The top floor was converted into office space while the basement and ground floor were refurbished according to plans sent by Hamza. Bench tops, sinks, and glass cabinets now lined the walls. In one corner, a large desk with bookshelves and an elaborate computer set up had been organised. An uninterrupted power supply system was in place to eliminate electricity interruption to all the expensive equipment—freezers, refrigerators, incubators, ovens, autoclaves, centrifuges, and DNA sequencers and synthesizers—that was due to be installed. A 20 kVA diesel-run generator was available for back up. An ISDN line was in place for high-speed Internet access.

'What's happening about the sub-basement?' Hamza wanted to know.

'Just started. It's very tricky. You've asked for separate access, air lock, negative pressure. It's going to take some time, you know.'

'It needs to be functional soon,' Hamza grumbled. 'We can't get going without it.'

'Right,' Malik responded, tight-lipped. He was fast learning that the best way to handle Hamza's air of assumption was to answer in monosyllables.

'What about the vacuum?'

'Soon,' said Malik.

The waiter stopped by and both men ordered more food. Hamza asked for a Diet Dr Pepper and made a face when he realised the waiter had never heard of it. He settled for a Diet Coke, instead.

Malik had never heard of a drink called Dr Pepper either, and figured it must be an American habit. He thought of making polite conversation—he was curious about Hamza's life in the US—but decided against trying to become too familiar this early.

As they waited for their order, Hamza returned to the lab catalogues. Apart from the hi-tech apparatus and appliances, a range of lab ware, reagents, and chemical supplies had also been flagged.

Malik went over the plans once again. These were not sensitive goods; any academic or industrial research laboratory could order them without arousing suspicion, but the Network was obsessed with hiding its tracks. The purchases were to be carefully spread over four different European cities and shipped to three separate locations—Riyadh, Johannesburg, and Singapore—before being forwarded to a warehouse in Dubai. A Pakistani freighter would then deliver everything to Gawadar, on Pakistan's western coast, where customs had been bribed to look the other way.

The waiter soon returned. Broiled swordfish, Döner kebab, and Coban salad were laid out on the table. Books were set aside and the two men began eating in silence. A light breeze blew across, gently ruffling the tablecloth.

The sun had dipped. Across the water, a grandly aged skyline dotted with proud minarets and domes signified a glorious Ottoman past.

Absorbed in the moment, Hamza allowed his mind to drift. The Turks were the only ones who had ever really stood up to the Western powers. Constantinople was finally wrested in 1453, followed by Hungary, Bosnia, Serbia, Albania and Bulgaria. Belgrade fell in 1521.

By 1529, Suleyman the Magnificent was knocking at the walls of Vienna, then capital of the Western empire. This was Islam's strongest foothold in Europe, but resistance in Vienna was fierce and that was as far as the Ottoman campaigns went. To this day, the flag of Islam had never flown over Western Europe or its evil progeny, the United States of America.

No doubt that will change, Hamza thought.

Malik's questioning voice broke through his reflections.

'Doctor Kadri...' Malik asked in a grave, hushed tone. 'Many hopes are riding on you. Can you do it?'

Hamza looked up but did not say anything.

It was getting dark, but out on the patio the lights had not yet come on. He looked straight into Malik's eyes, then peered off into the distance, letting his sight rest on the sky awash in gold and crimson.

'Yes,' he had said. 'I think I can.'

'Allah willing,' Malik had said.

Hamza had nodded. 'Allah willing.'

Fourteen

Having devoted nearly every waking minute for an entire week to researching the subject of encephalitis, it was only inevitable that Nadia would acquire a serious case of boyfriend trouble.

The secretive brain autopsy—in collusion with her role model neurologist, no less—had proved the most exhilarating experience. Asad's suggestion that she prepare a research paper based on the unusual encephalitis cases had ignited her. Intrepid detective work in the cause of advancing medical science, it was a thrill almost too much for Nadia to bear. Her need to organise and analyse all the teasing and provocative little details and convert them into a groundbreaking scientific report had rapidly become an obsession.

The boyfriend, a touchy sort, was finding it difficult to share this sudden new passion of hers. After Nadia had spent yet another day straight in the library devouring books and conducting online searches, his main concern was if she was trying to send him a message. Not that the relationship was a troubled one. His lanky body, shoulder-length hair and bohemian temperament had hooked Nadia; her friends knew that his ability to play bass guitar had also played a crucial role. Though they had been together for nearly a year now, he had a gloomy disposition and tended to see the negatives first.

For a while he had tried to keep up with her, pulling out *Harrison's Principles of Internal Medicine* from the shelf and sitting next to her as she took copious notes, her head buried in books on infections of the nervous system. His resolve had lasted about forty minutes. He became fidgety and Nadia told him to go away because he was making it hard for her to concentrate.

A row followed. Nadia was exasperated that he didn't share her priorities. He seemed to be begrudging her this shot at medical glory, she said. The boyfriend, for his part, wanted to know why she still hadn't unpacked the iPod he had given her on her birthday last week. Whispers turned to shrill exclamations, piercing the hanging silence of the vast library and its grave atmosphere. Heads turned. Maddeningly frustrated, Nadia slammed the book she was reading, gave the boyfriend a menacing look that said, 'Eat shit and die!' and stormed out.

That was enough to snap him out of his wallowing, leaving him to conclude that perhaps he had gone too far. An experienced campaigner, he had been here before. A predictable sequence of events would now play out. He knew what needed to be done—stay out of her hair for the next forty-eight hours and then invest in flowers and chocolate.

Nadia was engaged with more pressing concerns. For seven days now, Baba's brain had been sitting in a white plastic bucket in Asad's office, soaking in formaldehyde. It was hidden away in the bottom drawer of a filing cabinet, the lid tightly secured with several rounds of duct tape to prevent the noxious fumes from escaping. A denaturing chemical agent, formaldehyde altered biological tissue at the cellular level, fixing all the molecules in place and toughening up the tissue's consistency so it could be cut into vanishingly thin slices for microscopic study. The time had finally come for Nadia to retrieve the brain from Asad's office and deliver it to Dr Omar Javed, one of her pathology teachers and a friend of Asad's who had agreed to process the case.

Initially, Omar was reluctant to get involved. He had no appetite for controversy and balked at the thought of working with an autopsied brain that had been removed without family consent. Asad knew he had to respect his friend's wishes and worried that he might have reached a dead end.

But he was desperate for an answer to the diagnostic riddle. Eventually, after fretting alone in his office for a couple of hours exploring all options, he decided that the best way around this impasse was to forge a consent document and slip it into Baba's medical file. He told Nadia about it, and reassured her that he took sole responsibility. If he was found out, he would simply come clean to the hospital authorities and beg forgiveness in the name of science.

A blank Informed Consent form was filled in with the relevant details and Asad scrawled a phony signature at the bottom, making it look like permission for the autopsy had been granted by next of kin. He told Omar that the deceased's family had been reached after all, and consent documented. As he had expected, this proved good enough for Omar.

While the brain with the mystery illness marinated, Nadia assiduously scoured Avicenna's rather substantial library resources. Asad had given her two tasks. One was to learn as much as possible about whatever was currently known regarding encephalitis—its causes, clinical picture and variations, new epidemics reported from around the world, and any emerging treatments. She had quickly mastered the minutiae, rifling through the best textbooks and monographs, and digesting the most informative cutting-edge articles from the world's leading medical journals.

A star performer, Nadia already had a sound medical knowledgebase that was substantially advanced compared to the general competence of students in their final year of medical school. She had known enough to amaze Asad with her diagnostic acumen on rounds on the very first day of her neurology rotation. With her extensive reading on encephalitis, her command of the topic was rapidly approaching the level of an expert.

'Encephalo' is derived from the Greek word *enkephalos*, meaning the brain; 'itis' is a common medical suffix, also of Greek origin, signifying inflammation. The condition occurs sporadically (medical speak for randomly) but can also appear in epidemic form. Symptoms include mental confusion, fever and sometimes, epileptic seizures.

The illness is potentially life-threatening. Over thirty different kinds of viruses are responsible. *Herpes simplex* virus type 1, the commonest cause of encephalitis worldwide, is the same virus that causes cold sores, but if it finds its way into the brain, it can wreak havoc. (Genital sores are caused by another herpes virus, *Herpes simplex* virus type 2, a related but different agent.) Encephalitis from HSV-1 occurs randomly rather than as an epidemic. No one knows how the virus is picked up and how it manages to get into the brain, but it does produce certain characteristic signatures that can be detected by special tests such as spinal fluid analysis or EEG. Although it can kill, HSV-1 encephalitis is nevertheless curable if detected early. A drug called acyclovir, administered intravenously, inactivates the virus.

Encephalitis caused by other viruses tends to occur in epidemics. In Pakistan and the neighbouring region, the commonest cause is an entity called Japanese virus, but in other parts of the world, other viruses dominate. Collectively, they are all known as arboviruses (short for arthropod-borne viruses) because they are transmitted by the bites of mosquitoes, which are biologically classified as arthropods. Clinical symptoms tend to be the same as in *Herpes simplex* encephalitis, but the presence of arboviral infection is more difficult to diagnose, requiring highly specialised tests to detect antibodies to the virus (serology) or the presence of viral DNA (polymerase chain reaction or PCR) in blood or spinal fluid. These tests are neither reliable nor easily available, and certainly they were not available in Pakistan.

Asad had thought about trying to arrange for them overseas, but he didn't pursue it knowing it would have been prohibitively expensive. In any case, identifying which particular arbovirus is causing the encephalitis is of little practical value, since there is no cure for any of them. Diagnosis, therefore, is based on the patient's symptoms, on the absence of the characteristic features of HSV-1 infection, and on the exclusion of other causes of rapid mental deterioration, such as a stroke, hemorrhaging brain tumour, or toxic drugs or chemicals. Treatment is supportive, meaning that patients are kept well hydrated and the functioning of all the body's organs is closely monitored in the hope that the patient's innate immunity will be able to clear out the viral infection from the brain.

As she probed further into the topic, Nadia understood why Asad was convinced the encephalitis cases they had recently come across were extraordinary. Encephalitis produced confusion, clouding of consciousness, dullness, lethargy, drowsiness, stupor, and coma, but it did not make patients behave violently. Encephalitis was supposed to make people passive and unresponsive, not aggressive and ferocious.

There was really only one kind of viral brain infection that induced violent behaviour—rabies. But rabies was acquired through an animal bite, and in none of the three cases that they were aware of, had there been an animal bite of any sort. There had, mystifyingly, been a human bite in one case, but Nadia had no clue what to make of that. It depressed her that she had not managed to uncover any reliable details about the woman who was responsible for the bite.

A tantalising speculation was that the woman was suffering from a similar kind of illness, and she had passed the disease on to Baba by biting him. Asad had certainly suggested this but Nadia, a sharp and intuitive girl who took pride in being thorough and meticulous, was careful to avoid traps if the logic seemed too convenient. She felt the same way about the possibility that the violent behaviour present in the case histories was somehow precipitated by water—a finding that would favour the diagnosis of rabies. There was circumstantial evidence to suggest it, but that was far from any kind of scientific proof.

In any case, whatever this particular strain of encephalitis was, the important question was how the woman had picked it up in the first place. And there both Asad and Nadia had drawn a blank. Baba's friends could provide no address or identification for the woman in question, although they were clear that her husband had not mentioned any exposure to rabid dogs or any other kind of animal bite. Nadia had visited Baba's house twice to question people in the area, but her efforts had yielded nothing.

There were other uncertainties that Nadia's reading and research had failed to resolve. Did these cases, all appearing within a matter of a fortnight, constitute an epidemic? Encephalitis was an uncommon but by no means a rare disease. A computerised search of Avicenna University Hospital's patient database going back twenty years revealed that the hospital saw approximately 1.5 encephalitis cases every two months, or roughly one case every five weeks. But there was substantial variation in this frequency.

During an epidemic of Japanese encephalitis that had occurred in Karachi in late 1994, the hospital had admitted eleven cases in one month. At other times, it had gone as long as six months without seeing a single case. Certainly, this was the right season for an epidemic of arboviral encephalitis, which usually occurred in late summer or early fall following a heavy monsoon. But were two or three cases within a fortnight enough to be considered an epidemic? It was difficult to say.

Epidemics of encephalitis could be a funny business. Japanese encephalitis used to be limited to China and Southeast Asia, but at some point in the 1960s or 1970s it began to spread westward into India, Pakistan and Iran. Since the disease was transmitted by mosquito bites, expansion into adjoining geographic areas was explained by dispersing mosquito populations. In 1995, cases of Japanese encephalitis were detected for the first time in Australia, in an outbreak occurring in the continent's northernmost rim. Mosquitoes, naturally, don't cross the seas, so the whole thing was quite perplexing. Eventually, the virus was demonstrated in migrating birds. The logical explanation was that mosquitoes in Australia picked up the virus when they bit the infected birds, and passed it onto humans through inoculation.

In the United States, the Centers for Disease Control, a large government agency based in Atlanta, kept close tabs on encephalitis patterns, both locally in the US mainland, as well as around the world. Reviewing old issues of the CDC's *Morbidity and Mortality Weekly Report*, Nadia found that most epidemics of viral encephalitis in the US were attributable to one of three arboviruses: Eastern Equine Encephalitis virus, Western Equine Encephalitis virus, and St Louis Encephalitis virus. (As the names suggest, the first two viruses also cause encephalitis in horses, in addition to humans.)

For each virus, epidemics had been reported approximately every five to ten years. Their magnitudes seemed quite modest. A typical epidemic was anything from five to fifteen cases, occasionally going up to twenty or even thirty. They tended to occur in the same geographical locations. Outbreaks of Western Equine encephalitis, for instance, had been reported mainly from the western and midwestern United States and invariably occurred in the late summer or fall months. Eastern Equine encephalitis outbreaks, in contrast, were seen along the Atlantic and Gulf coasts, while St Louis encephalitis was restricted to Texas, the Ohio-Mississippi Valley, and Florida.

Although encephalitis viruses showed fairly consistent behaviour, every now and then something strange or unusual would be observed. As she sifted through the CDC's published reports, a series of items related to an entity called West Nile virus grabbed Nadia's attention. A well-recognised cause of encephalitis, West Nile virus was a mosquito-transmitted virus confined to Africa and the Middle East. But in 1999, an outbreak of West Nile encephalitis had been reported in New York City.

Nadia felt her pulse quicken as she absorbed the details. During a two-month period covering August-September 1999, fifty-nine people were hospitalised with severe encephalitis in Westchester and Nassau counties, as well as in the New York City boroughs of Queens and parts of the Bronx. Seven people died. Symptoms, including fever, lethargy, seizures, and mental deterioration often progressing to coma, were typical of any encephalitis infection.

The sudden appearance of a large number of these cases astounded the local health authorities. Intense diagnostic efforts were undertaken. For a while, no clues were forthcoming and everyone was mystified. Brain autopsies were performed on the fatal cases but the findings were non-specific, showing only diffuse inflammation and degenerating brain cells, without any unique or distinguishing features. In due course, the presence of West Nile virus infection had been confirmed by PCR and serology.

Experts were baffled as to why a virus known only to exist in Africa and Asia had suddenly showed up in North America. The eventual answer was that it had come along with a set of exotic birds from the Mediterranean region that had been imported into New York by collectors. The event triggered a major shift in local encephalitis patterns as the virus began to spread across the United States. In 2000, it was detected in twelve states along the Atlantic and Gulf coasts as well as in the District of Columbia. In 2002, it was seen in thirty-nine states and was responsible for nearly three thousand cases of severe encephalitis, of which twelve per cent died. From a small series of unexplained cases seen in New York City in 1999, the menace had grown inexorably.

Hypotheses began to form in Nadia's mind. Were the cases observed in Karachi the local emergence of an encephalitis virus normally found in some other part of the world? The thought-provoking example of the West Nile virus certainly suggested as much.

But which virus was the culprit? Could it be West Nile virus again, which was not known to occur in Pakistan?

Unlikely, thought Nadia. There was no evidence that West Nile virus infection made you aggressive. That, again, suggested rabies, but where were the animal bites? Nadia went around in circles.

Viruses could get up to great mischief in other ways, too. A virus is the simplest, most rudimentary form of biological matter, straddling the border between life and non-life. It consists of a coil of nucleic acid, DNA or RNA, encased in a protein coat. It is the protein coat that allows the virus access into living cells, as particular proteins on the viral surface recognise and attach to receptors on the surfaces of cells. Once inside, the nucleic acid uncoils itself and gets inserted into the cell's nucleus, which begins churning out millions and millions of copies of the virus. In a short time, the viral load overwhelms the cell and kills it.

Like any replicated piece of DNA or RNA, viral nucleic acid is prone to acquire mutations—unplanned and unexpected changes in the genetic message—over time. The right kind of mutation could make a virus alter its infectious behaviour, producing unexpected epidemics or even new clinical patterns of disease.

Influenza, for example, is caused by a virus with a tendency for rapid mutations. Normally a self-limited disease producing only a few days worth of fever and malaise, every now and then influenza would be transformed by a new mutation into a lethal and devastatingly contagious infection. In 1918, such genetic transformation unleashed an influenza pandemic, a worldwide epidemic that affected large populations throughout the world, in which an estimated twenty-five million people died. Pandemics reoccurred in 1957 and 1968, killing millions more.

For Nadia, a more obvious example was of a respiratory illness that had been making headlines in recent days. A sudden outbreak of unexplained pneumonia had been seen in Hong Kong. Symptoms would begin with cough and fever and quickly develop into a full-blown inflammation of the lungs. Many patients had to be placed on artificial ventilators and some cases were fatal. At a loss to define the disease, experts had been calling it SARS or Sudden Acute Respiratory Syndrome. Nadia had been following the story passively, but with her new interest she searched out all the details through Google. Something called coronavirus was responsible. It used to be a harmless virus with only nuisance value, producing nothing more threatening than the common cold. Then a mutation happened and it suddenly acquired the power to destroy human lungs. Sobering, thought Nadia. Very sobering.

Had the Japanese encephalitis virus—such a common cause of encephalitis in Pakistan—undergone a mutation that was making infected people show inappropriate hostility? The idea seemed like a reasonable hypothesis, and Nadia realised it could be investigated by doing PCR and serology on spinal fluid or blood drawn from affected cases.

Clinical laboratories sometimes saved biological specimens for a few days and, encouraged by Asad, Nadia had approached both the Avicenna and the Civil Hospital labs, hoping against hope. But the samples had been discarded. The tests, in any case, would have had to be done overseas, and at great expense. Nadia was determined to save adequate samples if another case showed up. Asad, meanwhile, had approached some former colleagues in Boston, hoping for a collaboration to take the project forward. He was yet to hear back.

Perhaps, in the end, they would have to conclude that they were standing eyeball to eyeball with a new disease altogether, a novel form of encephalitis caused by some deadly new virus that had come out of nowhere. As every medical student knew, the possibility was not at all fanciful.

In 1981, the sudden, unexplained appearance of two diseases in the United States—a weird pneumonia and a rare kind of skin cancer—was eventually traced to suppression of the immune system by a virus that had not previously been known to exist. From an epidemic initially confined to North America and Western Europe, HIV and AIDS had rapidly become a worldwide scourge affecting privileged and underprivileged alike, with infection rates continuing to rise at a staggering rate. No one had a clue where the virus came from.

Of course, there were theories. According to popular conjecture, it might have been a monkey virus that mutated and began infecting humans. But it was a mystery, really. No theoretical explanation properly accounted for the plain and undeniable observation that the virus had never made its presence felt, directly or indirectly, prior to 1981.

Nor was HIV unusual in this respect. It was the most obvious example, but in fact new infectious diseases were emerging all the time. One of the major texts Nadia consulted had a table listing twenty-six separate infections—Lyme disease, Legionnaire's disease, and Ebola among them—that had not been known to exist forty years ago.

At one point, Nadia also wondered if there might be some kind of foul play. Terrorism had become an almost chronic reality, especially in Pakistan, where hardly a week passed without some senseless episode of mass murder somewhere in the country. But all the incidents involved conventional weapons and explosives, used by gunmen or suicide bombers; there had been no suggestion of a biological attack of any kind. The militants, in any case, were operating out of undeveloped tribal lands and showed no sign of the technological sophistication required for biological work. She rubbished the thought.

Ultimately, Nadia had faith that in a medical mystery, the truth was to be found in the clinical details. Asad had been underscoring this point as well. As a budding clinician, Nadia had been indoctrinated in the principles of clinical methods and evaluation, which held that the quality and depth of clinical information—symptoms, associated features, physical examination findings—was the surest guarantee of a correct diagnosis.

The available clinical details of the three known cases—Zafar Majeed, Baba Sikander, and the case seen at Civil Hospital—had been thoroughly investigated and analysed, and provided some interesting leads. Not much had been learned about the woman who bit Baba, but several features in the other three case histories appeared common. They were all in previous good health, had developed rapid mental deterioration with fever, had displayed uncharacteristic violence that was possibly triggered by being confronted with water, and within two or three days of their illness, all three were dead. No cause had been identified by the standard diagnostic tests.

It was important to recognise that these were just the cases they knew about, Asad had told her. Karachi had no public health surveillance system in place, no mechanism for reporting unusual occurrences to health authorities. Whatever they were seeing could well be just the tip of the iceberg.

Comparing the cases had yielded another teasing feature as well. All three patients were from the same neighbourhood, a small lower to middle-income locality in Karachi's western district. Nadia thought this was significant, but wasn't sure in what way. Asad felt it could well be a coincidence. The neighbourhood was of modest size by Karachi standards, but in a city of fifteen million, that still meant thousands of residents. The houses of the three patients were not near one another. In fact, they were located several blocks apart, on streets that had no direct interconnections. Patients from this area not infrequently showed up at Avicenna, although because the income levels were low, they more often headed towards Civil Hospital or went to alternative practitioners such as homeopaths or faith healers.

By Thursday morning, it had been a full week since Baba Sikander's brain had been detached from his body and placed in a formaldehyde bath. Taking a mid-morning break from her library stakeout, Nadia walked over to Asad's office. It was time.

She knocked and waited. Hearing no answer, she allowed herself in using a duplicate key he had given her. As she had expected, the room was empty; Asad was probably on rounds in the hospital. She sniffed the air for formalin vapours but detected nothing. Clearly, the duct tape had been very effective.

A tall, gleaming white filing cabinet stood flush against the wall at the far end of the room. Nadia walked across and pulled the white plastic bucket out from the bottom drawer. It was heavy—she guessed maybe three kilograms, of which at least a kilo and a half was brain. The pathology building was not far and the walk proved mercifully short. One of the senior histopathology technicians received the bucket from her.

'This is for an unofficial project,' she said. 'Dr Omar knows about it.'

'Yes, he told me to expect this. How long has it been in formaldehyde?'

'Seven days.'

'Good. Is it already sliced? Have you done the gross?'

'No. We just took it straight out of the skull and dunked it in the liquid.'

'What are you suspecting?'

'Encephalitis. Of some kind. I think.'

'All right,' the technician said. 'Standard cuts, then. Coronal slices of the hemispheres and axial slices in the brainstem. Any special areas that are supposed to be sectioned?'

'Yes,' said Nadia, extracting a crumpled piece of paper from her pocket. She read off a list Asad had given her. 'Hippocampus, cerebellum, medulla, thalamus, putamen and frontal cortex.'

'OK,' said the technician, taking the paper from her. 'This should be ready overnight. You can check with Dr Omar around this time tomorrow.'

Nadia glanced at her watch. It was eleven o'clock.

Would the microscopic examination of Baba's brain provide some solid clues? Might it even, perhaps, yield a definitive answer? It was hard to say. Nadia knew that biopsies or autopsies of the brain have hallowed status as the ultimate investigative tool for diagnosing neurological mysteries. But she was also quickly learning that in medicine, things were never as cut-and-dried as you wanted them to be. Pathological findings in encephalitis could often be non-specific, showing only edema, neuronal destruction, and the presence of inflammatory cells around the walls of blood vessels. Would there be a conclusive diagnosis here? Nadia desperately hoped so. Was it likely? She knew it wasn't.

Fifteen

September mornings in Karachi are notoriously hot. Every year, summer reaches a peak in May and June, with temperatures crossing forty Celsius in the shade and humidity clinging like a wet skin. July and August bring the rains or, at the very least, two straight months of uninterrupted cloud cover. Temperatures drop and there is a general sense of a siege being lifted. With the monsoons, however, comes widespread paralysis when nothing works. The roads are destroyed and power gets cut off daily, usually for hours at a time. Still, it's cooler, and that's enough to keep everyone in good cheer.

September brings the heat back. It lasts through October, sometimes spilling into the early days of November too. In Karachi, they call it the second summer. Nadia could feel the second summer all around her when she got up on Friday morning. She had spent a restless night. The power went off in the early hours and although the standby generator—nowadays a domestic commonplace—had kicked in, it wouldn't run the air-conditioning. A whirling fan was better than nothing, but it was still oppressive.

At the breakfast table, a large bouquet of tube roses and a pretty little lavender-coloured box overflowing with chocolate truffles were waiting for her. They had been freshly delivered earlier that morning, and the sight charmed her right away. All of a sudden, the heat was irrelevant. A scented card sticking out from between the flowers said 'Sorry! Please forgive?' in her boyfriend's unmistakable scrawl. Feeling remorseful since her outburst, Nadia had been meaning to cut him some slack anyway. Now she softened completely. The guy knew his stuff.

That sorted, her mind returned to the task at hand. She was due to join Asad for a meeting with Dr Omar Javed in the pathology building at 11:30 am. The slides would be ready today. She was tired of waiting. Asad had asked her to come a little earlier so they could discuss her preparations for the medical case report. It had been a terribly busy week and he hadn't been able to see her. He was keen to know how she was getting along.

Traffic was light and the drive was swift and short. A little too short, thought Nadia, feeling utterly pampered by the chilly blast of her car's air-conditioner.

Asad was waiting in his office.

'Hi. Come in,' he said, motioning her to a seat. 'Sorry we haven't had a chance to meet this week. What's the progress?'

Nadia gave him a quick run down. She was animated and eager, and Asad couldn't help admiring her promise and ability yet again. She showed him a set of photocopied articles covering various aspects of encephalitis—epidemics, virology, clinical presentations, transmission. Underneath the pile was a five-page document full of bulleted text, in which she had summarised and referenced all the journal articles and book chapters she had found valuable and relevant. It appeared to be very thorough work.

'Have you started writing the paper?' Asad asked.

'Not yet. I wanted to be sure I had collected all the references and done sufficient background reading. Plus I wanted to get the pathology details.'

'We should have a draft ready by the end of next week. Is that doable?'

'Shouldn't be a problem. I'll email an initial draft to you latest by Friday. Where do you think we should send it?'

'Depends what the pathology shows. If we find something definitive and unusual, the sky's the limit. Maybe even *NEJM*.'

The suggestion grabbed Nadia in a surge of euphoria. Debuting with a research publication in the *New England Journal of Medicine* was like holding the very first recital of your life at Carnegie Hall. But she forced herself to sound sober and serious. It was just an idea. Talk was easy, she understood that only too well.

Asad continued. 'There's an infectious disease conference in Lahore in two weeks' time. That would be a good occasion to present our observations. A research paper will take time getting into print—at least a few months, I would think. But it's important to publicise this. This is the major ID forum in the country, so it's bound to be well attended. You should make the presentation, it'll be good exposure for you.'

'Wow!' said Nadia, immediately excited. 'But isn't it too late? I mean, will they accept an abstract this late?'

'Not to worry,' said Asad. Reaching over, he handed Nadia a publicity flyer for the conference. 'The deadline has passed but I've spoken with the chairman of the organising committee and he is keen to include our paper for a platform talk. You should write it as an abstract first. You know, background, methods, results, conclusions. Make it two hundred and fifty words max.'

The flyer was the size of a small poster. Nadia scanned it quickly.

'XIIth Annual Conference of the Infectious Diseases Society of Pakistan' was written boldly and colourfully across the top. A list of conference sessions and speakers, as well as website and email addresses, were provided underneath. Nadia folded and pocketed it for later consumption.

'That's a great idea,' she said. 'I'd love to do it.'

'Good,' said Asad. 'Let me check if Omar is ready for us.'

Dr Omar Javed told them things were in order and they were welcome to come over to the pathology building. The slides were ready but he hadn't seen them yet.

'So what's your hypothesis about these cases, then?' Asad asked Nadia as they walked out of his office and began heading towards pathology.

'Ummm...my best guess is it's a form of Japanese encephalitis. I think the virus may have undergone genetic transformation, which has resulted in a set of unexpected symptoms. At least that's what I think. Does that make sense?'

'Could be. I'm pretty confused myself. I have a feeling we're going to be surprised, though.'

They crossed the remaining distance in silence. The door to Dr Javed's office was ajar, and they walked right in. The pathologist was surrounded by his work. Files, books and papers rose in piles behind his desk. The desk itself was huge, but cluttered. In one corner sat a desktop computer, in the other a laptop. Boxes of microscope slides were strewn across the surface. In the middle of the desk, directly in front of him, sat a large microscope that dominated everything. Long black tubes extended horizontally from the microscope in both directions on which were perched teaching eyepieces for students and others to look in.

'Hello, Asad,' Dr Javed announced cheerfully, extending a hand. 'Come on in.'

He took the top slide out of a box marked '*Ref. Dr Asad Mirza, Neurology*' and placed it on the microscope's viewing platform.

'So what are you suspecting here?' he asked.

'Not entirely sure, Omar,' answered Asad. 'I think we've come across some unusual strain of viral encephalitis. But I don't want to bias you. We'd like to know what you think without skewing your judgment.'

'Okay, let's take a look,' Omar said, motioning for Asad to focus in on one of the teaching eyepieces. Nadia, used to the student's role, had already quietly placed herself in front of the other one.

'This is the frontal cortex,' Omar began, peering into the microscope. He moved the slide slowly around as he spoke. 'There's clearly some inflammation here. Can you see all that lymphocytic cuffing in the perivascular spaces? That's typical of encephalitis. It's not very specific, though.'

Both visitors stared intently into the microscope and strained to follow along. Not being trained pathologists, their eyes took time to adjust and pick up the details. They were aroused with anticipation. Asad realised his pulse was racing.

The first impression on looking through the microscope was just of various shades of blue and red against a light pink background. Omar moved an optical cursor around and the detailed features became more recognisable. As he scanned the slide for diagnostic clues, he began humming the tune from *Piano Man*, the popular Billy Joel melody.

'Adjust your focus please if you need to,' said the pathologist, in between rousing notes.

After almost a minute, he removed the frontal cortex slide and replaced it with a slide marked *Putamen*. 'Pretty much the same thing here,' he said, after moving the slide around for a while. 'I think there's some neuronal loss too.'

Reaching into the box, he next extracted a slide marked *Hippocampus*. The humming continued merrily. Omar was rather tuneful and his visitors were finding it quite agreeable.

'Are these all H & E sections?' asked Nadia. She was referring to the chemical dyes hematoxylin and eosin that are commonly used to stain biological tissues so their detail would be visible under microscopic view.

'Yes,' acknowledged Omar, looking up from the microscope. 'This first batch is H & E only, but there's enough tissue blocks, so we can do additional stains if needed.'

All three pairs of eyes focused on the viewing field again. The *Hippocampus* slide had been clipped in place and Omar was slowly moving it around. It was an easy, practiced motion, performed with the fluency of someone who had done it thousands of times.

The first thing to happen was that Omar stopped moving the slide. Asad asked him if he had seen anything, but Omar did not answer.

Then the humming stopped.

Asad and Nadia scrutinised the image intently, but could identify nothing extraordinary. Asad tried to get his attention again, but Omar held his hand up, palm facing flat outwards, motioning him to wait. It was close to three minutes before he finally spoke.

'There's your answer, Asad. Look.'

Asad's gaze followed the optical cursor as Omar moved it to a small round pink-purple spot. As Asad struggled to recognise it, he noticed the entire image was full of the same small spots, scattered randomly among the visible brain cells. It triggered a flash going off in his head. He'd seen pictures in books. The realisation took his breath away.

'Unbelievable,' he said, in a low, hushed tone.

'What? What is it?' asked Nadia, searchingly scanning the faces of both men.

'The *hippocampus* is full of Negri bodies,' Omar said. 'This is a case of rabies.'

Sixteen

Alice craned her neck to see the movie listings outside Chestnut Hill Cinema. She was driving down Route 9 at the end of a long day, headed to the four-room Colonial in Newton she was so proud of. With Justin's new position, they had finally managed the down payment that had seemed a vague and faraway dream when she was working two jobs to help put her husband through business school. Now Justin's Boston University MBA and six-figure starting salary with career prospects at Prudential Insurance had opened up a world of mortgage possibilities she could only have imagined.

A flashy sports car whizzed past, blazing a splash of red as it surged ahead in the late afternoon sun. Alice steadied her own car, trying to stay in lane. Her Volvo, another boon from Justin's accomplishments, performed like an obedient slave. It must be that dynamic stability traction control thing the sales guy at the Volvo dealership had so persuasively endorsed, when they couldn't decide between the S80 with its predictable looks and the SUV-style XC90. It wasn't the money anymore. At $389 per month give or take, they could afford either car comfortably.

Then the sales guy had uttered the magic phrase—that the S80 was the top safety pick—and Alice didn't need to hear another word. Justin saw that deep and tranquil look in her eyes and he knew the decision was made. It was the look she would get when she knew what she wanted. The look she had given him on their third date, after he had rattled on about the Red Sox. He knew she had scant interest in the subject but they had been talking about Alice's family all through the four-course meal, and there were things he needed to get off his chest as well.

And all of a sudden, as he went on about base hits and knuckle-ball pitchers and spring training, he felt this look from Alice, a serene, calm, transfixing look conveying intensity and assurance. A look that said I know what I want, and right now I want you.

The look at the Volvo dealership was exactly the same, but a different motivation was behind it. Justin knew very well what it was.

For almost a year, they had tried for a baby without success. Alice was a natural with children. For as long as she could remember, she had dreamt of becoming a mommy and cradling one of her own in her arms. Their financial circumstances had not permitted trying for a baby in the early years, but the day Justin had surprised her at work after landing seventeen interviews at the business school job seminar, she knew it was time.

Then the disappointment crept in. After the first three months of trying unsuccessfully, Alice had taken him through the rounds of infertility clinics—Prudential employees had a terrific health plan covering everything imaginable—and they had been told the same thing everywhere. Try for a year. Don't overthink it. Relax. Try for a year before you even start worrying about anything.

That year was coming to a close and all they had to show for it was a lot of tired, dissatisfying sex and a steady expenditure on home pregnancy kits that had been completely in vain.

It had come to the point where it was becoming a difficult topic in their marriage. Justin had been tested and found to have a normal sperm count. Alice had read up widely. She knew what the odds were for a woman who hadn't been able to conceive for a year. About half of these women got pregnant with treatment and time, but to Alice the overwhelming statistic was that about half did not. It was an unimaginable fate.

Justin heard her loud and clear when she decided for the S80 because of safety. She was saying that the car wasn't just for the two of them. It was her way of bringing up her baby anxiety once again. The XC90 was the car he truly desired. The body styling, the dark wood inlay, the sport watch dial instruments panel, the self-leveling rear suspension. But he knew not to get in the way of that look. Justin Ridley loved his wife deeply and devotedly. She was buying a car for a baby they didn't have, nor were they likely to anytime soon. If it settled some maternal urge in her, he was happy to make it happen.

Other than being childless, things could not have been better for Justin and Alice. After years of labouring as a dental hygienist, she had been made a manager. She had a friendly, respectful relationship with her boss, a kind and gentle dentist whom middle age had made even kinder and gentler. And after the windfall from Justin's new income, she had been able to give up her evening job answering phones at a teenagers' helpline.

The red speedster had distracted her and she couldn't get a good look at the movie listings. It was one of her passions. There was a new Holly Hunter flick she wanted to watch. Her mind drifted to Holly Hunter in *The Piano*. Alice remembered being mesmerised sitting in the dark theater as the credits rolled. Even after every one had left, she wanted to just stay there, letting the haunting music and the film's aftertaste consume her.

Would this new Holly Hunter movie be as captivating? Someone had said it was playing at Chestnut Hill. Or was it Cleveland Circle? She would look it up when she got home.

It was late evening by the time Justin returned. Alice had showered, made dinner ready, and was struggling with the *Globe* crossword when she heard the familiar ring of Justin's keys. He came up to her from behind and kissed the back of her neck. He was a different person now. The irritability and touchiness of his student days, the pangs of guilt watching his wife bend her back to pay the bills, were gone. Already his skills were being noticed at work. He was good with numbers, even better with people. It was a new job, but it was beginning to feel like a comfort zone.

After dinner, Alice suggested they go to the movies but Justin was too tired. It crossed her mind to go by herself, but she had had a busy day too, and they settled on the couch watching *Seinfeld* reruns. Within minutes, Justin was snoring. Alice wanted to have sex—they had gone nearly a week without it—but one look at Justin's deadweight form and she knew it was a lost battle.

Carefully extricating her legs from Justin's, she walked over to the kitchen and pulled out a small plastic bottle. 'Clomid 50 mg' read the label. Alice swallowed a tablet and hid the bottle away. Infertility was a very personal crisis for her and she wanted to deal with it in her own way. Justin was bound to come into the picture if her options kept getting exhausted, but she wished that day would never come.

She wanted to surprise Justin. So she had gone ahead and seen her gynaecologist, hoping to solve the problem on her own. Preliminary tests showed Alice was having anovulatory cycles—her ovaries were not releasing egg cells as they normally should. The doctor had prescribed medication that might do the trick. Alice didn't want to get her hopes up but her doctor had been encouraging.

It was her first cycle with Clomid and that weekend they went at it like rabbits. Her cycles were carefully marked on a calendar and she knew right away when her next period got delayed. For two days, she tried not to think about it too much and kept it at the back of her mind. Then hope and anticipation erupted in her head and she could think of little else.

What happiness, what joy that would be. A fulfilling career, a cozy house, a devoted husband, and adorable children. It was all part of the dream, a dream everyone had the right to hope for and deserved to attain. Did she dare to dream?

The third day she was overdue, Alice took a home pregnancy test. Justin was sprawled on the couch after a long day, eating a bowl of cereal and swearing at the Red Sox. She called out to him from the doorway, holding a strip of white that had turned blue.

Justin saw the same determined look on her face. Then he noticed the strip.

'Congratulations, Justiny,' she said. 'You're going to be a daddy.'

Justin couldn't remember ever being happier.

Seventeen

The most prominent feature of the façade was the razor wire. It snaked around the top of the walls, billowing out over the edges like clouds of smoke. Nadia strained for a better view, and saw it running the length of the perimeter as far as she could see. She found the sight imposing. The walls must have been twenty feet high. Dark and dusty red, they dominated her vision, commanding her eyes to look at nothing else.

It seemed a fortress. Or a prison.

Soon the bus came to a standstill and Nadia stepped out along with the others. A security guard with a helmet and a fancy machine gun motioned for everyone to gather to one side.

'Take out everything! Cell phones! Keys! Wallets! Handbags! Jewellery!' the guard yelled at the top of his lungs. He sounded like a sergeant ordering a battalion, but these circumstances were rather different.

The small group of people assembled before him looked at each other. They had already been through two detailed security searches and no longer possessed any of the things the guard was asking them to produce. Everyone stared back blankly.

'Cell phones! Keys! Wallets! Handbags! Jewellery! None of these things are not allowed inside!' the guard yelled once again. He walked up and down the length of the group as he bellowed, eyeing the gatherers from head to foot.

One or two patted their empty pockets, shook their heads, and shrugged their shoulders. No one said anything.

'Step forward single file and approach the gate!' the guard now shouted.

The group lined up in front of what appeared to be an impenetrable steel barricade.

'Single file! Single file!' he shouted again a few more times, evidently without any need to, as everyone had already come together into a neat little queue.

They stood facing the gate, which was painted a depressing gunmetal grey and was made up of closely spaced bars that allowed you to peer through if you looked at an angle. Nadia could see more security inside, each toting arms. Loops of razor wire were strewn on the ground and hung across the top of a doorway visible in the distance.

As she waited her turn to be let in, Nadia's eyes fell on a large and shiny metal engraving, gleaming beside the gate. It was a drawing of an eagle that was gripping a bunch of arrows in one set of talons, and what appeared to be an olive branch in the other.

'Embassy of the United States, Islamabad,' it said underneath, in boldly etched letters.

What a song and dance, thought Nadia to herself.

She had good reason to be irritated. After arriving exactly at six o'clock as per instructions, she had been made to wait an hour on a hard wooden bench, undergo a series of security checks at the hands of who she felt were some unnecessarily bossy guards, endure an uncomfortable ride in a bus with faulty air-conditioning and a rather officious driver, and was now being treated like a fresh military recruit. The only bright feature had been the nineteen other visa applicants with her, some of whom had gone through this routine before. The group had bonded quickly and easily, sharing jokes about 'these paranoid Americans.'

Soon, Nadia was led into a large hall with a series of windows. Behind the windows, which were thick plexiglass, sat consular officers interviewing applicants for visas to the United States. Closed-circuit TV cameras jutted from corners. Two security guards were present here, too, but they did not appear to be carrying arms. At least the air-conditioning was effective here and the seating comfortable. Nadia allowed her eyes to feast upon the captivating pictures decorating the walls. She had never been to America, but recognised the iconic images instantly: Statue of Liberty, Grand Canyon, Lincoln Memorial, Seattle Needle, a streetcar in San Francisco. All irritation was gone now. Her excitement returned.

She had good reason to be excited, too.

Asad had arranged for her to spend two months in the Hartmans' lab at Massachusetts General Hospital in Boston. They were a husband-and-wife team whom Asad knew from his Boston days, and they ran a cutting-edge lab with a successful research program focusing on viral infections of the brain. Nadia knew them by reputation. Sara and Joel Hartman had authored the chapter on viral diseases in one of the popular neurology textbooks.

It was a fortuitous arrangement, part of the windfall Nadia was enjoying since stumbling on the unusual encephalitis cases with Asad. Details had been worked out and her time in Boston was going to count as elective credit towards Nadia's medical degree.

It felt to her like an explosion of riches. Research experience at Mass General, one of the flagship Harvard hospitals, was great for her career prospects, adding lustre to her resume when the time came to apply for residency training.

It was also a powerful opportunity to try and solve the scientific mystery confronting Asad and Nadia. The Hartman lab was ideally placed to take their clinical observations to the next level. Nadia was going to assist in a molecular analysis of the rabies virus that had infected Baba's brain. The goal was to try and understand what, if anything, made this particular strain of virus different, because there was strong circumstantial evidence that it had been passed to humans in some unconventional manner. Asad had approached the Hartmans for a research collaboration and they had responded with keen interest. Over long email exchanges and telephone calls, a series of experiments had been carefully planned.

An electronic screen began flashing numbers. Nadia checked her ticket and was relieved to discover her turn would be coming soon. Applicants had lined up at each of the five windows and were communicating with their interviewers through microphones in the wall. Everyone was forced to speak loudly, creating a mélange of public conversations.

Nadia couldn't help but eavesdrop.

Farthest from her was a young couple. She couldn't make out what they were saying, but they seemed to be getting on fine with their interviewer. The man appeared confident and well-groomed, wearing a plaid American shirt and a pair of Dockers. The woman was shy, drowning in make-up, and weighed down with oversized bangles. Nadia guessed them to be newly-weds, the man probably employed in the US, headed back there with a new bride.

The next two windows were occupied by college-bound students—their age, eagerness, and low-slung jeans gave it away—and at the fourth window was a stern-looking man in a three-piece suit who Nadia guessed to be a businessman.

Right across from Nadia was a frail old lady. Nadia could hear everything she was saying. Her son was long settled in the US and she wanted to visit him. She held up pictures of her grandchildren but her interviewer, a dour blonde woman with an unsympathetic face, seemed unmoved. Their body language was off; clearly, the old woman and her interviewer weren't communicating well. It didn't help that the old lady's English was sketchy. Abruptly, the visa officer crossed her hands to indicate the interview was over. Visa had been denied. The applicant began pleading in Urdu, but the visa officer simply looked away. As the old woman turned to go, Nadia noticed she was in tears.

'Next!' shrieked the unfriendly woman behind the window.

A new number flashed on the electronic screen and Nadia realised her turn had come.

Oh, great, she thought. I'm going to be dealt with by this sourpuss.

Nadia stepped up to the window and put on her most charming smile.

The visa officer stared at her without expression. Nadia returned the look with a brilliant grin, but it had no visible effect on her interviewer.

'Nadia Fatima Khan?' the woman said, as she started to thumb through the application folder in front of her.

'Yes.'

'Have you been to the United States before?'

'No.'

'What is the purpose of your visit?'

'I've been invited for a short attachment at a medical research lab.'

'Are you a doctor?'

'Not yet. I'm a medical student.'

'Where is this invitation from?'

Nadia held up the letter she had received from Dr Sara Hartman. It was an impressive piece of paper, dark, formal typing standing out against an off-white background, with the crimson Harvard logo emblazoned across the top. Asad had predicted any visa officer would roll over after seeing it.

Nadia's interviewer took the letter and appeared to corroborate it with her own materials. Far from rolling over, however, she seemed quite indifferent.

'How long is this attachment?' she asked, continuing her aggressive tone.

'Two months,' said Nadia.

'How do we know you'll return?'

'Excuse me?' blurted Nadia. She had been warned to expect such blunt questioning, but it startled her all the same.

'How do we know you'll return to Pakistan and not become an illegal alien in the United States?'

'Of course, I'm going to return!' Nadia responded, feeling a touch affronted. 'I have to complete my medical degree. My family is here. My home is here.'

'Do you have any plans to settle in the United States?'

'No, of course not.'

'Do you really expect me to believe that?' the interviewer continued, without any discernible change in facial expression or tenor of voice.

'Yes, of course. I'm not lying. I have to return, my whole life is here.' She even thought of mentioning the boyfriend, but decided that was unnecessary.

'Are you married?'

'No.'

'Have you ever been married?'

'No.'

'Have you ever applied for a Green Card?'

'No.'

'Have you ever been denied a US visa?'

'No,' said Nadia. 'I've never applied before.'

'Have you been outside Pakistan in the last five years?'

These questions had already been answered on the application form. Nadia had an urge to mention that, but quickly determined it wouldn't help her case. 'Yes,' she said. 'I went to London three years ago on a family trip.'

'London, England?'

'Yes.'

'Do you have any relatives in the United States?'

'Ummm…there's a distant cousin on my father's side,' said Nadia. 'Settled in Florida, I think.'

'Any close relatives?'

'No.'

'Have you brought any evidence of your family's financial standing?'

Nadia had come prepared. The travel office at Avicenna had counseled that the key to her American visa wasn't the Harvard letter, as she was understandably inclined to believe, but private documents showing that her background was well-to-do. 'They have to establish you aren't some refugee escaping Third World poverty,' the travel specialist had explained. Nadia thought the man was exaggerating, but her instinct for thorough preparation had forced her to pay heed.

She produced a bundle of papers: bank statements, property deeds, investment certificates, and a letter from her father's employer confirming his status as vice-president at a leading bank.

The visa officer went over each page.

'You are being issued a six-month visa, single-entry,' she said. 'Your passport will be at our courier's office in Karachi after five working days.'

'Thank you,' said Nadia effusively, feeling a powerful rush of relief and flashing a perfect smile.

'Next!' shouted the officer.

Her journey seemed to go on forever. It had been God knows how many hours since she left Karachi. The stopover at Amsterdam had come and gone. She had mostly dozed through it. From what the map on her mini-screen was now indicating, they were somewhere over the middle of the Atlantic, still far away.

She looked out of the window again and tried to make out the features of the surface passing miles below. The clouds had cleared and she was able to discern a white expanse with small, indistinct dark patches. It took her some moments to figure out they were flying over Greenland.

Nadia had just been through a crazy two weeks. Now, she was

finally headed to the United States. Cloistered in an airplane out of contact from everyone, she felt she was in a sanctuary.

After obtaining her visa from the American Embassy in Islamabad, she had gone straight to Lahore, where she joined Asad for the infectious diseases conference and reported their unexpected clinical observations to a medical audience. She had been excited about her presentation but also very anxious. In fact, it went very well and produced the most stimulating Q&A of the entire conference. Many people had come up to her and Asad afterwards, praising the talk and offering suggestions for following up the work. In the concluding session, several panelists had cited it as the meeting's best scientific paper.

Asad hadn't said much other than a quiet 'good job,' but Nadia knew he was pleased with her performance. The senior author on the report, he sat beaming in the front row as Nadia touched all the right notes, and when he joined her at the podium for the Q&A, it was with an air of gratification and contentment. He was very proud of her. She could tell.

The best part about her talk had been to see it mentioned in the newspapers the next morning. It was a prominent national conference and Asad had commented on the possibility of media attention, but Nadia had been careful not to get her hopes up. Now she had made news, becoming a little celebrity in her family and with the other medical students. It delighted her enormously.

An email from Avicenna University's PR & Media department confirmed that Pakistan's top wire service had reported on the conference, with the story being carried by nine newspapers, including Pakistan's leading dailies in both English and Urdu. Each had opened with Nadia's talk and most had even headlined it. Vanity is crucial to an academic career, Asad had noted with a smiley, as he forwarded her the email.

The remaining days before her departure had been consumed by the manuscript. Asad was a demanding editor and had made her go through several drafts. Luckily, her ongoing medical school rotation was in community health sciences, with its famously light schedule and lots of free time, virtually all of which had been spent in front of a computer or buried among books and journals on a library desk. Her boyfriend grumbled a bit, but she handled him deftly with short, indulgent breaks and promised to get him something special from her trip to America.

To distract from the tedium of her long flight, she went over the article's summary yet again:

> ATYPICAL RABIES IN KARACHI, PAKISTAN by N.F. Khan, O.H. Javed and A. Mirza. Departments of Neurology and Pathology, Avicenna University Hospital, 29 Park Road, Karachi 84330, Pakistan.
>
> Rabies, a zoonosis endemic in many parts of the world, is spread to humans through animal bite inoculation and is uniformly lethal in symptomatic individuals. Nonbite acquisition of human rabies is rare and controversial. We report direct and indirect observations from four cases appearing within a short time span in Karachi, Pakistan's largest city. Cases 1 and 2 displayed clinical features of furious rabies with no history of animal bite. Case no. 3 presented with furious rabies and a history of human bite from a woman (case no. 4) who also reportedly displayed rabies features but had no history of animal bite herself (she died before coming to medical attention). Brain autopsy from case no. 3 confirmed the presence of Negri bodies in hippocampus, cerebellum, and brainstem. All four patients were residents of the same city district. Mortality was 100 per cent. We believe these cases may

> represent emergence of a nonbite form of human rabies. Molecular viral analysis from affected brain tissue is planned. Epidemiological surveillance for nonbite human rabies is warranted.

The body of the paper was organised in the standard manner, comprising an introduction, case reports, and discussion. Three photomicrographs showing inflammation, brain cell loss and Negri bodies—the diagnostic microscopic features of rabies—had been included. There were eleven scholarly references. A small addendum acknowledged the help of Dr Bashir Manzoor, the Civil Hospital neurologist who had provided details of case no 2, and the kind assistance of Drs. Sara and Joel Hartman, who had critiqued the manuscript. It was a crisp, articulate paper that the authors felt proud to have produced.

After a good deal of hand wringing, it was finally submitted to the *New England Journal of Medicine*. The *Journal of the American Medical Association* and the British journals *Lancet* and *British Medical Journal*, each a venerated medical publication with high professional visibility, were the other options considered. In the end, Asad decided for *NEJM* which was, after all, a Boston-based journal with Harvard origins. He considered the report groundbreaking, and was confident of a favourable response.

Going over the paper in her head had lulled Nadia to sleep. She woke up to find that the stewardess was handing out landing papers, a reassuring sign they would soon be in Boston. Nadia filled out the forms, an arrival and departure record called Form I-94 and a US Customs Declaration. As had been advised by Asad and endorsed by the Hartmans, she noted in the Customs form that she was carrying a biological specimen for medical research purposes. A letter from Asad explained that the sample was human brain tissue fixed in formalin that carried no infectious or biological risk whatsoever. Nadia also had a letter from Sara Hartman confirming that the specimen carried no biological risk and was intended for research purposes only.

Tired and groggy, Nadia disembarked from the plane and emerged into Logan airport's brightly lit Terminal E, the usual spot for international flights. A beaming, life-sized picture of President Barack H Obama and the First Lady greeted her. 'Welcome to the United States!' it said, in bold, oversized letters. Nadia followed the crowd towards immigration and customs.

At the passport counter, the immigration officer appeared to be taking longer with her case than he had for the others ahead of her. Nadia had flown American Airlines from Amsterdam to Boston and most of the passenger load had been Americans or Europeans. Her Pakistani passport seemed to have thrown the officer off.

For several minutes, he kept turning her passport over and rapidly clacked away on his computer, the frown on his forehead becoming more noticeable with every passing moment. Eventually, he took a deep breath, placed Nadia's passport in a coloured folder, and asked her to go through a door down the hall and wait.

'Is there something wrong?' asked Nadia, more puzzled than concerned.

'Please do as you're told,' he said sternly. 'Down the hall and to the right, through the double-doors. Take a seat there and wait.'

'What is the matter? Can you please tell me what's wrong?'

'Please do as you're told. This is not the time to cause trouble.' The words were spoken unsmilingly, and Nadia grasped their seriousness immediately. She walked off in the direction she had been pointed.

It must have been at least an hour before someone attended to her again, during which time Nadia's puzzlement had turned into frank anxiety. All kinds of thoughts went through her mind. What was the matter? Was there something wrong with her visa? Did the authorities know something she didn't? Perhaps she was being mistaken for someone else. Yes, that must be it. It'll all get sorted soon.

Finally, someone called out her name and motioned for her to stand before a very tall counter. Nadia had to crane her neck to meet her interviewer's gaze.

An interrogation followed. What is the purpose of your visit? Where will you be staying? Who is Dr Hartman? How long have you known her? What kind of research?

Nadia provided simple, clear answers. The immigration officer then moved into high gear.

Do you have any links with terrorist organisations? Now, or in the past? Do you know anyone who might have links with terrorist organisations? Either now or in the past? Have you ever visited Iran, Iraq, or Syria? What about Cuba or North Korea?

The officer kept peering at Nadia's face after each question, as if searching for tell-tale signs she might be concealing the truth. Nadia was bewildered. She kept answering the questions politely and patiently, but her frustration was piling up.

Just when she felt she had reached a tipping-point, the officer flashed a wide smile. Stapling the I-94 to her passport, he stamped her visa with a loud, banging flourish. 'Proceed to Customs, please. Back up the hall and to your right. Follow the signs.'

Stumbling out of the room, Nadia followed the overhead signs to the customs checkpoint. Hassled and stressed, she worried there might be a similar interrogation awaiting her there.

Her concern proved well founded.

The first thing the customs officer did when he saw 'Biological specimen: human brain tissue' written on the form that had just been handed to him was to make a bee-line for his supervisor.

He didn't even look at Nadia. One glance at the form and he did a 180 degree pirouette, walking straight through a doorway located right behind the counter. Nadia saw him place the form on a large desk that had a flat screen computer monitor on it but was otherwise devoid of any clutter.

From behind the desk, a heavyset man with a thick moustache and brooding eyes—the supervisor, evidently—peered intently at the form. Nadia watched him extract a pen and circle something on it. So far, the customs officer and his supervisor had not exchanged any words.

The supervisor looked at the officer, then back at the form. In a grave, painstaking motion, he repeated the circling a few times.

Then both of them looked towards Nadia, who had started to feel very helpless and lost.

The officer motioned with his hand that she should come in. The supervisor pointed to a chair and Nadia sat down, trying to gather her thoughts how best to negotiate this hurdle.

'Where is this biological specimen, miss?' the supervisor asked, carefully enunciating each word in a brogue, drawling accent that Nadia knew from movies and television to be a feature of the American South.

She produced a styrofoam box from her backpack and placed it on the desk.

'It's in here?' the supervisor asked, pointing a large, thick finger at the box.

'Yes. There's a metal flask inside, with pieces of brain tissue. They're immersed in formalin, which eliminates any biological hazard or risk.'

'Do you have any supporting documents?'

Nadia pushed Asad's official letter as well as the letter from Sara Hartman towards the supervisor. He went over them and shared them with his assistant. The letters confirmed that the specimen posed no biological risk and was meant for the purposes of medical research only.

'Do you have any other clearance?' asked the supervisor.

'Such as?'

'Such as permission from the USDA or CDC.'

'USDA or CDC?'

'United States Department of Agriculture or the Centers for Disease Control.'

'Er…no,' admitted Nadia, feeling disoriented and defeated.

The supervisor was silent. Pulling out a broad plastic tape from his desk drawer, he tossed it to his assistant. Within seconds, Nadia's Styrofoam box had been wrapped and sealed in a bright orange plastic covering that declared in loud, bold letters 'WARNING: BIOHAZARD.' The taped box was then covered in an even more brightly coloured orange biohazard bag and heat-sealed at the top. It was then placed in an unmarked bin behind the supervisor's desk.

Nadia watched helplessly, too tired and angry to speak.

'Please place your possessions on the desk to be searched,' the customs supervisor now said.

Without a word, Nadia dragged her suitcase onto the desk, and dumped her backpack, laptop and handbag on top of it. She sat seething as the two uniformed personnel slowly went through every item.

'Thank you, miss,' the supervisor said finally. He ran a line across her form in red, placed an official stamp on it, and handed it to Nadia. 'You may go now.'

'What about my specimen?'

'That is now the property of Unites States Customs and Border Control.'

'When will I get it back?'

'It has been confiscated. You're not getting it back.'

'No, no, you don't understand,' grumbled Nadia, visibly flustered. 'This is a very important specimen that I am bringing to Mass General for a medical research project. It poses no danger. We could be on the verge of a very important medical breakthrough here. I need that specimen. Please!'

The supervisor did not flinch. 'If you insist on demanding this specimen, miss, you may not be allowed inside the United States. You will be deported.'

That stopped Nadia dead in her tracks. But how could she give up on her precious cargo? It was the basis of her research project, the centrepiece of her whole trip to Boston. Asad would be so disappointed. And what about the Hartmans? What would they do with her for two months? Would they send her back early? Everything would be ruined.

Yet cold logic told her she could push it no further. The situation could not be salvaged and would have to be abandoned. She would have to find another way. Perhaps Asad could send more tissue by international courier? Surely Dr Hartman would be able to get whatever permission was needed from the USDA or CDC or whoever it was whose permission was needed.

Feeling battered, harassed and on the verge of tears, Nadia gathered her luggage and exited customs into the arrivals lounge.

The Hartmans had promised to receive her at the airport but it had taken her so long to get through the stupid delays at immigration and customs, that she didn't expect them to still be hanging around.

Yet there they were.

Most of the crowd had parted and Nadia spotted them easily, recognising them from pictures exchanged over email.

'Hi, you must be Nadia,' said Sara, stepping forward and embracing her in a hug.

Eighteen

The claws were back. This time they were digging into his temples. Malik held his hands up to the sides of his head and pressed down. There was nothing there but his flesh and hair, yet he could feel those dagger-like talons piercing through his skull, creating an agonising physical sensation.

He was seated in his apartment, surrounded by the midday heat and a sense of doom. Power was out. A battery-operated table fan blew air around the room but it wasn't enough. Sweat ran down Malik's face and trickled over his back.

In front of him, four newspapers were spread out. Each was opened to the same news item. Malik had read it again and again. He had been to a number of news stands already, trying to get his hands on as many different newspapers as he could. He had scoured the Internet looking for additional details. Massaging his temples, he looked down at the story yet again:

Doctors report new kind of rabies

Lahore, September 28: A new kind of rabies, transmitted by some means other than the bite of a rabid dog or animal, may have emerged in Pakistan, say doctors from Avicenna University Hospital in Karachi. They were presenting their observations at the XIIth annual conference of the Infectious Diseases Society of Pakistan that concluded at a local hotel yesterday. The authors of the study, Drs. Asad Mirza and Nadia Khan, say they have documented three recent cases of rabies and have indirect knowledge of a fourth one, in none of which was an animal bite involved. Through technical collaboration with a virology laboratory in the United States, they intend to test their hypothesis that they are dealing with a new variety of rabies virus that appears to have a nonbite mode of transmission. Rabies continues to be a substantial public health burden in developing countries, with the World Health Organization estimating 5,000 annual deaths from this scourge in Pakistan alone. The disease can be prevented by post-exposure prophylaxis (vaccine and antiserum injected after a dog bite), but is uniformly fatal once symptoms develop. Rare cases of nonbite rabies have been described, mostly spelunkers exploring bat-infested caves, who are believed to have acquired it through aerosolized bat droppings. However, the issue remains controversial and scientifically inconclusive. Dr Mirza stressed that their report is the first compelling account of rabies acquired in an urban setting through nonbite transmission. If confirmed, it poses an enormous public health risk, he said.

—Associated Press of Pakistan

So far, none of the international media had picked up on the story. Fighting anxiety and sharp jabs of headache, Malik carefully set up a series of Google alerts to monitor developments. He then closed his eyes and forced himself to breathe deeply, kneading his temples with the heels of his palms as he tried to recover some calm in the havoc raging inside his head.

The exchange with Hamza had gone as expected. Hamza had not seen the news and Malik berated him for it. A back-and-forth crescendo of sarcasm followed, soon evolving into yelled obscenities. Malik said they should never have done a field test. Hamza accused him of being a cretin with no understanding of scientific precision. Malik told Hamza off for being too obsessed with details and losing sight of the supreme goal. Hamza said if Malik was supposed to be such a fucking champion fixer, why couldn't he just troubleshoot his way out of this one. Finally, Malik told Hamza to get their virus arsenal ready immediately, because time was of the essence now and the Boston cell could ask for it at any minute. Hamza responded that Malik should just go fuck himself. 'I'm giving you forty-eight hours,' said Malik, which was the last thing he said before hanging up.

At least one difficult phone call had been made. But another, more challenging one, had yet to be made.

Malik had laid out his thoughts and concerns on a memo pad in front of him. He punched the number on his cell phone and waited. It was answered after three rings.

'Salaam, brother,' Malik began, with some trepidation. He was speaking to his contact node.

'Salaam,' responded the contact node.

'What is the guidance?' asked Malik.

'Why are you calling?' the contact node replied. 'The phone is not safe.' His voice was gravely and calm, contrasting sharply with the urgency and anxiety in Malik's.

'You haven't answered my email,' continued Malik nervously, betraying unease and apprehension.

'It does not need an answer.'

'But I will need guidance.'

'Proceed as you see best.'

'But which plan is being endorsed? The suicide martyr?'

'It is your decision to make,' the contact node said emphatically. 'You are on your own,'

Malik had received his guidance. There was no give. 'How long do we have?' he asked.

'Not long.'

There was little point in prolonging the conversation. His instructions were clear. The circumstances were becoming furious and frenzied. He had shepherded this impossible project, bringing it so far that they finally had a stealth bio-terror weapon with lethal effectiveness. He couldn't let it go wrong now.

After reasoning through the tactics from many angles, he had established that eliminating Dr Asad Mirza was necessary to arrest any further snooping into their project. The good doctor would be a martyr to Allah, and Malik planned to say a prayer for his soul. NF Khan, the other investigator, was just a female medical student and not expected to cause any trouble on her own. She would be left alone.

Flipping pages on his memo pad, Malik turned to the details of the plan that he had been working and reworking. Asad would be shadowed for two days to identify three potential locations, ranked in order of priority. With appropriate advance timing and disguised identity, Malik would cover his face and lift a car at gunpoint. A Chinese-made semiautomatic TT pistol would be used for the procedure. He will then use the car and gun to kill Asad, making it look like a botched robbery. The car would be abandoned in a suitable alley and Malik would disappear. This sort of thing was the stuff of standard street crime in Karachi. No one would know the difference. What mattered was that Asad would be dead and the snooping would stop.

ᘓᘐ

It had been a long and tiring day, full of challenging patients, demanding medical students, and irritable colleagues. Asad was relieved to be finally making his way to the parking lot. He got into the car, undid his tie and collar, and immediately relaxed. Dusk had fallen. The roads were still filled with commuters making their way home, but traffic had lightened. He was catching the fag end of the evening rush hour. The car stereo was playing REM's greatest hits. Asad tapped the steering wheel in tune with '*Man on the Moon*.'

As he turned off Jubilee Road into a narrow alley that had become his usual shortcut, Asad noticed another car enter the lane from the opposite end. It was a one-way lane, which meant the other car was coming down the wrong way, but respect for traffic rules in Karachi was modest at best, and Asad didn't give it much thought. He just steered his car as far to the side as he could and brought it to a stop, allowing the oncoming vehicle to squeeze past.

Yet the other car kept coming towards him, head-on. It was driven by a man who had his face covered and seemed to be pointing at something.

Unsure what to do, Asad stopped his car and motioned for the other driver to move past.

In that instant, he felt an explosion go off in his left shoulder. A hole had suddenly opened in his windscreen, and Asad realised he was being shot at. Another crack rang out and he felt a searing pain in the side of his neck, as if someone had slashed the skin with a white-hot knife.

Instantaneously, Asad's body went limp and he slumped onto the steering wheel. Blood flowed freely from his neck and shoulder. Two more shots rang out and the windscreen shattered completely, raining tiny shards of glass on his collapsed form.

The assailant stepped out of his car. He took a few steps towards Asad's automobile and stood there, gazing at Asad's body slumped motionless and soaked in blood from the neck down. Passers-by had entered the lane after hearing the shots. The assailant retreated. With a loud screech and a whoosh, he turned his car around, speeding off into a side-lane.

With the attacker gone, people rushed towards Asad's car. Two young men pulled him out and lay his body flat on the road. One of them felt for a pulse. The other fished around in Asad's pockets and removed his wallet and cell phone.

ജ൹

The surgery lasted four hours. There were two large wounds. Muscles were torn and the superficial veins had been damaged, but the shoulder joint had been spared and there were no fractures or bony injuries. The bullet in the neck had missed the jugular vein and the carotid artery by a whisker. Asad had come to within a few millimetres of his life.

On the second post-operative day, he was moved out of the ICU and into a private room. The first thing he did was call the two boys who had saved his life. They had quickly identified him from the contents of his wallet, called the Avicenna emergency room, and rushed him there within minutes. A trauma code was immediately called, the surgical team arriving speedily and taking over.

The head nurse in the ER had been full of praise for the boys. She insisted on taking down their phone numbers. The bullets had missed vital structures but if it hadn't been for these boys, Asad would have bled to death. The timely blood transfusion and fluid resuscitation he received in the emergency room is what saved him.

His saviours visited him in hospital the following day. Asad's wife had bought them each an ornate Persian carpet as a token of gratitude. There were also baskets full of fruits, chocolates, and gourmet snacks. The lads feigned objections about all the fuss and formality but they were made to feel as if they were Asad's younger brothers and accepted the gifts in that spirit.

They were nice lads. Computer technology trainees in their early twenties, they had been heading home from classes when they heard the shots. It turned out that one of them had even noted the registration plate on Asad's assailant's car. He passed on the number.

The advice from Avicenna's head of security, a seasoned ex-military man known for pragmatism and commonsense, was for Asad to move around with a security escort, at least for a while. The security chief had debriefed Asad at length, but failed to come up with any possible reason why anyone would make him a murder target. The most obvious motive appeared to be robbery. 'It's usually a deserted alley, but on this occasion a few people had gathered and that scared him away,' the chief concluded.

Asad wasn't convinced about the need for a security escort. It would be an added expense, not to mention a constant and inconvenient presence, and he dreaded the awkwardness. But his wife was having none of it, and the bodyguard detail was duly arranged.

Asad wanted to know if the matter was worth pursuing with the police.

'That won't help, Dr Mirza,' the security chief told him. 'The police are both incompetent and overworked, and you won't get anywhere with them. They'll register your report and go through the motions, but you can't get them interested in something like this.'

Asad knew the man was talking sense. The city government's services—electricity, water, roads, schools—were barely functioning. Why would the police service be any different?

Yet he wasn't ready to let go. He had been shot at. It may have been a robbery attempt, but he hadn't been robbed. He wanted answers, and he pressed the hospital security chief for assistance.

'How do we even go about investigating it, then?'

'You said his face was covered,' the chief responded. 'You didn't even get a good look at him. I hate to be so blunt, but such incidents are a dime a dozen in our city.'

Asad told him about the registration plate number noted down by the boys.

'I'm sure it's a stolen car,' the chief replied. 'That's the typical MO. Trust me, it won't lead to anything.'

Asad was persistent. 'I won't be satisfied until I've made some attempt to investigate this,' he said. 'It may lead to nothing, but I need to have the satisfaction that I tried.'

'If you're that keen on it,' said the security chief, 'I suggest you get in touch with Colonel Nabeel Mustafa.'

'All right. Who is he?'

'An old batch mate of mine from the Academy,' the chief replied. 'Ex-military intelligence. Retired about a year ago, and now has a business offering investigative services to private clients. I'll send you his card.'

Nineteen

Business was slow, and Col Mustafa was only too glad to engage a new client. The few commissions he had been able to attract were all soap opera stuff—husbands suspicious of cheating wives, siblings embroiled in family feuds, wealthy parents placing tabs on delinquent teenagers. There wasn't really a culture of private detective work in Pakistan, and the colonel sometimes wondered if he had retired from the army in haste. Yet with crime sky-rocketing and the police force in a state of near-total collapse, he knew a market existed for his services. It was exciting, not to mention reassuring, to finally land a criminal case.

Col Mustafa visited Asad in the hospital and took in all the details. He also spoke with the two boys who had brought Asad to the ER. They described the attacker's car, a black four-door Honda Civic with tinted windows, and passed on the license plate number. The attacker had his face covered but they thought he might have had a beard. He was wearing either a grey or a green shalwar kameez; in the fading light they couldn't judge the colour precisely.

The retired colonel pressed Asad for a list of potential enemies, but came up blank. Over the years, Asad had dealt with his share of acrimonious patients and relatives, and he knew one or two grumpy colleagues who harboured professional jealousies and occasionally expressed resentment, but he found it unthinkable that any of them would cross the line from mere incivility to crime.

Col Mustafa turned out to be one who wouldn't give up easily. He insisted Asad wrack his brains over every possible segment among his sphere of contacts. A domestic servant he had entangled with? Someone he owed money to? An affair gone wrong? In-laws? Anyone who might conceivably target him?

The answer was no, no, no, no, and no.

'So the license plate number is the only genuine lead we have,' the colonel mused. 'It's bound to be a stolen car, but I'll check it out. Give me a couple of days.'

The next day, Asad was discharged from the hospital. He came home weighed down by compelling concerns, and his narrow escape from death was just one part of it. He was worried about Nadia's research project at the Hartman lab, now in limbo after US Customs had confiscated the brain tissue specimen she was carrying. There was also the fallout from his unexpected absence from work, which had played havoc with the neurology call schedule, left one of his colleagues grousing about having to delay his vacation, and made his patients unhappy over cancelled clinic appointments.

Asad was deep in thought about Nadia's stalled research project when his phone rang. His pulse quickened at the sight of Col Mustafa's number lighting up his cell phone display.

'Hello, Dr Mirza?' The colonel sounded eager, almost thrilled.

'Yes?' said Asad.

'I have some news. It's important.'

Within the hour, the private detective was at Asad's house. He had been flexing his detective muscles looking into the license plate lead, and had unearthed a trophy.

The car was indeed a stolen vehicle. But the key revelation was that it was also involved in an accident the same evening. Apparently, a taxi had jumped out of a side lane and broadsided the car as it was making good its escape. The timeline suggested the collision happened very soon after the shooting, perhaps just minutes afterward, when the assailant must have been desperate to speed away.

Although the taxi driver was unscathed, Asad's attacker had been hurt. He was admitted at Holy Crescent Hospital and had undergone surgery to repair a fractured arm. Condition was reported as medically stable and he was due for discharge in twenty-four hours.

'Wow,' whistled Asad. He was blown away by the colonel's report. 'Are you serious?' he asked, incredulous and disbelieving.

'Yes, of course,' said the colonel.

'Have you seen him? What does he look like? Evil? Hateful?'

'From what I could make out, he looks pretty innocuous actually.'

Asad's heart was thumping. All he wanted to do was rush over to Crescent right then and rip open the man's belly. He took a deep breath to cool his rage.

'Are you sure it's him?' he asked. 'I mean, what's your source for all this information? Could there be a mistake?'

'Dr Mirza,' replied the colonel in a deliberate, measured tone, 'this information is very reliable. My detective work is based on a network of trusted contacts. This is the man who tried to kill you. I can assure you of that.'

'What about the fact that he stole that car? Doesn't anybody know about that?'

'He was booked as a police case at Crescent initially,' the colonel replied, 'but charges were thrown out the next day. He bribed them, I'm sure.'

'Well, then, what should we do? Can't you get the police to arrest him?'

'I would not advise going that route, Dr Mirza. The only thing the police are good at is asking for bribes. All you'll end up with is spinning your wheels in and out of court.'

Asad knew the man was right.

'What's your advice then?' he asked.

'We don't know anything about your attacker. He's provided virtually no personal information to the hospital. Gave his name as Waheed Khan, which could well be an alias. The motive was probably robbery, but we can't be sure. I suggest we shadow him.'

'Shadow him? How?'

'Leave that to me.'

'Am I in danger?'

'We have to assume that you are, Dr Mirza. But there's already an armed guard at your home, and so long as you travel with your security escort, you should be fine.'

Should? That was hardly comforting. 'What about my family?' asked Asad.

'I'm not worried about them. Unless, of course, it's a grudge motive. But from what you tell me, that's very unlikely, right?'

'That's right,' said Asad. He could think of no conceivable grudge that would make someone want to kill him.

ꕥ

A nurse tapped his shoulder and Malik stirred. She offered him a glass of water along with two pills. He looked up at her with questioning eyes.

'A painkiller and an antibiotic,' she said.

Malik gulped them down gratefully. The fracture was in his right arm. Midshaft humerus, the doctors had said. They said he was lucky not to have injured the radial nerve, which wraps around the arm bone and is vulnerable in such fractures. Wouldn't that have been icing on the cake, thought Malik. He had still not come to terms with the fact that he had fucked up so badly. It was something he needed to exorcise in private penance. But pressing matters awaited. He could afford no more digressions.

At least that idiot Avicenna neurologist was dead. Malik was pretty sure of that. He had got him in the neck and chest, he was quite certain. Chest wounds are often fatal and neck wounds almost invariably so, he remembered reading in the Network training manual. He could visualise Asad's flaccid body as he had left it, limp and listless, draped over the steering wheel, blood everywhere, the nosy parker breathing his last.

Yet Malik had to concede to himself that he left before confirming death. He had wanted to walk up and pump more bullets into the man, but people had started to gather. He had to run. Still, the death required confirmation. He would get to it the moment he left the hospital.

In his mind, the most difficult piece of the plan had been the timing. His best shot was in daylight, but the doctor did not emerge from the hospital until dusk. By the time Malik was ready to ensnare him in the narrow shortcut lane, the bastard had switched his headlights on. Still, Malik had got a few good shots in, firing from almost point-blank range.

He wanted to get in even closer. He had planned to empty a cartridge into the motherfucker's head, and empty his pockets too, so it would look like a mugging. But with a small crowd forming, he had to make a snap decision. He did the right thing, Malik reassured himself.

Technically speaking, a variance had occurred in the protocol, but Malik decided against reporting it further up the hierarchy. His decision violated the Command Manual, but what was he to do? The bastard was certainly dead. Even if he wasn't, he was definitely in a coma, strapped to a breathing machine. He won't be causing any more trouble, and that had been the whole idea.

He never saw the taxi. It sped out of a side lane from his right. Darkness had fallen but the moron didn't even have his lights on. Malik couldn't believe the fragile doors on the blasted Honda. Made of plastic, they were. Collapsed right in and crushed his arm. But it was a lucky escape—Malik was profoundly grateful for that. Allah had seen to it that he was still able to walk. The fracture was also healing nicely and already the pain, brutal and unforgiving when it started, had receded to a nagging ache that could almost be ignored. As he had done numerous times before, Malik marvelled yet again how Allah was guiding him to the grand destiny, to carry this great project to fruition.

The best part was the ease with which he had handled the police. What excellent judgment on the part of the Network to situate the project in a country like Pakistan. Where else could you always bribe the authorities to look the other way?

ഇ൬

'I have...important...meet you...' the caller was saying.

It was Col Mustafa on the line, but the connection was terrible and Asad could barely make any sense of it. He turned around and craned his neck hoping for a better signal.

The call got disconnected.

Within a minute, the colonel had called back. He sounded breathless. There was vital news to share, he said, and asked to meet urgently.

Twenty minutes later, Asad greeted him at home and took him into the study. Col Mustafa was bubbling with excitement. There had been developments, he said. It was something quite unexpected, bizarre even. The colonel's hands moved every which way as he talked, his speech coming in pressured gasps. He was having a hard time being coherent or coming to a point, and it was beginning to make Asad more than a little frustrated.

A maid came in and placed a cup of tea in front of Col Mustafa. Oblivious to its hot temperature, he gulped it down. Asad quietly urged his guest to relax.

The pause helped the colonel gather his thoughts, and he finally began to narrate a coherent story. He had shadowed Elvis—the codename he had given Asad's attacker—and caught him visiting what looked to be an abandoned warehouse in Korangi, one of the industrial districts. The colonel undertook a stakeout, and managed to gain access using a lock decoding tool. What he found inside took his breath away—all manner of complicated machinery and appliances; shelves full of scientific books, manuals and catalogues; lots of glassware and gadgets; and a thick notebook crammed with handmade figures and complex notations.

'I took some pictures,' said the colonel, handing Asad a computer thumb drive carrying images captured on a digital camera.

Asad fired up his laptop and inserted the memory stick. A folder of photographs opened. He began clicking on them one by one.

'I thought it was some kind of sophisticated medical laboratory,' said Col Mustafa.

Taking in the images, Asad concurred.

When he came to a series of scanned notebook pages, he slowed down. Zooming in to the maximum, he poured over their contents. Everything was handwritten. There were diagrams, algorithms, tables, lists. Flowcharts described plans for experiments in molecular biology. The scrawl was only half-legible, but Asad was able to read much of what he saw.

The realisation hit him like a bolt of lightning, and washed over his body giving him goose bumps. After a few minutes of careful browsing, he realised he had seen enough.

'You need go to Avicenna right away,' he said, turning towards Col Mustafa.

'Avicenna?' asked the colonel, puzzled. 'You mean Avicenna Hospital? Why?'

'Go right away, please. Ask for my resident Dr Farida Rasool, she can be paged from the main reception. I'm calling her right now to let her know what needs to be done.'

Col Mustafa kept looking at Asad quizzically.

'What do you mean?' he asked. 'What are you talking about? What needs to be done?'

'What you've uncovered is more than some souped up medical laboratory,' replied Asad, looking the colonel squarely in the eye. 'There is a serious risk you were exposed to a bio-terror agent in there. You need to be administered rabies immunoglobulin and the human diploid cell vaccine for rabies.'

'Shit. What do you want me to do?'

'Go now! Please.'

Twenty

All of a sudden, Asad feels very, very alone. He is embroiled in a battle whose enormity he has finally realised.

The problems are mounting. His immediate frustration is a letter that has just been delivered to his home. It is a bill for professional services from Col Mustafa. Tacked on to the bill is a small handwritten note. Although the bill has induced mild sticker shock, it is the scribbled note that makes Asad truly distraught.

'Unable to continue further with case,' it says, in a heavily slanted scrawl. 'Please accept regrets.'

Asad calls the colonel on his cell phone. The investigative expert is evasive at first, but Asad is persistent. Has the colonel been threatened? Is there something he isn't sharing with Asad?

No, says the colonel. He is simply putting two and two together. This is not the sort of case he ever imagined getting mixed up with. A bio-terror plot being hatched in a clandestine laboratory in a place like Karachi—it is just a matter of time before all hell breaks loose. All instruments of state within Pakistan, and soon the FBI, the CIA, the United States military, and God knows who else, will be involved. He is thankful that Asad has expeditiously arranged for him to receive the rabies vaccination. As he understands it, this act has saved his life. He wants to keep it that way.

'I'll be grateful if you'll just clear my bill,' he says, trying to sound professional as he suppresses his sense of dread. 'I'll be most obliged if you'll just leave me out of this whole business.'

'What is your advice for me?' asks Asad. He feels abandoned and angry. It is a real effort to retain composure.

The colonel does not mince words. 'Walk away from it,' he says. 'Count your blessings. You have no idea what you could be getting into.'

'I think I do,' Asad replies, irritated that the colonel all of a sudden is having cold feet. He had sounded eager for a commission on crime investigation, Asad reflects. Now that he's seen the scope of the mess, he wants out. What a baby.

To hell with him, thought Asad. If I'm on my own, I'm on my own.

He takes stock of where things stand. It's not looking pretty. After sending the colonel off to get vaccinated, Asad has been labouring over the digital images of notebooks and documents. He has found some clues to the intended use of the lethal rabies aerosol. There are notes in the margins, scattered scribbles that have been circled and underlined. The lynchpin is what appears to be a one-page algorithm for a terror plot. But he cannot see completely because a portion of the page has been left out by the camera angle.

'I think the plan is to unleash the virus in the United States,' he continues with the colonel, affecting a tone that says look, I'm having to do your job for you. 'I found specific references in the material you've uncovered,' he says. 'There's mention of releasing the virus in movie theaters in and around Boston.'

'In the name of Allah, Dr Mirza, you're an educated, intelligent man. Don't get involved with this muddle,' the colonel pleads. 'Count yourself lucky to be alive.'

'I'm really surprised to hear you say that,' says Asad, with more than a trace of condescension. He is fuming, but his voice remains measured and composed. 'Don't you feel we have a responsibility to expose the plot? Many lives could be saved.'

'Leave me out of it, sir. I beg of you,' says the colonel, after which he quickly hangs up.

Asad contemplates his options, as he has been doing since last night when he finally realised what murderous game was afoot. His next calls are to Omar and Bilal, his two most trusted colleagues. Each reacts with incredulity to the news but, after they have calmed down and absorbed the horrible significance of what they are being told, they are in unanimous agreement with Asad: he has no choice but to blow the whistle.

'You have to do it now,' says Bilal. 'ASAP! Sounds like they've already got a field-tested product. Why would they wait? It's an aerosol, for fuck's sake. They could pull it off tomorrow. They could pull it off any minute!'

Frustratingly, neither friend offers any practical help. They are sorry for Asad's predicament, but want no part of it themselves. Asad hadn't really expected them to provide anything more than reasoned advice, but their reluctance to step into the hole with him nevertheless stings. It is patently obvious no one would touch this issue with a ten-foot pole. Still, when his friends beg off, he is unable to hide the hurt in his voice.

Omar turns philosophical. 'Allah has put this hurdle in front of you,' he tells Asad, speaking almost in a whisper. 'Surely, there is some divine logic in it. The responsibility is yours. You have been chosen for this test. It is for you to pass. And you can do it, my friend.'

Ignoring the theological conundrums such analysis raises, Asad focuses on the hard conclusion—he is all alone. Him and this pile of shit he has fallen into. He can't share any of this with his wife and family, who will certainly panic and become a needless hindrance, only adding to his worries. He is clear that there is no point going to the Pakistani authorities, who would never take him seriously and, if he really persisted, would only come up with ingenious ways to harass and extort money from him. His only chance to elicit a meaningful response from local law-enforcement is if he directly approaches some high-ranking politician or government official. But Asad, a midde-class professional who keeps to himself and has no patience for hobnobbing, can boast of no such connections.

What is he to do? His mind races. He is frightened. He feels the urge to go for a long walk along the seaside in the hope it will clear his head, but he is in no state to do it. The shoulder is still bandaged up and neck movements remain tender. He feels like sitting forever in a warm bath, but his surgeon has cautioned against getting the bandages wet. Smoke and drink are out of the question because he's an avowed non-smoker and hasn't touched alcohol in nearly a decade, not since getting miserably drunk on a cold winter night in Boston and embarrassing himself with the wife of one of his Harvard attendings.

Instead, he simply gets up and has a good sit on the toilet. By the time he is done, he has subdued his panic, the panic that lapped at him excitedly like angry, frothy surf charging a beach. The panic that has now receded and settled.

Asad draws up a list of possible strategies. Number one is to call Avicenna's director of security and solicit the hospital's assistance with the local authorities. Number two is to communicate his concern to the American embassy in Islamabad. Number three is to call Sarah and Joel in Boston. Number four is to do nothing.

He stares at the list pensively, contemplating pros and cons for each option, calculating risks, trying to think several moves down. After a while, a scheme forms in his head. He picks up his pencil and underlines the first three options. Then he scratches out number four.

ᏇᏃ

The website for the US embassy in Islamabad lists a street address, a telephone number, a fax number, and an email address. The email option seems the least encouraging. Asad punches in the telephone number and waits for the call to go through.

He has arrived at this option because his employer, a major university hospital, a corporate entity with enormous local influence and regional fame, has turned its back on him. 'I am sorry, Dr Mirza, but you're on your own,' uttered Avicenna's security director coldly, and Asad wanted to smash his face in. 'We cannot get involved in something like this, which you must deal with in your private capacity,' the security chief continued. He advised Asad not to take the matter any further with Avicenna administration. 'No point coming across as a trouble-maker, Dr Mirza. I am sure you'll understand.' The director intended it to be a subtle hint, but it hit Asad like an arrow between the eyes.

The call to the US embassy has been rehearsed several times. For all purposes, Asad is approaching it blind. He has searched hard among his chain of acquaintances but found no one with direct links or connections to the embassy staff. Not even a friend of a friend of a friend. He has scoured the website of this and other United States embassies around the world. He knows the answers to all FAQs by heart—Can you get married at the embassy?

Can you staple the photo on your passport application? Does the embassy accept credit cards? All negative. Exasperatingly, there is nothing about how to call in a bio-terror alert.

Sensing a pause in the ringing, Asad prepares himself to speak. An automated menu plays out instead. Dial 1 for this, 2 for that, 3 for this…Asad waits patiently until he hears it all through, and punches 0 for the operator.

'Embassy of the United States. May I help you?' The voice is female, accent educated Pakistani.

'I need to speak to someone about a security matter please,' says Asad, his heart thumping, his voice tense and stiff.

'Certainly, sir. I'll connect you.'

A few seconds pass. He is greeted by another voice. 'Office of the RSO. May I help you?' This one is female too, though the accent is distinctly American.

'Yes, hello. I'm trying to report a security concern. Is this the right place?'

'This is the office of the Regional Security Officer, sir. What is this regarding?'

Asad had expected his call might get routed this way. The RSO is a special security agent assigned to US diplomatic missions overseas, he remembered reading on one of the web pages. The position serves as a personal advisor to the ambassador on all security issues, and involves liaison with US Marines, Navy Seabees, and the Department of Homeland Security. 'I believe I have some critical information about a bio-terrorism plot aimed at American interests,' says Asad, in as clear and measured a tone as he can manage.

'Certainly, sir,' replies the voice at the other end. The woman sounds unflappable, almost casual, as if Asad has just told her the time of day or the price of apples. 'I'll take down the details, and the RSO will get back to you if required.'

'If required? I don't think you understand. I need to speak with the RSO myself.'

'Are you a United States citizen, sir?'

'No.'

'I'm sorry, sir,' the woman says, still with no hint of emotion in her voice. 'State department policy does not permit unsolicited contact of non-citizens with the RSO.'

'I need to report something of grave concern,' says Asad, feeling agitated. His voice has taken on a contentious tone that he is unable to control.

'Have you gone to the Pakistani authorities, sir? You are advised to do that if you need to speak with an officer directly.'

'No, I don't believe that will help matters,' responds Asad, realising he has no option but to relent.

He is asked to report his full name, location, and contact information. He is then asked to share his concerns, and proceeds to provide the woman a summary. She asks for some clarifications, which pleases Asad, because it shows she is being responsible and not just blowing him off. Asad is well prepared and summarises the matter in a handful of points. From what he can tell, the woman takes careful notes. When he finishes, she reads them back to him and confirms everything. Her tone remains flat and unvarying.

Asad asks for her name. 'Carol', she replies. He asks for a complaint or reference number of some kind, a numerical authenticity that his worries have been heard. 'I will assign it a log number', says Carol, 'but that is classified.' Asad goes on marking the paper in front of him, checking boxes as he reads off the list he has made. He asks for a direct telephone number, but is told to call the switchboard again if needed. He asks for assurance that his concern will be urgently reviewed by the RSO. 'I can assure you it will be, sir', says Carol.

After Asad hangs up, the RSO's secretary dutifully logs the call and writes up a memo that she sends her boss via internal email.

The RSO is having a busy day. A team of American businessman is in Islamabad to explore acquisition of state-owned heavy mechanical industries, and the RSO is spending the day taking them through a security briefing. During a break between meetings, he checks his email and notices the memo. He scans it quickly. The content intrigues him, but in this line of work he has to deal with his share of cranks and eccentrics, so he is sceptical. Nevertheless, he flags it for later review.

The ambassador has hosted a high-profile dinner that evening for the American businessmen, along with top officials from Pakistan's ministry of finance. It is at a private club for which the Americans will have to venture outside the diplomatic enclave, and the expedition keeps the RSO fully occupied. He is not able to return to the memo until late.

By the time dinner is over, he is tired, ill-tempered, and desperate to hit the sack. Yet he has a habit of not leaving memos unattended into the next day, and he wants to clear his inbox tonight.

He goes through his secretary's email carefully and absorbs everything. Then he scans his bookshelf for resources on bio-terrorism. Lying on the bottom shelf, sandwiched between a book on criminal court procedure and a manual on fire safety, is a classified bio-terrorism booklet prepared jointly by the Department of Homeland Security and the Centers for Disease Control. He starts thumbing through it.

The document is neatly organised and easy to peruse. It lists twenty-five key biological threats and the RSO reads them cautiously, running his finger down the table, careful not to miss anything. Weird maladies are mentioned. In a column titled 'Bacteria', he reads anthrax, brucellosis, plague, tularemia, cholera, Q fever. Under viruses he finds small pox, yellow fever, ebola, dengue, lassa, hantavirus. There is also a column listing toxins—botulism, ricin, and staphylococcal enterotoxin B. None of this interests him.

Then the RSO notices a small box titled 'Encephalitis' which startles him. But he doesn't find what he's looking for. The chapter mentions Eastern Equine Enecepahlitis, Western Equine Encephalitis, and Venezuelan Encephalitis. He has combed through the booklet from cover to cover. There is no reference to rabies.

Yet his professional training demands exhaustive thoroughness. Not willing to let go until he has settled his concerns, the RSO logs on to the Internet and pulls up the website for the CDC, America's famous and formidable Centers for Disease Control and Prevention. Under the section on emergency preparedness, he finds a link to bio-terrorism. There is a table titled 'A-Z list of bio-terror agents'. He clicks on it.

It is a more comprehensive list. Several bacteria, viruses and toxins are mentioned for each letter of the alphabet. The RSO quickly scrolls down to 'R'. It lists ricin and rickettsia. No rabies.

So, he thinks, another hoax. He replies to his secretary's email, telling her to take no further action unless the caller re-establishes contact. Then he switches off his computer, turns the light off in his office, and heads home.

Twenty One

As THE SUN rises over New England, a thin shaft of light breaks through the curtains and slowly snakes its way across the room. Gradually it traces a path over the closet, the dresser, the wood paneling, and the nightstand. When it finally falls on Nadia's face, she stirs.

It is nearly eleven o'clock on a cloudless Boston morning. Nadia has woken up with the pleasant feeling that comes from having slept off your fatigue. She realises she has been dreaming, but cannot remember exactly what. Perhaps it was a replay of the nightmare she had experienced at immigration and customs.

What she feels now is simply relief. Sarah and Joel have been amazing. They sensed her mood immediately, comforting and reassuring her that a fresh shipment of the all-important brain tissue will be arranged. In the meantime, they said, they'll get her involved in an ongoing project so she doesn't waste any time during her short stay in their lab.

Nadia has taken an instant liking to them. They are both friendly and converse easily. Sarah is ash-blond, wears a sensible haircut with glasses to match, and smiles effortlessly. Joel has receding hair, clever eyes, a reddish beard, and a paunch that he makes no attempt to hide. There is a pensive air about him, but it seems more casual than cultivated, as though he were engrossed in things just for the fun of it. Nadia had expected both doctors to be a bit reserved, thinking that Harvard professors would naturally keep a distance from medical students, especially one from a foreign country. But after receiving a comfortable embrace from Sarah and a warm handshake from Joel, she had gratefully returned their welcoming smiles and relaxed.

The drive back from the airport had relaxed her even more. Sarah and Joel indulged in some friendly bickering over which music CD to play, eventually giving up and settling on WBUR, an FM radio station that was broadcasting a cello recital. Joel asked Nadia if she was hungry, and they stopped for Thai food at a corner bistro on Commonwealth Avenue. Over dinner, they spoke about Asad and compared notes about life in Karachi and Boston. Joel was startled to learn that Karachi boasted a population of fifteen million and counting. That triggered discussion about outsized urban settlements around the world. Nadia wanted to ask them about New York, Los Angeles, Hollywood, Washington DC, the places glamorised in the media she had been exposed to halfway across the globe. But she felt shy, and instead asked practical questions about living and getting around in Boston. Joel had given her a quick tutorial.

Traffic was heavy, and it had become dark by the time they reached the Hartmans' residence in Brookline. Sarah showed Nadia around the house. Joel checked the mailbox, took out the garbage, and brought Nadia's luggage in. The couple had no children and lived by themselves. The interior of the house was dominated by bookshelves, wicker chairs, armoires, and indoor plants. Nadia was surprised to see a huge exercise machine sitting in the middle of the study, a jarring eyesore in a room that was otherwise full of books, computers, and reclining furniture. Joel said apologetically it needed to be taken down to the basement and he would get to it one of these days.

As Sarah was orienting her to the kitchen, Nadia's eyes began to feel heavy. More instructions followed—the washer and dryer, the house alarm system—but Nadia by this time was struggling to stay awake. Sensing her exhaustion, Sarah quickly showed her to the guest room, handed her a set of fresh towels, and wished her good night. The last thought Nadia had before succumbing to sleep was that the Hartmans had made no mention of anything related to the lab or to the work she would be doing during her four-week stay.

Now, as she sits up and looks around the room, she spots an envelope marked 'Nadia' propped up on the small table beside her bed. It is a hand-written note from Sarah. She has suggested that Nadia can either spend the day resting or, if she has woken up in good time and feels up to it, may come to the lab. A subway pass and directions to the nearest T stop are attached.

Eager to get cracking in the lab, Nadia wastes no time showering and getting dressed. She scans the refrigerator and settles on yogurt and fruit for a quick breakfast. The little anxiety she has about negotiating the subway vanishes once she has studied the map and realised that the route to Mass General is straightforward.

Shortly after noontime, Nadia makes an appearance at the Hartman lab. It is a spacious set-up on the fifth floor of the Founders Building, overlooking the Charles River and, beyond it, the town of Cambridge. Nadia can see a few sailboats dotting the river, which glitters like a mirror under the radiant sun. As she enters, she is greeted by a man who introduces himself as Victor.

'You must be the girl from Pa-kis-tan,' he says, pronouncing the country's name with a distinct stress on each syllable.

Nadia is startled, but quickly recovers. Victor has surprised her coming from the side as she was gingerly stepping into the lab, trying to get a sense of the surroundings. Nadia takes in his appearance—ragged jeans, faded t-shirt, sharp features, two-day stubble, piercing eyes. Then she realises that he has extended a hand, and she rushes to shake it.

'Yes, I'm Nadia,' she replies, as she continues to study Victor. From what she can make out, he is probably in his late twenties, a prototype specimen no doubt of the bohemian presence that was a staple of American research laboratories.

'Sorry, it's my first day,' she continues. 'Just feeling a little lost.'

'I'm the lab manager,' says Victor. 'That's your spot, over there.'

Nadia's gaze follows in the direction he is pointing. An area about four feet across has been cleared on one of the lab benches. Glassware and some technical equipment she does not recognise is piled on shelves in front of the bench space. There is also a swivel stool, with a white lab coat draped over it.

'My spot?' asks Nadia, flattered and excited that a space has been set out for her, that she is already part of the rhythm of the lab.

'It's the bench space for rotating med students,' says Victor. 'You're lucky there are no Harvard medical students in the lab right now. That would've made things a bit crowded for you.'

As she stands chatting with Victor, Nadia is spotted by Sarah, who comes over and takes her by the hand. 'I see you've already made friends with Victor,' she says. 'Let me introduce you to the others.'

Everyone has noticed Nadia's presence by now and a hush has

fallen over the lab. People have interrupted their activities and are waiting for Sarah and Nadia to stop by their corner of the lab. Nadia greets Yan, the graduate student, Dolores and Rita, the two lab techs and Jorge, who is introduced as a visiting neurologist from Chile. Sarah then takes her down the hall to a computer cluster, where Nadia meets three more members of the lab—Ravi, Cheryl, and Xiao-Fan, all postdoctoral fellows. Each offers her a bright smile and words of welcome. Nadia asks about Joel, and is told he is finishing rounds in the hospital.

'You've come at a good time,' says Sarah brightly. 'Our weekly lab meeting is about to start. Join us in the seminar room. Afterwards, we'll go over your project.'

The seminar room is brilliantly lit, with a large blond wood table running down its length. Textbooks, monographs, and leather-bound volumes of scientific journals line the walls. A window at one end gives a picturesque view of Charles River, framing Longfellow Bridge in one corner. Nadia takes a spot by the window and watches as the room fills up. Joel is the last to enter, flashing a quick smile to Nadia as he takes his place next to Sarah at the head of the table.

The meeting begins with Sarah asking Cheryl for an update on the gene knockout experiment she has been working on. As Cheryl adjusts her papers and begins to speak, Nadia lets her eyes wander around the room. Except for Joel, who has been seeing patients in the hospital and has come wearing a tie, and Sarah, who Nadia guesses is never to be seen in anything other than sensible outfits, everyone cuts a picture of being carefree and casual. Many people even have soda cans in front of them, while a few others are seated sipping bottled water.

Yet once the discussion begins, the room becomes enveloped in intensity. Sarah goes around the table asking people to give updates on their research projects. Each report generates a series of queries from the others. Technical points are debated, experimental data are flashed on an overhead projector. Sarah and Joel are mostly supportive and keep nodding gently. Once or twice Nadia feels she has detected a hint of reproach or reprimand in Joel's voice, but only very briefly, and Sarah always follows these moments with a word of encouragement for the person whom Joel has targeted.

The experimental details are all Latin and Greek to Nadia, but the meeting's atmosphere makes her giddy with delight. Here she is, in the company of bright and dynamic scientists operating at the frontiers of knowledge, in an institution occupying the pinnacle of academic inquiry. It is a long way from Karachi, and it is simply intoxicating. She wants nothing more than to be like them, to have her own projects and make headway in important scientific problems. To one day sit at the head of the table at the weekly meeting of her own lab, creating new knowledge and enriching human life.

After the meeting adjourns, Sarah takes Nadia to an outdoor cafeteria where they discuss her assignment over sparkling Perrier and chicken-avocado sandwiches. Nadia is to be included in an ongoing project that has emerged as an offshoot from Yan's PhD thesis. It involves determining the microscopic location of a novel gene product in thinly cut slices of mouse brain. The gene product in question is a byproduct from Yan's cloning experiments. Its function is unknown but, based on some indirect evidence, Sarah and Joel think it could be a receptor for viral entry into neurons. Nadia is being charged with testing this hypothesis and seeing whether the gene product would be found in the same brain regions that are typically damaged in viral encephalitis.

Because her prior lab experience is limited, for the first week Nadia will be shadowing Victor, who will introduce her to the techniques involved. Sarah also assigns several papers for background reading. When they finish lunch, she tells Nadia to seek out Victor and get started.

'What part of Pa-kis-tan?' asks Victor, as soon as he sees Nadia.

'Excuse me?' responds Nadia in surprise. Approaching her from the side and blurting out his question even before she had a chance to see him, Victor has managed to startle her once again.

'What part of the country are you from?' he asks once again. He stands facing her now, a Pyrex flask in one hand, notebook in the other. His manner is pleasant enough, but Nadia cannot escape the feeling that there is just the tiniest hint of something confrontational about it.

'Karachi,' she replies. 'It's a big city, in the south, on the coast.'

'I know about Karachi,' Victor says. 'It's supposed to be a lawless place with lots of crime and overpopulation. But it's really Pa-kis-tan's premier city, isn't it?'

Nadia takes a moment to absorb that. She isn't sure if Victor has just complimented Karachi or insulted Pakistan. She decides to assume it is the former. 'Well, it's home for me,' she says with a shrug, hoping to end this line of conversation and move on to the lab work. 'Sarah wants me to do in situ hybridisation with Yan's T0971 orphan cDNA. She told me you could get me started.'

'Yeah, sure,' says Victor. 'Let me put these things away.'

Over the next hour and a half, Victor leads Nadia through a tour of the animal facility, going over the basics of sacrificing mice and harvesting their brains. He introduces her to the people in the Supply Room and goes over policies and procedures for waste disposal. As they get into the elevator to head back to the lab, he manages yet again to catch her unawares.

'Why isn't Pakistan doing more in the war on terror?' he asks bluntly. They have been riding quietly in the elevator with no other occupants present. Victor's question springs out like a jack-in-the-box.

'Excuse me?' Nadia utters with a frown. She has found the question intrusive. She is irritated, and makes no attempt to hide it.

'Musharraf should have done more to fight Al-Qaeda,' continues Victor, oblivious to Nadia's discomfort. 'We'd nearly finished them in Afghanistan but he went soft on them and now they're reorganising in Pakistan's tribal areas.'

Isn't the typical American supposed to have no interest in current affairs? Nadia wonders to herself. At least that is what she has read and heard. But perhaps like all stereotypes, this one too is inaccurate. Victor certainly appears a radical departure from that label.

'You're up with the latest,' she remarks. Her intent is to pay a compliment, but the words sound as if she is making some curious observation. 'I'd heard Americans didn't care so much about current affairs.'

'I'm a news junkie,' says Victor, pushing out the palms of his hands in a gesture that says, well, there you have it. He continues with his justification, telling Nadia that Pakistan is a controversial American ally that has been forced into a difficult role on the world stage. Ever since he heard that a medical student from Pakistan would be visiting the lab, he has looked forward to indulging his appetite for news and analysis.

Nadia has never considered herself a news junkie. But she is knowledgeable about what is going on in her country and the world. She has grown up in an upper middle-class Karachi household. It is a universe in which news and politics are conversation staples. She also belongs to a restless nuclear-armed country that by most accounts is located in the world's toughest neighbourhood—a country where everyone has made it their business to know what is happening and why, and where everybody always has theories and opinions about the forces shaping the world. If Victor wants to talk politics with a Pakistani, he's certainly found one who is more than up for it.

'The person who really dropped the ball is Bush,' Nadia says, taking the bait. 'He was fighting the war on terror in the wrong place. If Al-Qaeda is resurgent, it's because Bush diverted precious fighting resources into Iraq, which is such an unnecessary war.'

'It wasn't unnecessary,' Victor replies. He is leaning against the lab bench that has been demarcated as Nadia's area. 'Saddam Hussein was a horrible dictator who had to be removed. He was a threat to world peace.'

'Was he really such a threat?' Nadia asks rhetorically. 'Or was American thirsty for oil?' She has perched herself on the stool at her bench, her lab coat thrown over her shoulder. 'He had no weapons of mass destruction, so that rationale clearly was wrong.'

'Okay, so maybe we overreacted a little,' says Victor. 'But all great countries tend to overreact. Before 9/11, America had never been threatened on its soil.'

'And that allows you to go and bomb a country that had done you no harm?' asks Nadia pointedly, raising her eyebrows.

'There was credible intelligence about Iraq's war capabilities. That made Iraq a threat and that's what Bush acted on,' Victor says. His manner remains casual, his tone non-threatening and matter-of-fact.

'Well, it's an even bigger threat now,' says Nadia, trying to resist a rising intensity in her voice. 'George Bush made the problem worse.'

'Interesting,' replies Victor. 'So that's what people are thinking in Pakistan.' He gives a little laugh. It sounds to Nadia like a private laugh, as though he is laughing to himself.

'It's what people are thinking all over the world,' continues Nadia. She breaks into a smile. Victor's laugh has put her at ease.

'Let's go over to microscopy,' says Victor, changing the topic effortlessly. 'I have a lot more to show you before you can get started.'

Nadia trots off behind him, only too pleased that they will be getting back to business.

Twenty Two

The moment has finally arrived.

The password-encrypted signal Malik has so desperately waited for has been received. The weapon is ready, it has been successfully tested, and must be used immediately. No distractions are permitted. It is now or never.

Malik calls Hamza to review details. The viral particles have been suspended in phosphate-buffered saline, ready for use as an aerosol. Their shelf life at room temperature is approximately seven days. The cargo sits on the lab bench next to the PCR machine, a clear, concentrated, odourless liquid. It is stored in a 100 ml bottle that at one point contained Burberry aftershave and has since been autoclaved to serve as a receptacle for viral culture. There is enough there to cover twenty theatres, and then some.

After hanging up, Malik packs his valise and locks the apartment. He then takes a taxi to Korangi and gets dropped off half a kilometre from his destination, completing the remaining distance on foot. He enters Pentagon for what he knows will be the last time. It is the lab, coyly named by Hamza, where they created their masterpiece. Malik's bags are packed and his travelling documents—a US passport and airplane tickets on Lufthansa (Karachi-Frankfurt-Boston)—are in order. Hamza has already left the country. It is twelve minutes past midnight.

Malik checks the Burberry bottle's cellophane seal. He shakes the liquid about. It jiggles and splashes with the viscosity of water. It is colourless and unremarkable. He is satisfied. He douses the interior of the laboratory liberally with a mixture of kerosene and diesel. Then he places a homemade acetone-fertilizer bomb in the middle of the room and activates its timing device. He takes one last look at the lab. There is a pang of sentimentality but it is short-lived, perhaps lasting not even a second. The door shuts and Malik steps out onto the road to hail a taxi.

Thirty minutes later, when he is checking in at Jinnah International, the laboratory goes up in flames. By the time he gets to the departure lounge, a local news channel is showing footage of the terrific fire raging in Korangi Industrial Area. Instinctively, Malik pulls out the Burberry bottle from his bag and cradles it.

Everyone in the lounge is transfixed by the coverage and people gather around the television sets. There is a fire in a factory, the news anchor says; details are just coming in. Flames are seen rising into the night sky. A fire engine has reached and can be seen spewing water from its snorkel. A reporter comes into view, speaking excitedly in the foreground. Passers-by report hearing an explosion, he says. The place was supposed to be a quality control centre for pharmaceutical products. It is now gutted and unrecognisable.

The visual ends and the presenter moves on to other news. There has been a bank heist, a rape, a protest rally, and a murder-suicide in which a woman has shot her ex-fiancé before turning the gun on herself.

All par for the course in the psychodrama of Karachi.

Malik boards the plane and settles into his window seat. The space beside him is empty. He lifts the handrest and stretches out. His fracture has recovered well but the arm is sometimes uncomfortable in certain positions, and he props it on a pillow. A stewardess walks by handing out scented face towels and he takes one. The bottle marked Burberry sits in his carry-on bag, which is wedged securely under the seat in front of him.

ꙮ

Hours have passed and there has been no response from the US embassy. Asad thinks of calling them again but decides against it. The dispassionate and impersonal exchange with the RSO's secretary has left him despondent. He has no faith that the RSO's office is taking him seriously. The thought leaves him fighting fury and frustration.

His mood is shattered for another reason too—he has just received an email from the *New England Journal of Medicine* that they have rejected his paper. It is a form email toting the usual excuses: too many submissions, too competitive, not an editorial priority at the moment, blah, blah, blah. They have provided no proper critique of the work, no specific commentary or explanation.

Asad knows what has happened. The paper has been rejected because it is from Pakistan. Having inhaled the rarefied atmosphere of Harvard Medical School, he has a good idea of how sceptical the American medical elite are that reliable medical data could come from a developing country. What was I thinking, he asks himself in retrospect. He didn't even have an American or European co-author on the report, a trick that developing country authors often employ to get their papers accepted in the leading Western journals. Asad worries about breaking the news to Nadia, who had worked so hard on the paper and does not deserve to have her innocence smashed so soon.

But there is this other, far more pressing worry and it returns to consume him. He is down to option number 3. The last thing he wanted to do was to drag his friends Joel and Sarah into this. He is also petrified he might end up jeopardising Nadia's stay in the United States. Yet what choice does he have? He sits down to compose a short, pithy email to Joel and Sarah.

At approximately the same moment that Sarah is opening Asad's email, Lufthansa's flight 422 is landing at Boston's Logan Airport. Malik has had a comfortable flight. The Frankfurt-Boston leg was fairly deserted, and he napped soundly lying flat across the centre seats.

As he steps off the plane, his mind is a powerful mix of forced composure and a state of hyper-vigilant attention. It is a sensation that inevitably takes over when he is approaching the crux of an operation. Malik has arrived in America looking the part. He wears a purple Polo shirt on a pair of Dockers' khakis. To complete the ensemble, Hugo Boss sunglasses are positioned on his forehead. He is clean-shaven and his hair is trim and neat.

At the immigration counter, Malik is breezed through, the officer taking less than a minute to examine and stamp his passport. At customs, he is asked to open his bag, and the officer politely goes through it, sifting trousers, t-shirts, underwear, toiletries, a pair of sandals, a AAA road atlas, a copy of Dave Barry's *Guide to Guys*, and a bottle of Burberry aftershave. It could be any American's luggage. The official zips up the bag and says a brisk 'thank you, sir.' Malik responds with a soft smile and begins walking towards the exit.

Inside the arrivals lounge, he buys a Turkey club and an orange juice from Au Bon Pain, and picks up a copy of the *Globe* from a news stand. Then he steps out and rides the shuttle bus to the airport subway stop. Extracting a slip of paper from his shirt pocket, he goes over the directions once again. Blue Line inbound to Government Center, then Green Line westbound to Park Street. Change to Red Line outbound to Davis Square, exit from the College Avenue side, walk about fifty paces to the left, and sit on the stone steps. Leave the Burberry bottle a few inches from your left ankle and begin consuming your Au Bon Pain fare and reading the *Globe*.

The train arrives. It is not crowded. Malik boards and takes a seat.

Twenty Three

Alice has been looking forward to this evening. Her due date is still a week ahead, but the maternity leave has started. Justin has planned a celebratory night out. He comes home early from work and greets Alice with a bear hug and a wet kiss. Then he proceeds to give her a shampoo and a massage.

At seven o'clock they set out for Legal Sea Foods in the Chestnut Hill shopping area. Seafood is Alice's weakness—she has craved it through much of her pregnancy. Justin has carefully chosen this particular location because the restaurant offers a fresh fish market. They are ushered to a private dining booth. Alice relaxes in the restful setting accented by rich mahogany.

The meal begins with clam chowder for both, followed by steamed Maine lobster for him and wood-grilled salmon for her. She drinks soda; Justin has a beer. Dessert is a generous portion of Boston cream pie that they share with the same spoon. Conversation is easy and soothing. They reminisce about the early days of their relationship, about the things Alice liked in Justin before she really knew him, and what Justin saw in her that left him besotted. The lighting is soft and romantic, the atmosphere pleasant and warm. A floating candle flickers in the middle of the table.

Justin wonders if they should have coffee, but it is getting late. Alice glances at her watch and decides against it. She wants to be in time for their movie. Denzel Washington is starring in it, which is enough for Alice to want to see it, but Justin has been relieved to note that the reviews have been good, too. Tickets have already been purchased. The cinema neighbours the shopping complex. Justin takes his wife by the hand and they walk across.

They have arrived in good time. The theatre is just beginning to fill up. Justin spots two seats at the aisle about halfway down and nudges Alice. They walk over and settle in. Alice blows her nose and adjusts her dress. Justin squeezes her hand and wet-smacks her cheek. The lights are dimmed and the screen comes to life.

She noticed him because his curly hair was silhouetted against the brightness of the screen, Alice would later recall. He wore an usher's uniform. His face was hard to see. These thoughts came to her later, of course, when all was said and done, when the dust settled.

For now, all she notices is a curly-haired man walking up the aisle spraying something from a can. Must be air-freshener. She doesn't give it another thought. Later, when Justin is asked, he confesses not having noticed the activity at all.

The previews have started. Clips from a sentimental romance set during a leafy fall in Vermont are followed by scenes from an animated feature about frogs in a pond fighting to save their habitat from intruders. In theatres now! The message is flashed loud and clear after each preview. There are also two early sneak peeks—a biopic of Albert Einstein directed by Steven Spielberg, and *Seinfeld: the movie*, both scheduled for a Christmas release.

The baby kicks. Alice moves in her seat seeking comfort. They have known for a while it is a girl. The ultrasound pictures have been laminated and pasted on the refrigerator door.

Copies have been sent off to all grandparents, aunts-, and uncles-to-be. There is a shortlist of names that Alice and Justin are not sharing with anyone.

Assiduous preparations have been made to welcome this miracle into their lives. The nursery is ready—crib, mobile, baby gym, diaper station, night light, linens, toy chest. A few things are still left. Alice plans to shop for a video baby night monitor tomorrow.

The fetal movements have triggered a fresh craving in Alice. She wants popcorn like she has never wanted it before. Buttered, soft, and lightly salted. It has to be just so. Justin gets up and dutifully obliges. By the time he is back, the main feature has begun. The story hits the ground running. There is Denzel, stretched out on a beach. Trim waist, attractive pecs, dusky good looks. 'My kind of movie,' whispers Alice. Justin smiles and squeezes her hand, smacking another wet one.

ᘓ

As soon as she reads Asad's email, Sarah takes a printout and walks quickly from her lab to the Wang outpatient building where Joel is busy doing his clinic. She knocks on his door and hands him the email as he is stepping out. A frown creases his forehead and he adjusts his glasses. 'Go back to the lab and wait there,' he tells Sarah. 'I'm almost done here.'

She has barely re-entered her office when Joel bursts in. He is out of breath after scampering across the hospital and, too impatient to wait for elevators, running up four flights of stairs. After pulling out a Diet Pepsi from the office fridge, he jumps on to Sarah's desk. They go over the email again and ponder what to do.

Joel's phone call catches Asad bright and early. It is six o'clock, Karachi time. Blinking at his cell phone screen, Asad recognises

Karachi time. Blinking at his cell phone screen, Asad recognises the Boston number. He gets up quickly and takes it in the hallway, speaking in low tones, anxious not to alarm his wife.

The authorities have been notified, Joel assures Asad. One of Sarah's medical school classmates is a division director at the CDC, and through him the Coordinating Office for Terrorism Preparedness and Emergency Response has been activated.

'Fully activated?' asks Asad. 'They won't blow this off?' He wants so desperately to believe that he has finally been heard.

Fully activated, Joel assures him. Thanks to Sarah's contacts they are treating this as a highly credible threat. The data provided by Asad is gripping. Once someone in authority took proper notice, the complete anti-terror machinery was immediately activated. The head of the CDC has been summoned to Washington. An urgent meeting has been scheduled with the Secretary for Homeland Security and the White House chief of staff. Anti-rabies immunoglobulin and vaccine stores are being looked into. A media strategy is being developed. 'They're all over it,' Joel tells Asad.

'You realise the attack may have already taken place?' says Asad.

'I know,' Joel replies. 'There's going to be a mass vaccination strategy. Hopefully not much time has passed.'

'The typical incubation is several days, but who knows what it is with aerosol.'

'Right,' says Joel. 'I am told you'll be contacted soon. Sit tight, pal. And thanks.'

Twenty Four

Sandra had just taken her first steps and Alice's joy knew no bounds. It wasn't even a proper walk, barely a wobble really, starting from the edge of the couch and falling just short of the coffee table. But it was a milestone, and as every parent knows, milestones unleash maternal pride like none other.

There were also the usual regrets. Justin wasn't home to witness it. It hadn't been caught on camera. And wouldn't it have been great if she had actually made it all the way to the table?

The camcorder was brought out, but Sandra refused to perform. What a stubborn and moody girl, thought Alice indulgently, knowing well that these traits had passed on from mother to daughter. She loved her daughter to bits, but she also felt twinges of guilt and confusion.

Months had passed, and Alice had hoped that time would settle her nerves. But it took a while for the news cycle to finally change. At the time it hadn't seemed possible, but eventually they did get back to their old familiar routine. Now an article had appeared in *The Boston Globe* that threatened to reopen her wounds and make her relive the panic and fright of that difficult, inexplicable episode.

It was Sandra's nap time. Alice read to her from *Make Way for Ducklings*, the timeless Boston story of Mr and Mrs Mallard that Alice remembered well from her own childhood. Sandra fell asleep easily and quietly.

Lying in a silent room with the shades down and her precious daughter by her side, Alice let her mind wander. Her inner voice said whatever had happened was part of her life and always would be. She couldn't run away from it. It was nothing short of a supernatural marvel that she, Justin and Sandra had come away physically unhurt. Sure, it had left an ugly mental scar, which made her a victim, but the way to exorcise her victimhood was to bravely face the reality of what she had been through.

She picked up the newspaper, thumbed over to the article about the rabies bio-terror plot, and read the introductory blurb. It promised to be a comprehensive, intelligent piece. Virtually all the mainstream media coverage had been steeped in hysteria and jingoism. For a while Alice had gone along with it. It had appealed to her sense of anger and outrage. But that quickly wore thin.

As she read on, she realised she had been longing for a sophisticated and thoughtful account. It seemed she had finally found one.

The Massachusetts Department of Public Health eventually recorded twelve cases of rabies, the article began. None of them had suffered any animal bites. Their sole common exposure had been presence inside a Boston area movie theatre on that fateful evening. Nine different theatres were implicated, and at each theatre witnesses had seen someone walking through the aisles spraying something from a can. This observation was in keeping with the tip-off that the CDC had received from Pakistan, where the aerosolized rabies virus was believed to have been clandestinely developed.

Two leading Harvard scientists, a microbiologist and a clinical infectious disease specialist, had been interviewed for the article, and both were quoted as being amazed at the ingenious plot. Cases of rabies acquired through inhalation were a medical curiosity. No one, not even the CDC with its comprehensive resources and expertise, had anticipated this virus as a weapon of bio-terrorism.

One of the reasons, the article continued, why the attack could not be prevented was because the initial tip-off, received at the US Embassy in Islamabad, had been ignored. Alice remembered fuss being made about this by the White House press corps, and during the Senate hearings that had followed belatedly. The embassy's Regional Security Officer did not find rabies listed in the official manual and had dismissed it as a hoax, the article explained. The man had since been disciplined.

A key point in the article was that the death toll could have been much, much worse, no less than a medical Armageddon. Seating capacity in the nine theaters involved ranged from 150-400 each, and they were occupied on average between 50-90 per cent at the time of the coordinated aerosol attack. Approximately 2,000 individuals had been exposed, give or take. Had the CDC not acted on its tip-off and raised alarm bells in Washington, hundreds of men, women and children would have begun showing up at area hospitals with rabies, an illness that is almost never seen in the United States. It would have been the breath of death. There is no cure, and once symptoms develop, rabies kills with certainty.

Fortunately, the advance warning gave an opportunity to mount a defense. Carefully coordinated media messages and warnings identified exposed individuals, and prompt administration of anti-rabies immunoglobulin and vaccine saved countless lives.

According to the *Globe* article, the tip-off was credited to one Dr Asad Mirza, a Pakistani neurologist whose name Alice was coming